DEPTH

DEPTH

LEV AC ROSEN

Regan Arts.

NEW YORK

Regan Arts.

65 Bleecker Street
New York, NY 10012

First Regan Arts hardcover edition, April 2015.

Library of Congress Control Number: 2014955529

ISBN 978-1-941393-07-9

Interior design by Kris Tobiassen of Matchbook Digital
Jacket design by Richard Ljoenes
Jacket art by Vladimir Krizan

Printed in the United States of America

10 9 8 7 6 5 4 3 2 1

FOR JOY

ONE

—

SHE HAD THE SHOT. It was lined up. She just needed to wait for the fog to clear. And it was going to clear in a moment. She could read the swirls of it, how it breathed and parted. New York City fog was lazy, like cigarette smoke.

A small vibration in her right ear. She clenched her jaw and waited. The fog didn't clear. Her ear vibrated again. She sighed and whispered, "Phone ID." A holo-projection beamed out from her earpiece, displaying a small screen in the corner of her vision. She glanced at it, and as she did the fog swirled open for less than a heartbeat, then closed like a lover's kiss. She ground her teeth. *Caroline Khan*, read the display. "Answer," she told the phone.

"I'm working," Simone said softly. She was on a rooftop, four stories above her targets, and they were in a boat below her, but she was careful—voices could carry out here.

"I sent you a present," Caroline said, her low voice smug. "You're going to want to thank me."

"You just made me miss my shot," Simone said, "so let's call it even."

"No," Caroline responded without a hint of guilt, "it's not my fault you don't turn your phone off while stalking."

"Stalking is what people do for fun," Simone said. "Following a cheating husband to get photos of him with his special friend is business."

"Don't try to convince me it isn't fun for you, too."

Simone rolled her eyes and squatted down, letting the camera hang low in her arm. She leaned against the railing enclosing the roof.

"Why am I going to owe you?" Simone asked.

"I sent some business your way. Attractive business."

"The business, or the client?"

"The client is attractive, the business is lucrative and easy."

"Is this going to be a long conversation?"

"Maybe," Caroline said after a moment. "But only because I'll be laughing a lot."

"Can I call you later, then?"

"Just meet me at Undertow when you've got the money shot. Call if you still don't have it by eleven."

"Will do," Simone said, rising back up and trying to point her camera in what she thought was the right direction. "Later."

Simone touched the earpiece to turn it off. The fog rolled out for a moment, and the boat below her became perfectly clear. It was a floating restaurant, permanently moored, with a large, open deck made of wood, covered with tables and chairs. Fancy, too: white linens, low lighting, and waiters in tuxes. The couple she was looking for was sitting in a corner, far from the entry bridge. He, Simone knew, was Henry St. Michel, whose wife had hired Simone to tail him. She was a blonde and definitely not Henry's wife. Most cheating spouses cheated with blondes.

She snapped a photo, her camera silently capturing Henry and The Blonde. The fog rolled back in, blocking her view. Simone looked at the photo she had just taken. They were sitting across a round table from each other. The Blonde's back was to Simone, but Henry was fairly clear in the shot. He didn't have a romantic expression; he had a nervous one. Simone zoomed on the camera's display, taking a closer look at Henry. He was in his fifties, pudgy, balding, goatee, glasses. In the photo, his brow was furrowed into a stack of skittish creases. Simone aimed her camera again and waited for the fog to clear. When it did, she held down the release, taking about a dozen more shots before the fog closed around her. The images in her camera did not become any more romantic. They showed Henry taking an envelope out of his jacket and passing it across the table to The Blonde. She slipped it into her purse without looking inside. Then the waiter came over and took their order.

Simone rubbed at the back of her neck. Ms. St. Michel had only suspected an affair when she hired Simone. Her exact request was to find out what her husband was up to. From the look of it, it wasn't an affair, but it was still suspicious. Even if the envelope was just cash, no one used cash anymore unless they had to, and passing it across the table in an unmarked envelope didn't exactly make it seem aboveboard.

Simone squatted down and leaned on the rail again. She needed a shot of The Blonde's face, but she couldn't get it from this angle. She pressed a button, and the camera shrank down to the size of a business card, which she slipped into her trenchcoat sleeve. Then she stood and walked to the stairs at the other end of the roof, glancing out briefly before heading down.

She was on the roof of a twenty-four-story building, so the ocean lay four stories down, churning just below the twenty-first floor. The fog was thick, but she could hear the waves lapping at the other buildings around her, and the worn wooden bridges that connected them to one another and to the permanently moored boats that made up New York City. New York, city of bridges and boats. The green light of algae generators pulsed through the fog here and there, giving the view an eerie glow and, through it, the silhouette of the skyline bursting from the sea. It wasn't the iconic skyline of the past—just the top, with wide plains of ocean between crumbling towers, and large boats floating low on the horizon, like a steel ar-chipelago. Waves left streaks of yellowed foam like a sea chart against the buildings and boats. Everything smelled and tasted of salt.

Simone walked down to the twenty-first floor and stepped onto a bridge via a large window that had been converted into a door. Most of the city's bridges clung to the buildings, wrapped around their exterior walls and branching off into "streets" that connected nearby buildings or boats. Sometimes the bridges were nice, well kept, wide enough for many people. Sometimes, they were like the bridge Simone was walking on now—creaking wood planks hovering over a hungrily lapping ocean. The banisters were splintery, so Simone didn't touch them. Waves splashed at her ankles, but she had grown up here. She was used to it.

New York, though technically still part of the United States, had long begun to consider itself its own country, hundreds of miles from the Chicago coastline and the conservative, religious mainland. The Washington Monument and Lincoln Memorial had been airlifted to Salt Lake City, but no one tried moving New York. All the other drowned cities, like DC and Boston, were graveyards now—spires and flat tops of buildings tilting out unevenly from under the water like old headstones. Not New York. Though some older buildings had been worn away by the waves, others, retrofitted and laminated in that technological wonder Glassteel, stayed where they were as the ocean rose, closing off the bottom floors as they filled with water. There were newer buildings, too, designed to withstand the water, and decommissioned boats clever entrepreneurs had bought and moored around the city. There were a million New Yorkers left, and they were stubborn. They built the bridges themselves, and everyone bought personal algae generators and desalination filters for their apartments, stringing them out the windows into the sea. They reassembled their city. They stayed.

Simone walked the bridges that took her to the boat-restaurant's entrance, a well-preserved metal ramp that connected the bridge to the deck of the ship. The bridge here was wider and had a few lamps rising up and over it, like old street lamps, but with tubes that went down into the ocean to small algae generators that pulled the bright green stuff up and converted it to electricity. The railings were high enough, and solid metal, so the waves seldom splashed on the bridge in calm weather. A taxi-boat stand bobbed just down the bridge. This was a nice area. Well kept.

Strands of violin music came from the boat. Simone stood on the bridge, lit a cigarette, and waited. It was an early dinner, only six thirty, but the sky was darkening, and the fog was at its thickest. Maybe they chose the time because of the fog, Simone thought. The cigarette tasted dry and acidic in her mouth. It wasn't her preferred brand. If she had them, she smoked the old-fashioned ones that killed slowly, but those were hard to find, so she had settled for the non-cancerous ones that cleared out your sinuses, left your teeth whiter, and were just as addictive as real nicotine.

Simone settled in to wait. Waiting was a large part of being a private detective. She smoked two cigarettes and wondered what the envelope Henry had handed The Blonde contained. He wasn't a big deal, as far as she knew. Not in politics. Just an export-import guy. His wife had the money. She was from the European Union, the part that was still dry thanks to the dikes, not the part that was all gondolas and canals. They had met when he was traveling, and decided to settle in New York because she loved the ocean. Not that there wasn't a lot of ocean everywhere else. He ran the business with a partner, mostly bringing stuff out of mainland America as it became illegal (banned books, birth control, "scandalous" art) and sold it in Canada or the EU. Simone couldn't think of anything he could have come across that would require shady dealings outside the office—maybe looted art from before the flood, but that stuff was sold pretty openly in the city. It could be smuggling, but with the amount of money his wife seemed to have, he didn't need to.

They came down the ramp a little after seven. Not a long dinner. Not the sort of dinner where a couple gazed into one another's eyes over crème brulée and sighed. They weren't holding hands as they came down the ramp, either. Simone flicked her cigarette into the ocean and pretended to study the menu posted next to the restaurant's ramp. Henry and The Blonde walked down the bridge and stopped at the taxi-boat stand. Henry nodded an awkward-looking goodbye and got into a waiting yellow boat. The Blonde waved goodbye after him. Simone watched The Blonde walk farther down the bridge and wondered whom to follow. She still hadn't gotten a good shot of The Blonde, and her instincts told her Henry was on his way home, so she walked down the bridge, trailing The Blonde, her shoulders hunched, head down slightly. The Blonde turned onto one of the main bridges—huge things, reinforced, with suspension lines holding them up. Always crowded. Sometimes you might even see an old gas-powered car on one of them.

Simone followed The Blonde, picking out details of her through the fog. She was petite, wearing a blue jacket and knee-length skirt. Her hair hung pin-straight to just above her shoulders, as if afraid to make contact, and it swayed when she walked. When she turned, it covered her profile. Simone couldn't get a good look at her face.

The Blonde didn't look like a New Yorker. Her boots were tall, and waterproof, but they had heels. Her dress was short enough to move in, but tight. And if she were a major player in the city, Simone would have known her face already. Simone guessed they were headed for a hotel, probably the Four Seasons. It was down this street and off another—and The Blonde looked like she could afford it. She pulled her camera out of her sleeve, turning it on without the zoom, so it stayed small. The Four Seasons was in front of them, the white-painted steps up to its marble terrace built right onto the bridge. The doors had originally been the wide glass doors from a suite to a balcony, and they hadn't been changed much—except now the glass was tinted for privacy. They shone black in the fog, a doorman standing in front of them like a dark mast. He nodded at The Blonde, who nodded back and then turned as if aware of someone following her. Simone tilted her head down to hide her face but raised the camera and took as many photos as she could. The Blonde's eyes scanned the horizon but didn't seem to find Simone. She turned back around and went inside. Simone eyed the doorman, wondering if he would tell her who The Blonde was, but he had the look of an old dog about him, the kind who would stay loyal even if bribed, if only out of sheer laziness. Simone turned away. It was enough for one night. She'd call Ms. St. Michel and find out if she knew The Blonde.

Simone looked at the photos she had just taken. She was a blonde who could refreeze the ice caps—one of those pretty but cold, ageless faces that could be twenty-one or forty. Long bangs, a stylish haircut if Simone could judge by advertisements. She rubbed the back of her neck where it had started to ache and put the camera back in her sleeve. Then she took off down the street, walking to the bar to find out what sort of attractive client or job Caroline had found for her.

TWO

—

SIMONE WALKED INTO UNDERTOW, a seedy little bar right over the water with brick walls that were constantly being worn away by the waves. The ocean lapped at the windows with the regularity of a ticking clock, and the narrow bridge leading to the door was always slippery. The bartender was a guy named Perske. He knew Simone and Caroline well enough that he didn't water down their drinks.

Caroline was curved over at the bar, drinking a G&T through a straw. Her hair was a mass of black waves, like a storm rolling off her forehead, forever frizz-less from the FluoriSeal products she used. She was still dressed for work, in an expensive white DrySkin suit, and seemed to still *be* at work, staring into the screen on her wrist-piece, her right hand tapping at the keyboard projected onto her left forearm like a very methodical gull pecking at scraps. To anyone who didn't know her, she might have seemed a woman letting her hair down after a long day of work—sending personal messages, checking her feeds—but Simone knew better. The curls were carefully sculpted to look effortless and make her seem more easygoing than she was. And that was work she was doing on her wristpiece. It was why she didn't use any dicta-stuff, like the glasses, or the type of earpiece Simone used. She couldn't say anything aloud—people might hear, and then there'd be trouble.

Deputy Mayor Caroline Khan came from one of the most powerful families in New York. The Khans were a Korean American family that had lived in New York since before the water started rising and now owned several decommissioned luxury ships around the city, renting them out as apartments, offices, stores, hotels, and factories. They had ties to the EU, Korea, Japan, Canada, and the mainland, were involved in local politics, and were known as avid art collectors. They were on the Board of Trustees for the American Museum of Natural History and the city's Art Reclamation Fund. They personally had found over eighty paintings thought to be lost to looting or left underwater during the flood, and had donated them to museums. They employed a vast number of New Yorkers, were well respected, and those who crossed them always lost. They existed to be wealthy, powerful, and perfect. Caroline hated that about them.

"What'll ya have, Red?" Perske asked Simone as she sat down next to Caroline.

"Don't call her that," Caroline said in an irritated tone without looking up or removing her mouth from the straw. Simone grinned, took her coat and hat off, and unpinned her hair so it fell in a dark-red wave over one eye—Caroline also kept Simone well stocked in FluoriSeal.

"Something strong and sour," Simone said. Perske nodded and turned to the row of bottles behind the bar. "So what do you have for me?" she asked Caroline. Caroline turned for the first time, her mouth still biting down on the straw. She smiled and looked back at her wristpiece, then gave it a tap. The keyboard projected onto her forearm vanished, and the screen went dark.

"I don't know if you deserve it anymore," she said flatly. Caroline always sounded unimpressed. Her humor was the driest thing in New York. Anyone listening might have thought that Caroline didn't like whomever she was talking to. But Simone knew better: if Caroline didn't like someone, she didn't talk to them at all.

At thirty-seven, Caroline had been New York's deputy mayor for several years. She was Mayor Seward's mouthpiece and gatekeeper, and a shoo-in to replace him when he retired. She was also, to Simone's constant surprise, a very good friend—intervening on her behalf when the police rattled her, sending business her way. Simone liked Caroline, even trusted her, which was an unusual feeling for her—one that actually made her feel queasy every time she saw Caroline, as though she were looking down from very high up, waiting for someone to push her. But she'd grown used to liking Caroline. Enjoyed it. She was her only friend. And having a deputy mayor as a friend was always a nice advantage for a PI.

"Why don't I deserve it? Because I said I was on a stakeout?"

"Because you didn't seem very grateful."

"I don't know what it is yet."

Caroline pursed her lips and looked forward again, nodding. She leaned back and stretched, her hands clasped above her head, her back arched. In the white suit, she looked like a cold crescent moon.

"Fair enough. It's an anthropologist. Or archeologist. I don't remember. I met him at some party my parents threw two weeks ago, just for five minutes, but then he came into the office this morning, saying he needed a tour guide."

"I'm not a tour guide," Simone said.

"Slash bodyguard," Caroline continued, ignoring her. "He's good looking. Extremely good looking. From the EU, Spain I'd imagine, beautiful body, slight accent. Tell me you don't owe me one." Caroline smiled for the first time since Simone had sat down, a small upward curve so subtle that it almost didn't exist.

"What does he want me to do?"

"He's looking for places where the buildings are dry down past the twenty-first floor." Caroline's laugh came in a short, sudden burst, like the single rotation of a siren. It harmonized well with

Simone's own low chuckle, like the rumbling of a building about to collapse into the sea.

"Is this a joke?" Simone asked. She'd heard rumors, of course—everyone had—about buildings that were so airtight and advanced that you could walk down to the bottom of the ocean. When the water was first rising, scuba companies had done good business offering to rappel down the sides of buildings with airtanks, going into submerged apartments to bring back old heirlooms. As the water got higher, though, buildings began to crumble, and algae bloomed everywhere, making it impossible to see below the surface. Crumbling cement could land on your head without your ever seeing it falling towards you, or an adventurous shark could take you from an alley. These days, if you were foolish enough to go into the water, you didn't come back out. People still went in, now and then, not searching for waterlogged heirlooms but for the mythical airtight buildings—the Atlantis under New York. No one ever found anything because it was all nonsense. Simone had lived there thirty-six years and knew the city as well as anyone, and she didn't know of anywhere where the water stopped below the twenty-first floor.

"No joke," Caroline said, though she let out another laugh.

"And he's a real anthro-archo-whatever?"

"His papers were legit. But that's the best part. You basically get to spend time with a good-looking guy and get paid for it, and, since what he's looking for doesn't exist, he'll be with you a while."

"I have other cases, Caroline. I don't have time to babysit some pearl diver."

"I know you find the idea of work that doesn't involve you skulking alone in the shadows to be a personal insult, but you need the money, and you could stand to get laid, judging by the fact that you've cracked your neck twice since coming in. Haven't called up Peter for a quick-and-dirty evening of heartbreak lately?"

"We broke up years ago," Simone said, trying not to sound too bothered and failing. "And I haven't seen him in almost a month."

She looked over at Perske, willing him to mix the drink faster. "And even then, we didn't fuck."

"Exactly. Take the job, take the money, and take any bonuses that come with it. If only so I don't have to watch you roll your head around like some MouthFoamer who just found a stash the size of the ocean. You're doing it again."

Simone stopped rolling her head and glared. Perske put a yellow drink down in front of her and walked off to another customer. She drank deeply.

"Okay," Simone said, "but I'm not agreeing that I owe you one till I see him."

"Fair enough. I gave him your info; he'll probably stop by tomorrow."

"But he'd better not be full-time. I have to at least finish up this case I'm on."

"What is it?"

"Wife thought it was a cheating spouse, now it looks like more."

"More?" Caroline cocked her body on the stool, turning slightly closer to Simone.

"I can't tell you," Simone said, smiling. "You know that."

"Hmmm," Caroline said, and locked her mouth onto her straw again. "You're no fun," she said.

"I'm lots of fun," Simone said, "but only when water pistols are involved."

Caroline snorted into her straw. What was left of her drink bubbled in the glass.

"I'll be sure to tell Alejandro that."

"That the hot client?"

"Yep. Alejandro deCostas."

"Are you sure you don't want to tour him yourself?"

"Nah," Caroline said. "I don't like them stupid."

"Ah, but you have no problem with the stupid ones for me?"

"If you don't, I don't . . . and judging from your dating history, you really, really don't."

Simone finished her drink and raised an eyebrow at Caroline. Caroline stared back, eyes wide with a false innocence.

"Okay, gotta drift. Have to call a woman and tell her about a blonde."

"Why is it always a blonde?" Caroline asked.

"I've been asking myself that for years," Simone said, getting up and putting her coat on.

"Let me walk out with you," Caroline said, standing. "I have way too much work to do tonight."

"Something interesting happening at City Hall?" Simone put on her hat. Caroline put on her long overcoat, then pulled her hair out from under the collar in one quick motion. For a moment, it haloed out around her, like dark, churning water.

"You know I can't tell you that," Caroline said, her voice rising slightly with amusement.

"We still on for the weekend? Going to finally try that VR bowling place?"

"Yeah," Caroline said. They walked out the door. Sea froth whipped up over their ankles, occasionally up to their knees, as they walked the rickety walkway from Undertow back to a more solid bridge.

"You'll have to have a real conversation while bowling, you know, so you better come up with something interesting to talk about," Caroline said.

"Yeah," Simone said, nodding. They parted ways at the next bridge, a steady one with rusted metal railings, and Simone headed home.

She lived on the sixth floor above sea level of an old thirty-story building, its brick walls mirror-smooth from the waves. The rent was cheap because there was a chance it could fall into the sea at any moment. But Simone liked that.

It was in an area of town her dad used to call Alphabet City, but which most people now called Cartarojo for the large tanker in the center of the neighborhood. It was a relatively peaceful neighborhood, with plenty of bars below the various decks. People were quiet, or at least not too loud. It wasn't like the touristy area to the west, or the expensive places uptown. It was just the city: cool, wet, uncaring. She had large picture windows that she'd had to reinforce against the ocean storms but which gave her a nice view of a flat expanse of water and the buildings just beyond it. On bright days, when the sun was at the right angle, she could see a building maybe ten or so feet below the water, like a reflection of what the city once was. The water was too shallow to dock a large boat over the building but too deep to build anything on top. Small taxi boats and private yachts sailed over the empty water at all hours. Sometimes it was a lake. Sometimes it was an intersection.

Simone's apartment had been huge once, with high ceilings and decorative wooden beams that gave it a slightly rustic feel. She had turned the front part into her offices—an old-fashioned front door with *Simone Pierce Investigations* carefully lettered across the frosted-glass window. Inside was a waiting room, with chairs and a desk for a receptionist (if she could ever afford one) and behind that a table and sofa. From there, through another, more tightly locked, door was a hallway leading to her office, the kitchen, and a bathroom. Her bedroom was past her office and had its own bathroom. No one was waiting for her, so she locked the front door for the night, shut the light, and went into her office.

Simone lived in the office, and it showed. What money she made was spent here. She had a relatively up-to-date touchdesk, the kind that looked like a long curve of black glass that curled up into a wave on one side, ending in a flat screen. She placed her palm on the desk to turn it on, the black glass becoming a series of images. She shrugged off her coat and hat, put them on the coatrack by the door, and sat down at the desk. She slid the small inbox symbol up to the flat screen and tapped it once so it expanded. She had six new messages, but nothing pressing. If she were like Caroline, she'd have an expensive wristpiece connected to her phone and her home office through a high-security cloud, and she could check all her messages from one place, but when she was out, she was usually working, and preferred as few distractions as possible. Her phone and office were cloud-connected, so she could always have messages that came through her touchdesk dictated to her by her phone. She just didn't want a screen on her wrist. It affected her aim.

She lifted her left leg to take her gun out of its ankle holster and put it on the desk. The images under the gun twitched, realizing something was covering them, and reorganized themselves to another part of the desktop where they could be seen clearly.

Simone turned her earpiece back on while walking to the kitchen. It was only nine thirty. She called Ms. St. Michel's personal line.

"Hello?" Ms. St. Michel answered. She had an accent Simone couldn't place—some sort of European, maybe Scandinavian.

"Ms. St. Michel? It's Simone Pierce."

"Ah, yes, Ms. Pierce." She hesitated on the other end of the line. Simone switched on the light in the kitchen and turned on the coffeepot. "Do you have something to tell me?" Ms. St. Michel's voice wavered ever so slightly. If Simone hadn't known better, she might have thought it was part of her accent.

"Can I ask you first when your husband came home tonight?"

"Perhaps seven thirty, maybe a little later. Why do you ask?"

"Just checking a hunch. Ms. St. Michel—"

"If you are going to be the one to tell me my husband is cheating on me, you may as well call me Linnea. Being called Ms. St. Michel and then being told Mr. St. Michel is unfaithful makes it all seem like we're just actors in a play. This is my life."

"Linnea, then," Simone said, licking the bitterness off her lips. She hated it when clients got personal. "I took some photos tonight of your husband with another woman, but I don't think it's an affair.

I would appreciate it if you would look at some photos of the woman in question and tell me if you recognize her. May I send them to you?"

"No. Henry is home, and I don't want him to walk in on me and find me staring at photos of him that should not exist. I will come to you. Tell him I need some air."

Simone looked out the window. The only light now was coming from the city's buildings and algae generators, but she could make out some heavy clouds on the horizon.

"Linnea, it's going to storm soon. Maybe we should wait until tomorrow?"

"I could never sleep. I will come over now. That is okay, yes?"

"Yes . . . I just don't want you to drown on your way."

"Don't worry about that," Linnea said, her voice a sigh. "I will be there soon."

"Sure thing."

Linnea hung up, and Simone shook her head as she poured herself a cup of coffee, took it with her to the waiting room. She unlocked the door again, and turned the light back on.

Simone went back to her desk to read her messages, sometimes glancing out the window at the approaching storm. Lightning flashed in the distance, and she could hear the wind on the windows. Walking around New York, even without the high waves and strong winds of a storm, was dangerous enough. The city was permanently slippery and poorly maintained, and try as they might, shoe companies couldn't make your soles completely slip-proof. Rip currents had taken up residence around all the buildings, a complex map of tides and undertow; struggling against them would drown you, but relaxing and letting them carry you would end with you miles out to sea, far from the city, if your head wasn't bashed into some debris on the way.

But during a storm, being outside went from merely deadly to suicidal. One wave could throw you against the side of a building and you'd fall off whatever narrow bridge you were on and into the water, unconscious. The next day, the recycling boats would find your body while dragging the water, and deliver it to the recycling center, where they'd look for your IRID or some other identification. If you were lucky, and your IRID hadn't floated off your body (or been taken along with your wallet by a particularly ambitious recycling boat worker), then notifications to your family would be made. But if you had no identification like most drowned people, and your fingertips, lips, and eyelids were too damaged from water and hungry fish to get a fingerprint or a facial scan, they took your photo, pinned it on their bulletin board, and posted it online. Your body would be kept at the recycling center, and if no one claimed you in two weeks, whatever nutrients could be harvested from your corpse were sucked out and the rest of you burned, the ashes poured back into the ocean. Simone tried to check the website regularly, just to make sure no one she knew was on it. On average, there were between a dozen and twenty new faces every week.

Simone's messages weren't anything interesting aside from an amusing bit of gossip from Danny about one of New York's elite coming in for a psychic reading to ask if his mistress was cheating on him. About half an hour and two cups of coffee later, there was a gentle rap at the door, and Simone walked out to the waiting room to open it. Linnea stood in the hall.

She was an attractive woman, somewhere in her fifties, the kind who aged gracefully, though whether that was natural or not, Simone couldn't tell. Her being well dressed wasn't a surprise, but still the richness of her clothes took Simone aback. She wore a fur-collared, brown-bronze trench coat that went down to her ankles, and under that a perfectly tailored golden sheath of a dress that ended just below her knees. That meant she'd had a ride over; dresses—anything that tangled your legs if you slipped—were idiotic in the city. That's why women were never fined for wearing pants, even though it was technically a federal offense.

Linnea took off her coat and handed it to Simone but left on her hat, a small bronze oval perched on her chocolate hair, from which hung a long veil, down to her shoulders. And it was all made of Dry-Skin. Even the veil, Simone was willing to bet, had thin layers of the stuff over the holes in the netting. It felt like nothing, stretched like spiderwebs, and breathed like air, but when water hit the fabric, it broke into a thousand droplets, never penetrating—just hanging there like diamonds until they dripped off or evaporated. It was the same stuff they used to waterproof electronics these days. Expensive. Even Caroline didn't have a complete wardrobe of it. Simone only had one coat made with the stuff. She went back to her office and carefully hung Linnea's coat.

"Linnea," Simone said, motioning for her to take a seat on the other side of the desk. Linnea did so and crossed her legs. She was wearing high heels—ridiculous to even own in the city, unless you never had to walk anywhere.

"I'm a bit nervous, Ms. Pierce," Linnea said, clasping her hands in her lap. "I have been wondering what you meant when you said you did not think it was an affair."

Simone nodded. She got up again and went to the coatrack to take her camera out of her coat sleeve, then turned it on and put it on her desk. The desk automatically started downloading the photos she had taken, displaying them as small images on the desk. Simone tapped them once so they grew, then slid them around so they were facing Linnea.

"You see, I've done plenty of cheating spouse cases. There's nothing romantic here. It looks more like a business deal. That's why I wanted to ask you if you knew the woman." Simone tapped a shot of The Blonde's face, enlarging the photo even more. "Have you ever seen her before?"

Linnea shook her head. "No . . . but they are at a restaurant together. Isn't that like a date?"

"I don't think so," Simone said. "They didn't touch, and they didn't go back to a hotel together or anything like that. Henry went right home to you after dinner."

"Did you hear their conversation?"

"No—but I can plant a bug next time, if you'd like." Simone scratched her chin.

Linnea nodded slowly. "So what does this mean?"

"I don't know. I was hoping she was just a business associate, and then I would tail him again tomorrow, but if you don't know her . . ."

"I want you to follow him again anyway," Linnea said resolutely. "He is not himself lately. A wife knows. Something is amiss. Even if it doesn't seem like an affair . . . perhaps it is something else. Perhaps the envelope had a payment for a girl for another time. The girl could be a, what do you call them, a dock mistress, who keeps a boat of sirens."

Simone shrugged.

"If you want me to, I'll keep tailing him."

"Please. I want to know what he's doing with . . . *her*," Linnea said with some distaste, tapping at The Blonde's photo, accidentally causing it to enlarge so that it took up almost the entire desk, her forehead and chin cut off by the edges.

"I can do that," Simone said.

"Thank you," Linnea said, standing up. "That is all, I assume?"

"Yes," Simone said. "I should mention, Linnea, that the longer I follow your husband the more expensive—"

"Money is of no concern," Linnea said with a wave, as she took her coat off the rack and slipped it on. She turned to look at Simone. "As I said, a wife knows when something is amiss," she said, her voice low, the dim lights of a boat outside the window running over her face. Raindrops began to hit the window with light thudding noises.

"Will you be all right to get home?" Simone asked.

LEV AC ROSEN / 21

"Yes. I have a yacht and a driver," she said. Simone nodded. Safest way to travel.

"I'll let you know as soon as I find out anything else," Simone said.

"And I will call you if I discover anything on my own," Linnea said. She looked Simone square in the eyes for a moment. The rain became heavier all at once, moving from light drops to a heavy drumming, thick rivers of water streaming down the windows. Thunder clapped. Linnea adjusted her veil and smiled at Simone, then nodded. "Good night," she said. She left the office and the waiting room, the clicking of her heels blending into the sound of the rain. Simone looked at her desk again. The giant face of The Blonde stared back at her. Simone lay her palm flat on the desk to turn it off. Then she turned off all the lights and went to her bedroom.

Her bedroom was in the corner of the building, with windows on two sides, looking out on New York and the heavy storm that had descended on it. It was almost completely black outside, except when lightning struck—for brief moments illuminating the city skyline and the surging waves devouring it. In one flash, Simone saw a yacht motoring swiftly away, like a white arrow in the darkness, pointing at the horizon. When the waves surged so high that the wind could carry the spray up to her window, blurring it with flecks of salt and algae, Simone closed the drapes, stripped, and got into bed. A large mirror hung opposite her bed, but when Simone tapped a screen on her nightstand, it turned into a video feed. Simone absentmindedly flipped through the shows, news programs, and old movies they sometimes ran. She sighed. Nothing interested her. She turned the video feed off and the screen turned back into a mirror. She shut off the light and rolled over on her pillow, falling asleep to the sound of waves, and rain, and the occasional shudder of thunder through her drapes.

THREE

——

THE MORNINGS AFTER STORMS were often bright and clear, the storm having somehow cancelled out the usual morning fog. The light, only slightly dampened by the closed shades, fell hard on Simone, waking her earlier than usual. She took a deep breath, pushing away the usual flickering remnants of her dreams—the red hole of an exit wound, ashes pouring into the sea. They faded away until she'd forgotten them, the edge between dream and reality becoming sharp again. She hit the button on her nightstand to lift the shades. Gulls soared above the city, cutting the air and looking for scraps that had churned to the water's surface. She got out of bed and showered, then dressed in a gray collared shirt and black pants, with her knee-high boots pulled over them. In her office, she turned on the touchdesk, checked her messages, and scanned the headlines: the European Union was condemning the US's "homosexual re-education" camps, lawsuits over the failed Mercury Imported Polar Ice Project were stalled again, Canada's virtual reality city had repaired the damage done by a hacker last month, and the United Nations Space Station seemed to be having a record number of health issues and was trying to hire top doctors from Earth. Nothing that concerned Simone. She went to the kitchen, turned her coffee maker

on, and lit a cigarette, then went out into the waiting room and unlocked the door. She hadn't even crossed back to the hall when it
opened behind her.

"Ah, hello?" came a voice behind her. She turned. Apparently,
he had been waiting. Caroline had been right about the handsome.
He had warm tan skin, roguish black hair, and full lips, and his
clothes clung to him well enough to show that he had the sort of
body that could inspire spontaneous sculpting in marble. He didn't
look older than thirty. "I'm supposed to meet a Ms. Pierce," he said
with a very faint accent.

"You've met her, then," Simone said. "You're Mr. deCostas?"

"Yes," he nodded. "Ms. Khan told me you were the best."

"It depends on what she meant I was the best at," Simone said.
She turned back to the hall. "Come into my office. Would you like
some coffee? It's not the fancy, genetically perfected stuff, but it's
coffee."

"Thank you," he said, following her. She pointed him into the
office, then went back to the kitchen to get the coffee. When she
got back to her office, holding two mugs, he was sitting, staring at her
desk. The Blonde's oversized face still stared back out of it. Simone
walked back to her chair and tapped The Blonde's face so it shrank
down again, then slid all the photos to one side and spun her finger
around to gray them out. She handed deCostas his coffee and swung
her legs up onto her desk.

"So you want a tour guide," she said, appraising him.

"No." He tilted his head slightly, as if considering, and blew on
his coffee. His lips were damp and shone pale pink like the inside of
a strawberry. "Tour guide makes it sound, ah, pedestrian. I am not
touring. I am researching. I need an escort. Someone who knows
the city and also can deal with any . . . trouble that may arise during my research."

"Do you anticipate a lot of trouble?"

"I try to be prepared for anything." He pushed his shoulders back, possibly in an attempt to look prepared, but the effect was of a teenager trying to look older.

"Then you'd be able to handle the trouble yourself," Simone said.

"A fair point," deCostas said with a curved smile. "Let's say then that hiring you would be part of my preparations. You look like you're capable of handling trouble." He let his eyes look her over slowly. She met his gaze and locked it.

"I suppose I'm used to it. I don't know if that makes me capable."

"*Asumiria.*"

"Pardon?"

"I mean that's ideal."

"So if I feel a drop, I get us out of wherever we are—that's what you're looking for?"

"If a drop means trouble, yes."

Simone nodded. "That I can do. Now, explain to me exactly what you're looking to find," Simone said, sipping her coffee. He had black eyes, mirrorlike. Seeing her drink apparently reminded deCostas that he also had coffee. He took a sip of his, then frowned.

"Used to the good stuff?"

"Used to the weak stuff." Simone raised an eyebrow. "I'm a student, Ms. Pierce, I can only afford weak coffee." He pursed his lips in a way that was probably supposed to suggest this was his lot, and he was used to it, but which Simone found incredibly sexual. "I am looking to find areas where the architectural strength of the buildings kept them watertight, so the buildings themselves are still inhabitable to street level. No water."

"I know New York, Mr. deCostas. That's all driftwood." He looked confused, so she explained: "Nonsense."

"I've done extensive research on architectural techniques used in New York over the past hundred years. Some buildings—and I have a list where we can begin—some buildings should have been strong enough, and used technology advanced enough, to keep out the floods."

"Even all these years later?"

"Yes." deCostas frowned. "Maybe. I think so. And it does not really matter if you don't think so. I just need you to help me locate these buildings and take me there. If I am wrong, you've been paid for what will most likely be an easy job. If I am right, you get to see a secret side of the city you claim to know so well. You get to be part of a great discovery." He raised his eyebrows slightly.

"If these buildings did exist, don't you think someone would know?"

"Maybe. But they might want to keep it a secret."

"Ah, and now we come to the trouble you predicted."

"Yes. Some inhabitants of these possibly watertight buildings might not take well to having what they consider their private spaces invaded."

Simone swung her legs off the desk and opened the drawer in a cabinet to her left.

"I'm not some exterminator, Mr. deCostas. If you find some place you want to move in, you need to take care of current occupants some other way." She took out a business card for Dash Ormond, another private detective in the city whom Simone sometimes sent business to. He had what Simone would call a different set of ethics, but he'd been around as long as she had, and he sometimes sent her stuff that he didn't want. "This guy can probably do the job better." She handed him the card. He stared at it but didn't take it.

"No, I think you misunderstand," he said. "I don't mean for you to harm anyone who does not pose a threat." Simone stared at him. She was fairly certain that that was exactly what he had meant. He stared back, a small smile forming. "Please, Ms. Pierce. The mayor's office said you were the best in the city. Said you knew every inch of it, because you'd grown up here."

"Okay," she said, "I'm a thousand a day, in advance, on my schedule, and I'm no tour guide; you find out which buildings fit your structural integrity criteria, tell me what they are, and I'll take you there, and get you in, if getting in isn't as easy as walking in the front door. I still think you're not going to find anything, but I'll take your money just the same."

deCostas stood and nodded, then drank the last of his coffee.

"When do we begin?"

"Tomorrow," Simone said, "if you can get me your credit information and the names of some buildings today. At least two buildings ASAP. I'll handle the rest."

"You won't just take me to the nearby buildings and say they're the ones I asked for?" he asked, smiling.

"You'll have to trust me, angel," she said, smiling coyly.

"Then I will do so. Until tomorrow, then. Thank you for the coffee."

They shook hands and he turned and walked out. Simone caught herself staring at his ass. She would have to think of reasons to walk behind him. Easy money and eye candy. She did owe Caroline.

Trying not to linger on deCostas' curves, Simone decided on the rest of her day. She needed a way of hearing what Mr. St. Michel was talking about with The Blonde, which meant a bug, which meant meeting him, which meant a cover, which meant Danny. That was fine. She hadn't seen Danny in a while. She brought up the photo of The Blonde again and printed it out. She could send it to Danny, but if she was going to him anyway, a hard copy seemed safer. She had another cup of coffee, locked the office up, and headed out.

Danny's office, if it could be called that, was only a few bridges from the *Rialto*, the old freighter moored where Union Square used to be, filled with shops and street performers who docked motorboats around the bridges and played guitar in neon-piped scuba suits or juggled. It was a good location for his business—the top floor of a twenty-two-story building, just barely above the water, accessible by the old fire escape that led up to the window he used as a door. He had painted over the sliding glass door with images of crystal balls and pentagrams and had hung velvet curtains behind it. A neon sign proclaiming "Psychic" flickered in the window, and above that another sign: "The Great Yanai, Seer of the Future, Teller of Fortunes." It looked like crap, but Danny did a decent business. Simone climbed the steps and walked into the shop. The waiting room up front smelled of sandalwood and had old gray carpeting and glass cases displaying various occult accouterments. The curtain leading to Danny's "reading chamber" was closed, so Simone sat down in one of the old chairs and picked up a digital magazine called *Horoscope Weekly*.

Simone was an Aries, born March 29. "Now is a great time for love," her horoscope read. "You're letting out a seductive energy no one can resist. Use it wisely, but beware of fair-haired women." Simone raised an eyebrow. Those were words to live by. She put down the magazine, a thin sheet of white polymer that scrolled through pages as you brushed a finger on the bottom. Originally, people had had entire libraries on small screens like that, subscriptions to magazines downloaded every day or week, but then advertisers and publishers had realized they could make more money by selling each magazine and book individually. Simone's bookshelves were lined with the thin, folded white sheets, their titles and authors stamped across the front in black.

The curtains to the back parted and a well-dressed, wealthy-looking woman stepped out. She was pale, and her eyes were red. Behind her, Danny stepped out, wearing a ridiculous feathered turban and cape over what were probably black pajamas. His eyes met with Simone's for a moment, and Simone winked. Danny raised his eyebrows, then turned back to the woman, clasped his hands together, and bowed slightly. The feather on his turban bobbed.

"Thank you again, Mrs. Seward," he said. "The spirits appreciate your business."

"Thank you, Yanai," Mrs. Seward said, tapping something out on her wristpiece—her payment, Simone assumed. "I'll be back again next week."

"Of course," he said, flourishing his cape to disguise his surreptitiously checking his own wristpiece to confirm payment. Mrs. Seward sniffed and walked out the door, her heels making metallic clicks on the fire escape outside. Danny looked at Simone and wiggled his eyebrows.

"The mayor's wife," Simone said, impressed.

"Shall we consult the spirits in my private chambers?" Danny asked in an overwrought imitation of a vampire from an old movie. Simone rolled her eyes, stood, and followed him into the back room.

The back room was much like the front, but smaller, and even more ridiculous. A circular table had a heavy black cloth over it with a crystal ball in the center, and various crystals hung from the low ceiling. In the back were a few steps leading up to an old-looking wooden door. Simone walked through the room and opened the door. Beyond that was Danny's real office. Metal walls and an old sofa and coffee table. A desk covered in gadgets. Printers, screens, and other large electronics Simone couldn't place lined the walls. Danny took off his turban, set it on the desk, and flung his cape over the sofa arm before sitting down.

"So what are you in the market for today?" he asked.

"I need a fake IRID. Canadian importer. Net-backing to go with it. And . . ." Sitting next to him on the sofa, Simone took the photo of The Blonde out of her jacket and asked, "Know her?" Danny stared at it, his eyes narrowing.

"No. . . . Do you think they found me?" He looked up at her, worried. Simone smiled.

"Nothing to do with you; just a case."

Danny took a deep breath and nodded. "Want me to keep my eyes open, or a full-on search?"

"Just keep your eyes open."

"No problem." Danny grinned, pushing his shaggy brown hair back, revealing a metal plate just over the ear. Danny was somewhere in his early twenties, and had come to New York five years ago, running from the mainland. The US was no longer the world's superpower. China had taken on that role ages ago, and with the various laws in the US forbidding most scientific research, all the experiments the US military did had to be kept secret. Danny was one of those.

Raised with nineteen others, he was genetically created in an underground lab near Chicago. As a child, he'd had various electronics implanted in his head. He was supposed to be the perfect spy—a hacker who didn't even need access to a computer, because he *was* a computer. Danny was trained from birth to use the computer in his mind, as well as the wireless signals that were constantly swimming around him. At thirteen, he and the others could all sit quietly in a corner and surf the net to their hearts' content, bashing down encryptions and security systems as fast as they could blink. They were always kept in small white rooms and never interacted with anyone besides each other and a woman they called "Mother," who gave them their assignments and took their reports. At fourteen, they could hack into most classified government sites— any government. At fifteen, they were taken on field trips to the South China Sea, where they logged onto local signals and hacked into Chinese military clouds and databases.

Also at fifteen, during a routine check of what Danny (then called Odin 17) had been looking at online, his supervisors found that Danny was gay, or at least looking at gay pornography. In the US, under normal circumstances, they would have sent him to a re-education camp, but with Danny that would be a problem. The camps were outside, in the real world, where they wouldn't be able to control his movements as easily, and where the metal plate on his head would get some attention. If the Odin Program, with its genetic modification and hacking, were to go public, it would be a disaster, both internationally and at home. And besides, they had nineteen others. They decided killing him would be easiest. But Danny beat them to the punch, hacking onto the facility servers and finding the orders for his termination.

Simone was never exactly sure what Danny had done to escape, or how he had gotten to New York, but he had shown up one night in her waiting room—wet and miserable, begging her to hide him. She had done it, without payment. She'd showed him how to create the new identity of Danny Fray and how he could easily forge his own IRID, helped him find a place to work and live under the radar, taught him how to use his skills for more petty criminal enterprises than those he'd been instructed in. Mainland troops had only come looking once, and Simone had gotten them off his back by making it look like he had gone to South America.

Simone and Danny had been close since. The mass of cloud networks over New York allowed him to access the web without being found by anyone looking for his particular ISP. He changed networks and ran through other servers in the blink of an eye. He could set up a web page and download secure information all while taking a deep breath. It looked like magic. Which is why he had become a successful psychic, telling people what they already knew: that his spouse had booked a room at a hotel a few nights ago (hotel databases were very easy to access); that her father was living in Canada. He did a lot of what Simone could do, but much faster. And he owed her. So she used him. But she didn't kid herself; if it had been Dash Ormond's or some other PI's doorstep Danny had shown up on that night, he'd be here instead of Simone, using him like the mainlanders had hoped to.

"Any particular importing?" he asked, leaning back into the sofa. His eyes had the slightly glazed look they got when he was working on the Internet in his head.

"Art. Antiques. Furniture. Keep it vague."

"Done and done," he said, smiling, "You want the IRID?"

"It would help."

He opened a drawer in a cabinet and took out a small thumb-print scanner and an infrared chip, which he then put into a nearby 3D printer. It began to print, oozing plastic over the infrared chip and sensor to create the infrared identification card—the IRID. It was a slow process, so he turned back to the photo of The Blonde.

"Who is she?"

"Possible mistress, possible business partner, possible pro siren."

"Sounds sexy."

"Could be. Hey . . . can you check something else out, actually?"

"Anything for you."

"Alejandro deCostas."

He nodded.

"Alejandro deCostas," he read from a screen only he could see, "PhD in archeology, master's in physics, up until a month ago worked for StableCorp in the EU. Oh, and there's a picture. Nice. I don't suppose this is a blind date you want to set me up on . . ."

"Sorry, no such luck. Just wanted to make sure he was legit be-fore I took him on as a client."

"If you get him naked, take photos. And if you don't get him naked, bring him around sometime for me to seduce."

Simone laughed. "Of course." As long as she'd known him, Danny had never been on a date, had never had a boyfriend. For all she knew, he was a virgin. She probably would be, too, if every man she met could be a mainland agent sent to kill her.

"He looks legit. Everything checks out."

"Good."

Danny stood and walked over to the printer. "What're you do-ing for him?"

"He wants to explore the city, looking for places where the build-ings have held so that you can go down below the twenty-first floor," Simone said with a grin.

"A tunnel hunter?" Danny said, sounding excited.

Simone arched an eyebrow. "Don't get enthusiastic about the idiot stuff, Danny."

"So I should be like you and save my enthusiasm for cigarettes and silly hats?" he asked with a smirk. He looked down at the printer and tapped it idly with his finger as it oozed plastic into a neat white sheet. Simone folded her arms. Danny was terrible at keeping anything to himself, you just had to wait. He looked up again suddenly. "But it's not so stupid, you know."

"Yes it is," Simone fired back before the last syllable had left his mouth.

"There were all these companies when the waters first started rising," Danny said, waving his hands—a gesture that looked particularly absurd as he was still in costume. "Aquatube, C-Rail, the Waide Corporation—they were all working on building tunnels so they could control trade between here and the mainland. I read all about them when I was coming here. They knew that—"

"I grew up in the city, Danny," Simone interrupted. "If there were some underground pipeline to the mainland, I'd know about it. No one could keep that secret." Danny shrugged and looked back at the printer. It was nearly done, the card baking in a red light. "OK, then, you're the one who literally has information on any server or cloud. Can you genuinely tell me that, with all that information, you believe there is a working pipeline?"

Danny turned one corner of his mouth up as if both amused and sad. "No, of course not. It doesn't exist. But it would be cool, though, wouldn't it? An underwater train?"

"It would make our connection to the mainland much stronger; they'd have more control, could enforce all those federal decency laws no one obeys out here, and find you a lot more easily. Be happy there's no pipeline. And I'll be happy there are people dumb enough to pay me to help them find it anyway."

"Yeah," Danny said, his shoulders slumping. "Still. It would be cool to ride an underwater train. I wonder if it would have windows."

Simone patted him lightly on the back. "I'll take to you the Carnival Ship sometime. They have a little train ride for kids that goes through a tunnel that's also an aquarium—water all around. I rode it once. It was pretty cool."

"How is Peter these days?" Danny asked with a sudden smile. Simone narrowed her eyes. She had, in fact, been on the Carnival Ship with Peter.

"Is that ready yet?" Simone asked, pointing at the IRID in the printer. Danny took it out and fanned it in the air to dry.

"What, we can talk about my stupid excitement over a train, but not your stupid decisions with men?" Simone stayed silent, her arms refolding in fluid motions. "Fine, fine," he said, grinning. He held out the IRID to her. "Here, press down with your thumb so it can get the initial scan." She did so, placing her thumb on the small square next to her face on the card. The scanner on the card lit up for a moment and then buzzed gently. "All done. Here you are, Alexis Foyle, of Maple Leaf Importing. All your data is in order."

"Fantastic," Simone said, standing and taking them.

"What does tunnel hunting have to do with Canadian importing, anyway?" he asked.

"Nothing. Different cases."

"Don't overwork yourself."

"I'll be fine."

"Are you still using your infrared-blocking wallet?" he asked.

"Sure, of course."

"I can feel your real IRID's signature. It must have a hole. You should get a new one if you're going to carry two IRIDs around."

"Thanks. I'll do that when I have a moment. You want to come out with Caroline and me this weekend? I think we're finally trying that VR bowling thing."

"Sure, I'm in. Now scram, I have another client in ten minutes, and I have to check what year her dear departed Grandma Elsie died.

I always forget. Hard to pretend to be a dead woman if you don't know when she died."

Simone smirked. "Some business you got."

"Same as yours, just different wrapping," Danny said with an amused look. "It's why we work so well together."

"Is that why?" Simone asked, raising an eyebrow. "I thought it was because you didn't charge me."

"I'm sure that helps. As do my phenomenally good looks. Keep you coming back for another glance. Got anything else? I don't wanna have to do any work for you in front of Caroline. It weirds her out; she always thinks we're doing something damp and dirty."

"Just keep an eye out for The Blonde, if she pops up anywhere." Simone put her finger to her lips, deciding. "Yeah, and if you could check out the finances of Henry St. Michel and send them to me when you get a second, that could be useful."

Danny put the turban and cape back on as she spoke.

"St. Michel?" he asked.

"Yeah, M-I-C-H-E-L. Saint."

"Funny name for this city," Danny said.

"Funny name for anywhere, these days. Thanks again." They walked back through Danny's inner sanctum to the waiting room, where a young girl with honey-colored curls was waiting, her eyes already wet. Simone turned back to Danny and clasped his hands.

"Oh, thank you," Simone said, in a voice wrought with tears. "Thank you so much, Yanai. You are as great as they say you are."

Danny glared but bowed with a flourish. Simone walked quickly from the room, trying to stifle her snickering.

False IRID in her leaky wallet, Simone strolled the bridges of New York towards St. Michel's place of business. The day was blue, but the clear skies from early morning were clouding over, and the wind was picking up. Still, it was a nice day, and Simone enjoyed the walk, even stopping at one of the cart vendors on the decommissioned tanker *Guandong* for a quick lunch of warm noodles. *Guandong* and the neighboring cruise ship, *Fu*, were what was left of Chinatown. *Fu* was mostly residential, but *Guandong* was filled with carts that sold cheap electronics or fresh noodles or fish caught that morning from the deck. It was hung with red lanterns and streamers and was often crowded. Simone liked that. She ate her noodles on a stool by the cart, surrounded by throngs of strangers, feeling like calm water— invisible and safe.

When she got to Above Water Exports/Imports, it was nearly two, and the skies were steel and chilly. St. Michel's business was operated out of an old masonry building, nearly twenty stories above sea level. He was on the thirty-fourth floor, but thankfully, they had put in a new algae-powered elevator in the building, so Simone didn't have to hike. The offices were marked only by a small plaque. Simone knocked once and went in without an answer. The room was barren: concrete walls, metal desks, one large touchtable in the center of the room, and a few cheap chairs lining the walls. The room was empty except for an older woman leaning over the touchtable, apparently tracking something on a map.

"Yes?" she asked, without looking up. Simone walked up to her.

"My name is Alex Foyle," Simone said, "From Maple Leaf Imports. I was hoping to talk to a Mr. St. Michel?" The woman turned to look at Simone. She was easily eighty and her gray hair was tied back in a tight bun. She was tall and had good posture without looking like a tin soldier. She appraised Simone with the look of someone who hadn't been impressed by anything a young person had done in several decades.

"I'm Ms. Freth," she said, "I'm Mr. St. Michel's partner. What can we do for you?" Her voice was low and rough but had the tone of a woman used to getting what she wanted. She walked to one of the metal desks and opened a drawer to take out a pack of cigarettes and a lighter. Real tobacco cigarettes, Simone noted. Maybe being

LEV AC ROSEN / 37

in importing made them easier to get. She lit one and began to smoke, waiting for Simone.

"We're interested in doing business with you," Simone said carefully. "I was told Mr. St. Michel was the one to talk to about exporting American antiques to Canada."

"He's in the john, you'll have to talk to me."

"Of course, it's just that—"

"I handpicked everything in our inventory and know all our dealers," Ms. Freth interrupted, "so don't think I'm old and absentminded. I started this company with my husband, and I can still remember everything we've ever bought. I have a whole catalogue of our stuff up here," she said, tapping the side of her head and giving Simone a hard look. Simone nodded, accepting.

Ms. Freth sat down at her desk and motioned for Simone to sit opposite her. Simone did so, her eyes scanning the room for the toilets, hoping St. Michel would show himself before she got in over her head.

"We sell to several major furnishing stores in Canada," Simone said, "and several chains. American antiques are going to be the next big thing in Canadian interior design. Some of our stores want actual antiques to sell, but several are also looking for archetypal antiques from which to draw inspiration for products they design themselves for the virtual shops."

"I see," Ms. Freth said, blowing smoke out her nose. "And what furnishings, specifically, are you looking for?"

"One of our clients is most anxious for table lamps," Simone said, "but most of the others are looking for basic furniture sets: couches, chairs, tables, and so on."

From the back of the room came the sound of a door creaking closed and then Henry St. Michel appeared from behind a column, wiping his hands on his pants.

"Henry," Ms. Freth said, "this is Ms . . ."

"Foyle," Simone said, standing.

"She's looking for antique American furniture."

"Ah, good to meet you," Henry said, stepping forward and extending his hand. It was still damp, but Simone shook it anyway, her face a mask of professional friendliness. "Has Lou been helping you?"

"She said she was told to speak to you," Ms. Freth said, "but I talked to her anyway."

"Ah, well, anything you would say to me you can say to Lou, here," Henry said. "She's my partner."

"Right," Simone said. With a flick of her thumb she removed the small bug from her inner sleeve and transferred it to her index finger. "Yours was just the name I was given," she said, gesturing at Henry, her palm up. "I didn't mean to cause any offense." She closed her hands slightly, then opened them again, sending the small bug flying off her finger and landing on Henry's jacket, where it quickly faded into the fabric. It was a good bug, fairly advanced, a clear circle that faded into fabric and then transferred sound up to fifty miles away for forty-eight hours, after which time it would dissolve.

"I'm sure you didn't," Henry said, looking at Ms. Freth.

"No, you didn't," Ms. Freth said. "Now tell me more about what you're looking for. What period antique, exactly?"

"Oh," Simone said, "the 2090s, or thereabouts."

"The nineties?" Ms. Freth said. "There's a style I was hoping wouldn't come back." Simone smiled politely. "Everyone thought it was so cute, wearing rain boots all the time. My husband had a pair—bright blue with ducks all over them. Ridiculous."

"Does he still have them?" Simone asked politely.

"He's dead." A thin curtain of smoke fell from her lips as she said it.

"I'm sorry."

"It's been a few years. But thank you. Still don't know why anyone would want to bring the nineties back. Rubber boots and umbrellas. Chairs made to look like rising waves. It would just be depressing now." She sighed, as if the idea bored her. "Give us your information, and we'll send you what we have on hand, and if you'd like, what we think we can get. Tell us what you want to look at and then we can set up a viewing."

"That would be wonderful," Simone said, as she took out her false IRID and touched her thumb to the thumb-scanner, releasing the information on the infrared chip into the local network. Lou glanced at the screen of her table briefly, then nodded. "Hope to hear from you soon," Simone said standing. She gave them another cheerful look, pivoted, and walked out the door, not wanting to shake Henry's hand again. In the elevator down, she tuned her earpiece to the frequency of the bug she had just planted.

"The nineties?" Lou Freth's voice came in clearly. "I tell you, every time I think of retiring to Canada, they go and do something to make me want to stay right here."

"More business for us, Lou," Henry's voice said. "Don't complain."

A small tone played over the bug's feed, indicating a message in Simone's cloud. Simone set the earpiece to record the feed from the bug and pressed another button. A sensually inhuman voice read her new message aloud to her: "To: Simone Pierce. From: Alejandro de-Costas. Subject: Buildings. Text: It was a pleasure meeting with you today, Ms. Pierce. I look forward to exploring with you. As requested, here are two buildings I would like to examine: The Broecker Building and the Hearst Tower. See you tomorrow."

Simone pressed a button, ending the message dictation. The Broecker Building she knew; it had been one of the last built when they still thought they could re-freeze the polar caps with the Mercury ice and lower the sea level again. Some developers had built a whole bunch of buildings like it in Long Island City, hoping to make the area the new business center of the city and partially succeeding. It was an office building, so getting in would be easy. Getting past the lobby would require some finesse. The Hearst Tower sounded older. She'd have to look it up. But not now. Now she wanted a drink.

It was approaching four, and the wind had picked up, the sky gone pewter. The fog would come down soon. She would find a nearby bar where she could listen to the bug feed and wait until Henry was leaving work. Then she'd follow him again.

THE BAR IN THE Icewater Hotel was clever. The building itself was huge, built in 2045 or so with a giant atrium. Twenty-one stories up, the large hole in the middle of the building that once looked down on the lobby now looked down onto the ocean. And not very far down. It was a clever aesthetic, not unlike having a koi pond in the middle of the room, but less tranquil. The management had opened up the rest of the twenty-first floor, so there was a small desk for a concierge and a very large bar. It was decorated in old-style deco, with rusted bronze finishes and statues of angels. On one side of the bar, a holographic rendition of a singer with long pink hair in a white dress sang in low, romantic tones. Over the bar hung a large, classical-looking painting of a woman in a pink dress sitting at a loom, cutting a piece of thread with her teeth while just beyond the stone wall behind her, men tried to get her attention, holding out flowers and gifts. Simone liked the bar and stopped by whenever she was in the area. It was as good a place as any to wait and listen in on Henry and Lou. She ordered a Manhattan and drank slowly, her earpiece tuned back to the bug.

The conversations at Above Water Exports/Imports were generally pretty dull, Simone discovered over the next few hours, and peppered with inside jokes she didn't understand. Lou seemed to forever play the part of grump, while Henry was her doting, optimistic kid brother. Simone had just begun her second Manhattan when she felt a hand on her back and spun quickly.

"Get your hands off me, you—" She looked up into familiar eyes. "Peter." Lieutenant Peter Weiss smiled at her.

"Hey soldier," he said. "No offense meant, just saying hi." He was handsome, of course, but it was his voice that always sparked the kindling. His mother was Anabel Acevedo, a lounge singer at The Blue Boat—not really famous, but New York famous—and he had her smooth intonations, her lilts and pauses like murmuring waves. His voice was as alluring as the ocean.

"Sorry," she said, reminding herself she was on a case, and she had no time for distractions. "How are you?"

He shrugged and smiled that half-smile, where only one side of his mouth went up. "I'm all right. How about you?"

She shrugged back and took a sip of her drink. Their families had been close, when her family was still around. Both she and Peter had had fathers who were NYPD, but where Peter had followed in his father's footsteps, Simone had skipped over actually becoming a cop and had gone straight to taking over her father's detective agency. They had been childhood friends, then adult friends; then they fell into an inevitable romance that lasted a year and a half. Then she broke his heart—and maybe her own a little, too. She kept doing that for a while, re-breaking them both every few weeks or so, but she hadn't seen him in over a month now.

"What are you doing here?" Simone asked. "Some dry out-of-towner get held up by a sea rat, and you're here to take the statement?"

"Apparent suicide in room 3307."

"Oh. Sorry." Simone turned back to her drink. The ice fell against her lips, bitter and cold. She put the empty glass down.

"I didn't know the guy, nothing to apologize for. How about you? Little early to be on your second."

"You watch me finish my first?"

"Took time to get the nerve up to come over."

"Since when do you lack for nerve?"

"Since you came into the picture."

He smiled, then creased his brow, realizing what he had just said. Then he looked down and ran his hand through his brown curls.

"So," he asked after a beat, as if pretending there hadn't been a moment of unsaid things, "working on a case?"

"Yeah," she said, "can't live off salt."

"Something interesting?" he asked, sitting on the stool next to her.

"Not at the moment," she said with a shrug. In her ear, Lou was complaining about how stingy traders from the EU were and asking Henry to close up. The door slammed, leaving Henry alone. Simone shifted uncomfortably in her seat.

"Anything you can talk about?"

"Usual wife thinks husband is cheating story."

"And do you think he's cheating?"

"I try not to think anything until I know for certain."

He nodded, looking steadily into her eyes. She noticed his chest inflate slightly and knew he was going to start a real conversation. But in her ear, the door slammed again and locked. Henry had left.

"I gotta go," Simone said before Peter could speak.

"Oh," he said, exhaling.

"Case," she said, trying to look disappointed they couldn't talk. "It's walking out the door." Peter turned to the door of the hotel. It was empty. In her ear, Henry was out of the office and walking somewhere already. "Other door," she said. He looked at her as though she were trying to get rid of him. "Really," she said, trying to smile.

"Well, be careful, soldier," he said, standing. "I should get back to the station, anyway. Kluren doesn't like us taking time off to talk to . . ." He let his sentence fade.

"Take care," Simone said, smiling. Peter grinned at her. She didn't know if they should hug, but she didn't have time to find out, so she just nodded and put a hand on his shoulder for a moment before heading for the door. She had a flash of memory to their last time in bed together, the cool roundness of his thighs and the soft pressure of his nose against her neck as he kissed her. Then, her sneaking out in the middle of the night and not returning his calls. It could never have worked, of course. She was right to end it when she did. She missed him. But then she missed a lot of people. One more wasn't going to make much difference.

Outside, the mist had risen up like a soft wall, and the temperature had taken its usual early-evening plummet. The sensors in Simone's trench coat felt this, and the thin gel that lined her coat began warming up, but the initial shock of the cold scattered the little traces of inebriation that had muddled her head.

Henry was nowhere in sight, and there were a few directions he could have gone. If he was going straight home, he would be taking the bridge that went past the cruise ship *Xanadu*, but if he wasn't . . . Following her gut, she took off down the bridge towards downtown, where he had met The Blonde.

The sun had started to set, and the fog was getting heavier. Rose and gray mixed as darkness overtook the city. The buildings grew harder to see, but you could always hear the water rushing underfoot. She walked quickly, hoping Henry would come into sight through the mist. She should have hit him with a tracker, too, but then she would have needed to actually hide the bug on his jacket and get it back later. Or hit him with two dissolving bugs. She caught sight of a yellow jacket like the one he'd been wearing last night and took off after it. She was only a few steps behind him, but in the fog, no one would notice a tail. To make sure it was him, she coughed loudly. The cough echoed in her ear. She fell back a little, now that she'd found him. He walked down small winding backway bridges, where there were few people around. Some didn't have banisters, and the waves splashed over them onto her feet. She would be easier to notice now, so she hung back even more, speeding up occasionally to get a look at him, then falling back again.

She couldn't tell where he was heading. That worried her. They seemed to be moving farther and farther from central downtown, heading west and north. New York was always dangerous, but the more central areas of the city at least played at being civilized. The people who lived out in West Midtown were people who couldn't pretend anymore: MouthFoamers who would do anything for a fix when they weren't catatonic on a bridge; people who had given up everything but their own lives, hoping someone else would take them; people who had come to the city looking for an escape but found themselves completely trapped, clawing at anything they thought might offer some form of release. She could handle herself out here, but she didn't think Henry could, so the ease with which he walked felt wrong. She didn't think it was a trap—though that was always a possibility—but she sensed something off. She checked the small pistol inside her boot, making sure it was easy to reach.

Henry stopped. She heard his footsteps fall silent on her earpiece. His breathing seemed a little heavier, too. Wherever he was, it was where he was going to stay. She looked ahead. A short building, barely a full story above water, was in front of her. She couldn't see anywhere else he could be waiting. She quietly walked closer until she got a better read on the building. There was a large hole in the wall leading in and another hole at the other end. The building itself seemed to have been totally cleared out—just bare concrete walls and floor and fluorescent lighting making the place glow. No shadows. Nowhere to hide. A good place to meet someone you didn't totally trust. A bad place for Simone to eavesdrop.

She looked around for someplace higher, where she could see who came and went. She toyed with the idea of climbing to the top of the building itself, but there was no fire escape, and it would have been a noisy undertaking. She settled for a bridge a little ways away, but higher up. It faced the side of the building. She'd be able to see who came and went but not what happened inside.

She took her camera out again, watched the fog, and listened to Henry's heavy breathing in her ear. Someone else approached the building. All Simone could make out was a shadow, a hat, and a trench coat. She took some photos anyway, hoping she could enhance them later. Henry's voice came in clear on her earpiece.

"Why are *you* here?" he asked. Apparently, this wasn't the person he was waiting for. There was a long pause; she couldn't hear the other person's voice. "Yes," Henry said, "I did. You didn't care about it." Damn. Still nothing but Henry's voice. "Not yet." The other person must have been standing far away or talking softly—like he knew he was being observed. "No, I won't. I need it."

Then, all at once, the sound of Henry yelling "what?" and a gunshot. Simone ran for the building. Too fast—she slipped on a wet plank of the bridge and went skidding towards the edge. No railings. Once she hit the water, she'd be dead. She'd be sucked under by currents or thrown into underwater debris. She grabbed for the space between the slats, and caught one, but she was already dangling over the water, her toes just touching the surface, her chin and neck just barely higher than the bridge. Splinters dug into her fingers, and she could feel blood making her skin slippery. She took a deep breath. She wasn't falling anymore—not until her fingers slipped off—but a wrong move and the wood she clung to could snap off. She turned her head towards the building anyway. A shadow was leaving the building from the opposite exit, carrying something large. Carefully, she clawed her way back onto the bridge as quickly as she could, the rough wood gouging into her palms over and over. She pulled slowly, trying to test each moment of pressure so nothing cracked or snapped. It took far longer than she wanted, but soon she was back on the bridge. There was no time to catch her breath, to dwell on her near-death plunge, to pluck the splinters from her bloodied hands. She ran down the bridge and around another, heading for the building. The bug in her ear fizzled out into static. She reached the room, her heart pounding, and stepped slowly inside.

In the center of the room under the bright lights was a pool of blood, slowly creeping out towards the edges of the room.

FOUR

—

WHERE WAS THE BODY? Was there a body? Simone went out the opposite exit, careful not to step in the blood. No one in sight. She checked the water. It was dark now, and the fog was heavy, making it hard to tell, but she couldn't see anything besides a single plastic bag, a few feet below her like a boil on the water's skin. Gunshot, blood, no body.

Simone saw two possibilities: Someone was injured, but everyone had escaped, or someone was dead, and his body was bobbing somewhere just out of sight. She could hear her father's voice in her head, his old lessons drilled into her, telling her she couldn't be certain of anything.

She stared at the pool of blood as the light outside disappeared completely and the waves grew louder, angry. She could call the police, but she wasn't sure what to tell them, and they would definitely screw up her investigation. Kluren would see to that. She could call Peter. But he was a Boy Scout, he'd call it in. Instead, she called Linnea. Voicemail.

"Linnea, it's Simone Pierce. Please call me back as soon as you get this. Thanks."

Simone crouched down in front of the blood and took out a small piece of cotton from her pocket. She dabbed it in the blood until it was nearly red all over, then took out a metal vial and stuffed the cotton inside. She locked the vial and looked down at the top. The screen there was blank for a long moment. She felt the wind pick up and shivered. The vial finally beeped and Simone read, "O positive, male." Simone couldn't remember Henry's blood type, but O positive was common, and unhelpful. Making a mental note of the location, she headed out the way she'd come, winding slowly east over bridges, towards home. The wind blew her coat up around her, spraying her damp in the darkness.

At home she changed out of her wet things and toweled off her skin. She sent out Henry's photo to Danny and other contacts, asking them to keep an eye out. She had no other moves until Linnea called her back to say her husband was alive, or Henry's face showed up on the recycling website. She confirmed Henry's blood type was O positive. It didn't tell her anything. And the photos she'd taken of the shadow approaching the building were just blurs, even enhanced with the night filter.

Simone had seen many deaths in her years as a PI and had long ago learned to compartmentalize. The death of her client's husband was a mystery to be solved, not a loss to be mourned. She leaned back in her chair, put her feet on the desk, and tried calling Linnea again. Voicemail. Simone left another message. She stretched her arms out behind her head. A message from Danny came in on her touchdesk. It was a video with a note attached: "Is this her on the right?"

The video was taken off a security cam, but high quality, a clear image panning back and forth. It was the interior of Delmonico's, all dark-green carpets, brown leather, and dim chandeliers. Caroline had taken Simone there after the first big case she'd done for her. It was out of Simone's price range to even stop in there for a drink unless someone else was picking up the tab.

On the right side of the image, panning in and out of view, was a woman with blonde hair to just above her shoulders sitting alone at a table. But it was just the back of her head. Simone wasn't sure it was The Blonde, instead of a blonde. But she trusted Danny and kept her eyes on her and, sure enough, when she next panned into view, she stood and shook hands with another woman who had just walked over to the table. In profile, it was clearly The Blonde. She was shaking hands with a tall black woman in a sapphire-blue cape coat and a skirt to just below the knee. Simone couldn't make out her face before the camera panned away, though she had a guess. When the camera panned back, her guess was confirmed: Anika Bainbridge was sitting at the table.

She sent a thank-you back to Danny and then dialed up Anika. Straight to voicemail. Not unexpected. As a vice-president of Belleau, the second largest commercial cosmetics company in the world, she was a busy woman. Technically she oversaw foreign sales (which were most sales), but the city was considered outside the mainland, and Anika was a native New Yorker, so she'd set up her offices here. She'd once told Simone she went to the mainland only as long as she needed to. She didn't intend to live anywhere else again. But she was always flying around—the mainland, the EU, Africa—doing whatever it was that she did. Simone wasn't totally sure. But she had hired Simone for some corporate espionage on several occasions and paid well. Simone liked her. She was cold but sensible, and Simone liked to think that if she'd been more ambitious, she might have ended up like Anika. She wasn't sure Anika felt the same way—they'd never clicked, gone out for drinks or anything—but Simone thought maybe that was just because she had never asked.

Simone had never read Anika as the violent type, though. She'd always seemed to find violence distasteful; if she couldn't achieve what she wanted through scheming alone, she'd just walk away. But maybe Simone was wrong about that.

"Hi, Anika," Simone said into the voicemail. "It's Simone Pierce. I was hoping you could give me a call sometime soon. I have something I'd like to ask you. Thanks." Keep it vague. Hopefully Anika would call back. She was the closest thing Simone had to a lead on any of this.

There wasn't anything to do now, unless she wanted to call the cops. And she didn't. So she lit a cigarette and smoked it near the window, looking out at the darkness punctuated only by the sickly green of algae generators and their paler reflections, rippling as the water breathed. Then she turned to her other case: babysitting.

Two buildings: The Broecker Building and the Hearst Tower. Simone brought up all the intel she had on her touchdesk about each of them. The Broecker Building was finished just before the water reached the streets, built with the city's flooding in mind. An adjustable system with separated frames meant it was one of the few buildings with an elevator that never flooded or stalled, and the Glassteel and titanium carbon alloy frame had held, showing few signs of corrosion. It was a huge glass column of a thing, bulletproof and wave-proof, with a special repair team on-site daily, and it housed several of the more important businesses in the city, mostly ad agencies. They loved the city, as it was the one place left where ads could be suggestive or even lewd. There were a lot of accounting firms, too, because people still paid taxes, if they wanted to collect benefits. Companies with branches on the mainland paid because the mainland would use any excuse to shut them down, if they saw money in it.

So the Broecker was suits and probably fairly easy to break into. Make an appointment somewhere. Duck down a stairwell instead.

The Hearst Tower posed a larger problem. A much older building in midtown, retrofitted well enough to survive the water, it was privately owned. Sold a year before the water hit street level (and so at a low price), it had traded hands over the years and was now in the possession of Ned Sorenson, a Boro-Baptist minister and the church's head missionary to New York. The mainland had several

large branches of Christianity, but Boro-Baptism was the largest. Their ministers weren't just religious figures, but also political
ones. The current president, and the past several before him, were
all Boro-Baptists. The sect had been founded by a Baptist minister
who felt the rest of the conservative branches of Christianity weren't
responding to the rising waters seriously enough and started preach-
ing against them from his pulpit in the town of Boro, North
Dakota. It painted itself a religion of values and protection in this,
the time of the second flood. The religion that could get people
through. And people believed it, or pretended to. Simone, like most
New Yorkers, thought all religions were crap, and Boro-Baptism
was just the latest name for a generations-old addiction to fear and
an overwhelming hope that someone else could save you. But Boro-
Baptism had stalked further ahead than its antediluvian predeces-
sors, and the chaos of the flood and the loss of life that followed had
fed it like a fat toad. Pastor Sorenson was like the emissary from the
mainland: ambassador, spy, maybe even fist. Whatever you wanted
to call him, he was someone with lots of powerful connections.
Someone you did not want to get mixed up with. Getting into his
building would be much harder.

Simone glanced at the clock. Barely eight. She told the touchdesk to call Caroline.

"Do you want to get something to eat?" Caroline asked after a
ring.

"Sure," Simone said.

"I'm still at work, if you'd believe it."

"Well, I'm calling with a work-related question, so that's fine by
me." Simone stared down at the grayed-out photos of The Blonde,
still a small digital pile in the corner of the touchdesk.

"When I saw it was you calling, I picked up. I could have ignored
it. If I knew it was work-related, I would have."

"I'll let you pick the restaurant."

"Deal. Question?"

"One of the buildings deCostas wants to get into is the Hearst Tower."

"Why does that sound familiar?" Simone could hear Caroline's fingers tapping on her own desk, writing something else as she spoke.

"Owned by one Ned Sorenson."

"Oh, that's where Sorenson keeps his cult!" The sound of Caroline's typing stopped for a moment, then restarted.

"I don't think it's a cult if it's the majority."

"It's New York. He's not the majority. We heathens are the majority."

"Heathens?"

"Sorenson's favorite word. He's not a bad guy, aside from the religion."

"So, any thoughts on getting into the Tower? I was thinking we could go as curious potential converts—"

"No. Just ask him."

Simone stretched her legs out and put them up on the desk. "Really?"

"Tell him you're deCostas' personal assistant trying to set up an inspection to see the stairwell, see that the water is there. Drop my name, if you'd like. Don't mention the detective thing. There isn't going to be a dry stairwell, so Sorenson won't mind you seeing it."

"That easy?"

"He's really an okay guy. You'll probably get preached at a little. Tell him you're an occasional churchgoer. He knows that's the best they can hope for out here. Pick a church, though, he'll ask you which one."

"Great. I thought this one would be hard."

"Not with me on your side."

"Just don't tell deCostas. I don't want him figuring out he didn't need me for this."

"Fair deal. I'm putting on my jacket now. Meet me at Rosie's in twenty?" Simone sighed. Rosie's was a greasy diner Caroline loved and Simone tolerated. "I believe my information has earned me the right to a bloodstained meal of my choosing."

"Fair enough. I could do with a burger."

"See you in twenty."

She went back to the front office and began getting her coat on as she called deCostas.

"Hello, Ms. Pierce," deCostas purred.

"I got your message. I think I should be able to get us into the buildings tomorrow. I need to make some appointments for both of them, though, so I'll send you the exact time once I've made them. Don't be late."

"Thank you, that's very good news."

"They're both fairly conservative, so dress appropriately."

"What is appropriately?"

There was a pause as Simone finished shrugging her coat on and considered his question.

"Don't show too much cleavage," she said and hung up.

ONCE A LARGE YACHT, probably of serious luxury, Rosie's had been transformed into something approximating a nostalgic diner. The yacht was painted in green-and-white checks, which matched the plastic tablecloths inside, and a large neon sign hung over the sliding glass doors that worked as an entrance. On deck, there were some tables and chairs, but it was cool out, and most people were eating inside. It was a wide open space, with booths and servers who wore sailor hats. One of them recognized Simone and pointed her towards Caroline, already at a booth and halfway done with her mug of beer, sipping the rest through a straw.

Simone sat down, and Caroline regarded her with tired eyes.

"Rough day?" Simone asked with a half-smile.

"It started when some mainland yokel who'd won a decommissioned cruise ship in some auction sailed it into the city at about four this morning," she said. She finished the rest of her beer, the straw sucking dryly at the bottom of her glass. The server, with perfect timing, put down another in front of her, plus one for Simone, and a pair of menus. Simone glanced at hers but let Caroline continue. "He figured he was just going to anchor it in the city and start renting out rooms, like we're a city of flotsam. Who does that?" Caroline put her mug down hard on the table, in emphasis, then immediately picked it up again and took a long drink. Simone smirked. Mainlanders tried setting up shop once every other month or so, as if they didn't think New York was still a city, and they could just set up a boat, charge rent, and make a fortune. They didn't realize they needed an anchor permit, leasing contracts, inspections, and all the stuff that went along with owning real estate in any other city.

"Four a.m.," Caroline repeated. "I was paged to the office at ten after, got there at four thirty. After we dealt with him, and getting his boat back outside city limits where it belonged, and talking with all the residents whose homes his boat had rammed into, it was already six thirty, so I stayed. Then I had to deal with your boy, who I thought I was done with." Caroline glared at Simone over the beer.

"My boy?"

"deCostas. He's not being backed by just his university— apparently the EU, private investors, and some companies are funding part of it as well. He didn't mention that. But he headed over to the City Archives when they opened at eight and tried to look at all the city building records. From forever."

"And Tharp didn't bond with him as one of his own?" The head archivist, Martin Tharp, was a knot of conspiracy theories, hometown pride, and xenophobia, all in a shape and demeanor most closely resembling a deflated balloon. He was the president of several organizations, including the New York Society of Underwater Cartographers—essentially a club of pearl divers like deCostas. He'd written papers on the plausibility of the pipeline in the society newsletter. He was, in Simone's opinion, King of the Pearl Divers—a title only earned by a steadfast ability to speak so loudly that he could hear no one else. Which is probably why Caroline liked to keep him in the archives, where his combination of inflated ego and paranoia were kept at bay by the rows and rows of old papers and lack of people.

"No, the hatred of outsiders won. I'd sent him a message saying deCostas was legit, but good ol' Tharp has decided that deCostas, being a foreigner and with backing from a foreign government, is probably doing research to sell information to evangelical terrorists back on the mainland who want to sink the city for good." Caroline rolled her eyes and shook her head. Simone tried to hold it back but couldn't help firing off a gunshot of laughter. That sounded about right for Tharp. Caroline sighed. "And I have some crap family stuff to take care of while my folks are out of town, as my father keeps reminding me." Caroline put her forehead on the table and sighed again. Simone took the opportunity to read the menu and think about what she wanted to eat. "I know you're reading the menu," Caroline said into the table. "You should be empathizing with my pain."

"I am," Simone said. "But I'm also looking at the menu. I'm a multitasker."

"If you were a real friend, you'd stroke my hair and tell me that my hard work will not go unappreciated."

"Your hard work will not go unappreciated, and if I tried to touch your hair, you'd snap my fingers off. How about we order and then you can tell me more about your horrible day?"

Caroline lifted her head and gave a slight nod, and they spent a few minutes in silence considering their menus. They had beef here, but it was cheap, from the farm ships far uptown: big decommissioned ships where the cows would sleep below deck at night and then come up during the day, lowing at each other across the deck. Sometimes Simone liked to go watch the cows, who stared back at her and the city off the side of their boats, chewing their kelp, its long strands falling from their mouths like a MouthFoamer's saliva. There was something calming about them and their vacant gaze at the city, as if they had accepted their lot, and could accept yours, too. Simone thought they tasted okay but weren't nearly as good as the imported mainland stuff.

After they'd ordered and Caroline was onto her third beer, she continued with her woes: the water-taxi drivers were threatening a strike, plans for the main bridge over the Upper East Side were not coming together, and a reporter had called asking if it was true that the mayor's wife regularly consulted a psychic to check on her husband's extramarital affairs. By the time she finished, the food arrived, and Simone was picking at her fries.

"How about *your* day?" Caroline asked. Simone held her face carefully blank. She liked Caroline, considered her her best friend, if such a thing existed after age eleven, but Simone dealt in secrets, and Caroline was still deputy mayor, and she'd have to report something if Simone mentioned gunshots and blood. That might mean Linnea would hear from the police, instead of Simone, and that might mean Simone wouldn't get paid. She repressed the urge to tap her earpiece to see if she had any messages, but Caroline would see, and her phone had been with her since she called Linnea. She just needed Linnea to call her back. So in answer to Caroline she just shrugged and let out a long sigh.

"The usual," she said.

"Well, thanks for letting me rant, anyway. And of course, tell anyone any of this and no one will find you till you bob to the surface."

"Of course," Simone said. "I did bump into Peter today. But it was for five minutes."

"Fun," Caroline said dryly. "He get that puppy dog look?"

"Little bit. Had to brush him off to tail a guy, though."

"Feel bad about it?"

"Maybe."

"Well, don't bother. You ended it for a good reason, and you've finally stopped having those nights where you forgot that. Besides, now you're escorting deCostas around. That seems like more fun."

"Could be," Simone said, eating another fry and thinking of de-Costas' ass.

"Should be," Caroline said. She bit into her burger. "So what is the usual with you these days, anyway? Are you still working cases like the ones I used to hire you for?"

"Like the Meers case?" Simone asked. "Yeah, this could be like the Meers case, I guess—though I doubt I can get a confession right now."

Caroline sighed and took a long drink through her straw. Then she looked up and frowned. "Now, before I say this," she said, "you need to understand something."

"Mm?" Simone raised her eyebrows.

"I'm not just a pretty face," Caroline said in a low monotone.

"No?" Simone bit into another fry.

"No. I speak Korean, Mandarin, and every language used in the EU. I have a PhD in political science. From Oxford."

"I've seen the diploma," Simone nodded.

"So you understand, I'm very smart."

"OK," Simone said, smirking.

"Brilliant, some would say."

"I believe you."

"You've seen the evidence. So I need you to remember that when I tell you this . . ."

Simone nodded, but Caroline stopped speaking and took another strawful of beer. Then she looked back up at Simone, the closest thing to ashamed Simone had ever seen her. "I still don't understand the Meers case."

Simone stared at Caroline for a long while, then took a long drink and stared again.

"It was the first case you hired me on," she said, finally.

"Yeah."

"You were there when I got Meers to confess."

"Oh yeah, I understand he did it. I just don't know how you knew he would confess so quickly. I'd expected us to need mountains of evidence and copies of documents and all that. You just accused him, and he caved. How did you do that? Was there a trick I didn't understand? And more importantly, can you teach it to me so I can use it on the various people I have to deal with all day? I'd have so much more free time if people would just admit they're idiots."

Simone smiled. The Meers case had been a few years back, right after she and Caroline had settled into a friendship. Dustin Meers had been sent by the mainland government to retrieve "lost American treasures" for the mainland museums. "American treasures" meant art and artifacts that had been saved or taken during the looting. The problem was, most of this art was already in the city's remaining museums—and there were a few: The American Museum of Natural History was a huge freighter, the giant Apatosaurus skeleton crowning the bow; the Met operated out of four stories of an old, seashell-colored building; and the Guggenheim was on a decommissioned oil tanker, completely altered with strips of metal curved around in an attempt to recreate the original building's shape, but which had ended up becoming a rusted shadow of its former glory, forever crusting over with moss and barnacles no matter how often it was cleaned.

But the mainland hadn't shown much interest in the museums before Dustin Meers. Caroline theorized at the time that their interest developed because the world had stabilized and people had become used to living on the water. The decades since the flood had been all about learning to live again, about making technology that worked in the wet and salt, and the world had done that. Now, the mainland wanted to get back to restoring America's glory, and that apparently meant art. And New York was where they'd kept the good stuff. So they dispatched Meers to find some of that good stuff from the flooded city, buy it, and send it home where it would be appreciated by "true" American citizens.

Simone had gotten the call from Caroline minutes after Meers had left the mayor's office the first time. She didn't trust him, she told Simone, and since she knew Simone and trusted her, hiring her to find out if Meers was on the level seemed like a good investment. It wasn't that Caroline doubted he was official; she'd seen the paperwork and gotten messages and calls confirming he was there for what he said he was there for. But Caroline had good instincts, and she didn't like him.

It had been a fairly long case. Simone had gotten herself hired as part of Meers' small staff, working as a secretary to one of his "scouts"—the three people he'd hired to find art and confirm it was pre-flood. It wasn't as close as she would have liked, but it gave her access to the small office he'd set up. Once everyone had gone home, she'd call Caroline over, and together they'd dig through files. Caroline had insisted on being part of the investigation, which Simone hadn't minded. She understood the bureaucracy in the papers better than Simone did. But for the first month, they found nothing incriminating. True, Meers hadn't bought any art to send back to the mainland yet, but he hadn't been stealing art, or embezzling, either. He just didn't seem to be very good at his job.

"Okay," Simone said. "So a month and a half in, he bought his first painting, something the Guggenheim had but wasn't displaying. And he sent out a press release showing how the mainland was taking back lost treasures and what a boon it was for Boro-Baptism and everything."

"I remember. He used the phrase 'momentous undertaking' six times on one page."

"But the shipping crate that he sent back to the mainland was ten times larger than the piece itself. I filled out the manifest."

"Well, sure, it needed to be packed."

"Not *that* much. Even with all the packaging and foam and what-ever, it was too big and too heavy."

"That's how you knew he was smuggling. I get that."

"That and the amount of porn on his touchdesk."

Caroline barked a laugh. "What did that have to do with any-thing? I mean, it was funny. What was that one site he loved . . . GMILFs and their Doggy Boys?"

"GrandmasNaughtyDogTraining.com," Simone said, laughing with Caroline and remembering their mutual horror and amusement at finding the site on Meers' touchdesk.

"It was disgusting," Caroline said, the laughter dying down. "But what did that have to do with the smuggling?"

"It was a specific fetish. People with fetishes that specific often seek out others with similar fetishes—especially on the mainland, where all pornography is strictly illegal. If you want to find some-thing, you have to find the person who has it. That, combined with the budget for ink that the foundation was running up . . ."

"He was printing out Internet porn and shipping it back home to friends on the mainland?" Caroline asked. "I thought he was smug-gling other art, or maybe documents he'd compiled on the mayor."

"No," Simone said, "porn. Weird porn. That's why he was so quick to confess. Remember how I phrased it when I asked him if he was smuggling?"

"You called the art 'media,'" Caroline said, nodding.

"I said, 'You're using the art shipments to smuggle additional me-dia to the mainland. What that media is, we won't pry into if you confess now.'"

"He was embarrassed."

"You'd be amazed how many criminals are. It's the shameless ones you have to look out for."

Caroline shook her head. "So, do you think he found himself a grandma to punish him?" she asked after a moment, and the two of them burst out laughing again. The laughter faded into more stories and talk until it was late. They paid the bill and left, Caroline catching a taxi and wishing Simone good luck with Sorenson the next day.

At home, Henry's face still hadn't shown up on the recycling web page. Simone tapped her fingers on her desk and pursed her lips. Maybe it wasn't a murder. Maybe it wasn't Henry's blood. She stood, looking forward to sleep, but her earpiece buzzed. The ID said it was a call from Belleau Cosmetics. Probably Anika, though Simone couldn't be sure. Could be her secretary. Anika probably made her secretary stay as late as she did.

"Hello," Simone answered.

"Are you at home?" Anika asked. She had a deep voice that was smooth but unvaried. A concrete slab wrapped in velvet.

"Yeah," Simone said.

"Put me on vid," Anika said. Simone put her earpiece on the desk, and an image of Anika at her desk popped up. Anika always wanted to talk on vid, though Simone was never sure why. Her eyes always wandered from one document to another, and she was constantly rearranging things. She only sometimes looked up at the screen. Maybe she just wanted to advertise her company's products, which, Simone granted, were beautifully displayed on Anika's face.

"So," Anika said, "I think I have something I could use you for. A few experimental samples went missing from one of the labs here in the city. I was going to just ask security to handle it, but then you called, and I think I can justify that expense."

"What are you talking about?" Simone asked, leaning back in her chair. She put her feet up, away from the camera so it wouldn't block Anika's view.

Anika looked up from something she was reading off her desk and furrowed her brow at Simone.

"You called me," she said. "For work, I assume."

"Oh," Simone said. "No. Thank you, but that's not why I called."

Anika raised an eyebrow and folded her arms over her desk. She was wearing a blouse buttoned to the top button. Her wardrobe always followed mainland decency laws, but somehow, it always looked illegal on her.

"So what did you call about?"

"You came up in the course of an investigation. I was hoping you could help me."

Anika leaned back, studying Simone. "What do you need?"

"You met with a blonde woman at Delmonico's recently. I was hoping you could tell me why."

"That?" Anika shook her head. "That was total nonsense." She unfolded her arms and started reading something off her desk again. "If your case has anything to do with that, it's a dud." The thing about Anika's wandering eyes was that it made it hard for Simone to tell if she was lying.

"Humor me," Simone said.

"I really can't," Anika said. She glanced up. "Have you tried our new fall line, by the way? We have this new lipstick that would look great on you."

"The Blonde?" Simone asked, taking her feet down from the desk.

"I only took the meeting because Darren Keep asked me to," Anika said. Darren Keep was the president of Belleau. "He wanted me to take the meeting, give him my thoughts. My thoughts were that that woman was peddling bullshit. I told him as much. That was it."

"What exactly was she peddling?" Simone asked.

"I can't tell you that," Anika said, as though it were obvious.

"Why not?"

"It's a company meeting—therefore, it's a company secret."

"I'll sign a nondisclosure form, if you want," Simone said, but she slumped her shoulders back. Anika was all business all the time. She could see where this was going.

"I appreciate it, but still no. I'd have to have lawyers draw up the form, which means Darren would see it and ask why and I'd have to tell him it was because a private investigator was asking questions and I thought it would be okay to answer them. Sorry, Simone."

"C'mon, Anika. I've done some work for you. You know you can trust me."

"You've done great work for us," Anika said, looking right at Simone. "But right now, you're doing work for someone else."

"Can you at least tell me her name?"

"Honestly?" Anika said with a shrug. "I don't remember it. I'm telling you, Simone—she's not worth it. If she doesn't know she's peddling pure bullshit, then she's either an idiot or insane. It's not worth your time."

"Do you know Henry St. Michel?" Simone asked.

"No—should I?" Anika asked.

"No. Just . . . maybe he was buying this bullshit."

"Then I don't want to know him. I don't have time for stupid people, Simone. And you shouldn't waste yours on them, either. Anyway, I'm going to send you our fall sampler. Just pop the pack in your 3D printer and pick the sunset pearl lipstick. Trust me, you'll love it." She glanced up and away. "I have to go. Think about the lab job? Get back to me."

The screen went dark before Simone could answer. Simone leaned back, putting her hands behind her head. So The Blonde was selling something. Probably not women, if she thought Anika would buy. But what would you try to sell to both an export/import guy and a makeup VP? And why would it be worth firing bullets over to Henry, but not to Anika? Simone rubbed the back of her neck and shook her head. She didn't know enough yet.

SHE MET DECOSTAS AT the Broecker Building the next morning. As the building had been in Queens, the walk was across several ships floating over what was once the East River. Those ships now made up Little India, and the smell of frying pakoras and samosas from the food carts wafted on the early wind towards her. It smelled like smoke and spice.

She was wearing a suit and tie under her trench coat and carried her father's briefcase. She had made a ten-thirty appointment with a bank manager, saying she wanted to offer him corporate espionage services, but she had no intention of keeping it. When deCostas showed up, he was in a shabby brown suit, with a loose tie. Simone tightened his tie without saying anything, then walked into the building. Security men were posted at the elevator banks and behind the desks. Most of the businesses in the Broecker Building had branches on the mainland or the EU, but a New York branch was still important because of its lax enforcement of inconvenient laws, like the Tithe Rule or the Modesty Codes. When the water had first hit the streets, big business had started to flee the city, but seeing how many people stayed, they had come back. The Broecker Building welcomed them. The twenty-first floor had been expeditiously repurposed into a lobby after the waters rose, with working elevators, chic leather sofas, and a fully 3D directory server: a glowing woman made of holographic crystal who told you what floor each company was on.

Simone marched ahead of deCostas to the security desk and smiled, pushing her hair behind her ear so her face was clear. She told the security guard whom she had an appointment with, then showed her IRID and thumbscanned it to confirm her identity and motioned deCostas to do likewise. She was rewarded with two visitor's badges, one of which she handed to deCostas before leading him through the guard posts to the elevator banks. She waited until there was an empty elevator before boarding, then exited at the twenty-second floor. She smiled at deCostas, who still had said nothing, just followed her. She nodded down one of the hallways, and while they were walking, dialed the corporate account on her earpiece and spoke in a frantic tone when the secretary picked up.

"I'm so sorry," she told the secretary, "we were coming up in the elevator when we received a message that there's an emergency back at HQ. We're leaving now, but I'll reschedule when I'm back at the office."

She found the door to the stairwell as she hung up.

"Now it's your game," she told deCostas.

"I was wondering if I would be allowed to speak."

"I never said you couldn't speak."

"You didn't give me a chance," he said, walking downstairs. "I had plans to be charming."

"I had plans to get the job done. That's what you're paying me for, isn't it? And," she said, motioning down at where the water lapped at the stairs, "I've done it."

"Yes you have," he said, grinning at her. "But think of the fun we could have had in the elevator if I had thought I was allowed to talk."

Simone raised an eyebrow at him but grinned when he turned away towards the water. It was a large white stairwell, and the water seemed clearer here, a deep blue, swaying against the stairs and walls. DeCostas took a small metal marble out of his jacket pocket and dropped it into the water. It sank silently down the stairs. Then he turned on his wristpiece and began taking notes.

"What was that?" Simone asked.

"Depth measurement," he said, still looking at the water. "I have the monitor back at the hotel. It keeps track of the water pressure on the device so I know how deep it went. Stairwells are more free from debris, so they may be able to get clear readings."

"Think there are secret air pockets?" She was leaning back against the wall, her arms crossed. He turned around and shrugged.

"I didn't think that would be so fast. Are we ready for the next one yet?"

"Next one knows we're coming. He's given us special permission to see the stairwell, but you have to be on your best behavior."

"I thought I was."

"You smile too much to be on your best behavior." Simone headed for the door, deCostas following. No one raised an eyebrow as they handed their passes back and left the building.

"Who is it who runs this building?"

"Pastor Sorenson. It's the Boro-Baptism missionary. Like a cult and an embassy all rolled into one."

"He knows we're coming?" deCostas asked, trailing a little behind her as she walked towards a water-taxi stand. There were a few taxis lined up. It used to be that the taxis would just roam the city, waiting for someone to stick their hand off a bridge or whistle, but people fell off doing that more often than anyone wanted to admit, and half the time the drivers never saw them. So they put in stands—places where the taxis lined up to grab customers and places you could ask to be taken to, if you weren't quite sure of the address you were going to or didn't want to say it aloud. Generally, New York was still a walking city, and Simone had the legs to prove it, but the taxis were nice to have around. Especially if you had to get across the city and your client was footing the bill.

"I called this morning, said I was your assistant, asked if we could examine the stairwells as part of a study involving water depth. Didn't get more specific than that, but they okayed it. Keep in mind this is a church. Also a corporation, but mostly a church. Run by someone with powerful ties to the mainland."

She stepped into a waiting water-taxi and gave the driver the address of the taxi stand closest to the church. Like most taxis, it was a small solar motorboat with room for about four, plus the driver. It was painted yellow but had faded greenish.

"What does that mean?" deCostas asked. "Should I cross myself when we enter?"

"No," Simone sighed, "just be respectful."

"Did I do something to make you think I wouldn't be?"

The water sprayed them as they cut through it; the boat had a windshield but no roof—it was too small for that. Some fancier new models had little tarps over them, but Simone always thought those smelled like cheap plastic, and, besides, it was New York. Everyone was going to get wet.

"Most New Yorkers aren't very respectful of Boro-Baptists," she said to deCostas, leaning back in her seat. "It's sort of a joke. I doubt we'll talk to anyone besides a secretary, but if we do meet a pastor or something, just nod politely and pretend you believe in Jesus."

"I do believe in Jesus."

Simone gave him a sharp look to see if he was joking. She didn't think he was. Even the driver turned around for a moment before realizing it was none of his business.

"Well, I guess it's just as plausible as no water below the twenty-first floor," Simone said after a moment.

deCostas said nothing to this, and they finished their ride in silence, aside from the toddler wail of the motor and the sound of water being sliced like torn plastic. They stopped a bridge down from their destination, and Simone climbed out, leaving deCostas to pay the driver. She started walking, knowing he could catch up. The Hearst Tower had been retrofitted and painted in Glassteel about twenty years before the water hit the streets. It was a tall, mathematical building, all mirrors and triangles. The doors were once windows in a slightly indented section of the building, and they were spread wide open. A large cross hung over the doors. It was just on the edge of the bad part of town—west, but not too far west. The tall, needle-like buildings just down the bridge were bustling condos, but in the other direction was a trashed-looking yacht. The church was right on the border. Simone frowned to herself, then put on a ruthless smile and stepped forward.

The interior was clearly renovated post-flood. A wide room greeted them, carved from sunlight and heavy paneled wood, giving it a dark but airy feeling. Paintings of Bible stories hung behind a wooden desk, next to another cross. In the far corner was a bench that resembled an old wooden pew. A woman was sitting on the bench, legs crossed, a digital news page in front of her face. The legs seemed oddly familiar, but before Simone had time to give the woman a once-over, a secretary dressed in a modest skirt and long-sleeved jacket stood up, her face all bright hopefulness. "Hello, welcome to the Mission. How can I help you?"

"Hello, my name is Simone Pierce, and this is Alejandro deCostas. I called this morning about stopping by to see the stairwells?"

"Oh, of course!" the woman said, standing up. "It's exciting. You know, I've never seen the stairwells myself. I just use the elevator." She laughed a little and Simone forced a smile. "Let me just call Pastor Sorenson, and he can take us all over there."

"Pastor Sorenson?" Simone asked. She knew that he would have to approve their entry into the stairwell, but she didn't think he'd be showing it to them personally. He was too important for that.

"Oh yes," the secretary said, "he's eager to meet you." She pressed a button on her headset. "Ms. Pierce and Mr. deCostas are here," she said. "Of course, we'll wait right here for you." She pressed her headset again and looked at Simone. "He'll be right down. Would you like a pamphlet to read in the meanwhile?" She handed Simone a rectangle of blank white paper which shifted the moment Simone touched it, raising embossed letters telling her that now was the best time to accept Jesus. She ran her hand over it, and the embossing scattered under her fingers like ripples. Then it popped up again: new words, same message. It was a nice piece of work, probably from Brazil, or somewhere else in South America. The mainland didn't make stuff like this; they specialized in cosmetics. Not the genetic stuff, of course—that was outlawed—but the US owned the market on basic items like creams, shampoos, hair dye, and makeup. China did the genetic stuff, the Japanese fleet did robots and augmented reality, South America did smart polymers, Israel did defense, the EU did communications, Canada did VR. Everyone did guns.

Simone ran her hand over the pamphlet and pretended to look at it a moment before turning to deCostas. She took him by the arm and led him away from the secretary and spoke in a low voice.

"Pastor Sorenson is the head of the Mission," she told him. "Be very polite and very vague about what you're doing."

"Why?"

"I'll explain later." Simone furrowed her brow, wondering what it could mean that Sorenson himself was coming to see them. Did this job have implications she wasn't aware of? "Trust your instincts, but don't assume," her dad always said. Her instincts told her there was something going on here she couldn't see. The pastor wasn't just coming to see the stairwell.

The elevator at the end of the room opened, and Ned Sorenson stepped out. Simone had seen him in the papers and on the web but never in person. He was about sixty years old, but only just graying, and only slightly balding. His tight black curls made him look younger, but his face was more worn, as though to make up for it. The wrinkles were deep in his mahogany skin. His eyes had the look of someone used to being in control, and who was often amused. Simone wasn't sure what to think of him. He wore a plain black shirt and pants with a white pastor's collar, and walked with his hands behind his back. He smiled when he saw them. It was a kind smile, but Simone wasn't sure it was a genuine one.

"Hello," he said. "You must be Ms. Pierce and Mr. deCostas. I've been waitin' excitedly for you since I heard you were comin'." He spoke in the mainland accent, where words never really ended but just rose and fell into one another.

"Pleased to meet you, Pastor Sorenson," Simone said, extending her hand in what she hoped was a confident way. He shook it. His hands were rough and dry.

"Thank you for letting us do this," deCostas said, also shaking his hand.

"I'm always eager to help scientists," Sorenson said. Simone kept her face still and managed not to laugh. Sorenson was a representative of the mainland, and the mainland policy on science was generally not eager to help. "But I fear you'll be disappointed. I've been in our stairwell many a time. It's just water." He opened his arms, gesturing towards a wall. Simone walked towards the wall and noticed the seam in the wood paneling—a secret door.

"Why hide the stairs?" she asked, stopping next to the door.

"Looks nicer," Sorenson said with a shrug. He pressed his thumb onto a small square of wood, which lit up and scanned the imprint. The wall clicked open. Hidden and locked. Simone was even more curious now. But the stairwell was just as Sorenson said. Water lapped at gray-painted stairs. The walls were a dim yellow, the paint chipped away in many places, and a few pipes, painted bright red, thrust through the landing. The ceiling was rough, and moss grew in the corners. Just like any other stairwell.

"Sorry," Sorenson said.

deCostas reached into his jacket and took out a marble.

"What's that?" Sorenson asked. He still had a smile on his face, but his eyes were narrowed, the lines at the sides of them like needles.

"A depth-measurement device," deCostas said.

"I don't think we agreed to lettin' you use that." Sorenson said. He was still smiling, so much so that it looked painful, but his voice had become chillier.

"It's just part of Mr. deCostas' research," Simone said.

"And I'm sure it's harmless, but we don't give out information on our building willy-nilly. It could be used for terrorism."

"Mr. deCostas is here on an academic study. His funding comes from a major European university," Simone said, angling her body so that Sorenson was focused on her and not deCostas. Sorenson's smile finally faded, but only for a moment. He shook his head as though he were dealing with a child and sighed. When he spoke, his voice was warmer again.

"And as soon as I have a signed form sayin' he won't share any information about the building with anyone but us, I'll be happy to let him conduct his experiment."

"Do you have a form?"

Simone's back was to deCostas, but she hoped he was taking her cue and dropping his marble while she shielded him from Sorenson's view.

"No I don't, as you didn't fully apprise me of what he'd be doin'. I'll have our lawyers draft one. It should be ready in a few days. Then I'll be happy to let Mr. deCostas measure the depth." Sorenson motioned with his arms again, pointing them back to the lobby. deCostas sighed, and Simone watched him tuck the marble back into his pocket. She glared, wondering why he hadn't dropped it when she'd given him the chance. "I'll send you the documents as soon as they're ready," Sorenson said in the lobby. "Thank you for your patience."

"Of course," deCostas said. Simone nodded. Sorenson turned and got back into the elevator. Simone left the building, deCostas following. Outside, she walked a few bridges away before speaking.

"You should have just dropped it," Simone said.

"What?"

"Your depth measurer. You were right there. You could have dropped it. Said it was an accident."

"He wouldn't have liked that. You said to be polite."

"Yeah, but you could have gotten away with it. He would have insisted you turn it off, or not check the status until you signed his forms, and you could have agreed and gone home and done whatever you wanted."

"That wouldn't have been polite. I think that what I did—which was dropping the marble when you distracted him—thank you for that—and then taking another out and making it look like I was putting it away—I thought that was the polite thing to do."

Simone was silent for a moment. "Is that what you did?" she asked.

"It was."

"Well," Simone said, somewhat impressed. "Nicely done."

"Thank you. Would you like to get something to eat?"

Simone looked him up and down. He grinned at her, one eye-brow cocked.

"Sure," she said. There was a little café on the other side of the bridge next to one of the needle buildings where they ordered fish sandwiches and she had coffee and he had tea. They ate outside at a small table, the water a low rumble that stopped just short of making them both vibrate.

"You know this is pearl diving, right?" Simone asked. "I mean, I don't want to discourage you from paying me, but we're not going to find anything."

deCostas was silent for a moment, as if considering what she said. He looked like he was holding his breath. Simone wondered if she'd gone too far and lost the client.

"I know most people think it is a useless quest," he said finally, his voice even, "but I've done the research, and enough people agree with me to fund this expedition." He gestured firmly, almost violently, slapping his palm down on the table. Simone's hand involuntarily crept closer to her gun. "If I can find space below the water in New York, then others may ask me to find space below the other sunken cities. We could use what we find to build underwater and try to get life to like it was before the flood."

"And make your career in the process?" Simone asked, staring at him as she sipped her coffee.

"Well, yes." He pushed his hair out of his eyes. "It would make me famous. But I do really believe there must be somewhere the water stops." He was speaking loudly and jabbed his finger, pointing at her, then realized what he was doing and dropped his hand, but Simone had seen how his eyes had gotten brighter without focusing on anything. She'd seen a touch of rage and maybe something darker.

"I think you're crazy," she said. He laughed, and he seemed to shake off whatever it was that had possessed him a moment before. He was charming again, the storm over, the waves calm. He smiled, and Simone relaxed a bit, moving her hand from her pistol, where it had been resting.

"Maybe," he said. He sipped his tea. "So you have lived in the city your whole life?" Simone nodded. "Have you been to the EU?"

"No. Only left New York once, to visit the Appalachian Islands."

"The mainland?"

"Yeah, kinda. Eastern islands, connected to the Chicago coast by a giant bridge with a maglev train. Still takes a long time to get there from the mainland, though. So only the really wealthy have homes there. It's like a vacation spot that's still part of the mainland. Beaches and mansions and little hotels, but still well policed by the mainland, still safe from 'corrupt influences.' My dad took me there when I was little. We stayed at a B&B for a weekend and played on the beach a little. Then we got ticketed for indecency because his bathing suit rode down a little in the back. He didn't have one of those fancy no-slip kinds. Showed a little crack, and he got charged as much as the vacation cost altogether. That's mainland life."

"I've never been to the mainland. They say it's . . . unwelcoming. Make one social mistake and you're in prison."

"That's about right."

"So why is it different here?"

"Well, we're technically still the US, I guess, but everything is decentralized here. We have our own government, and while the mainland decency and morality laws apply to us, no one enforces them. Which makes it a great place for foreign businesses to set up shop. Still America, but with none of the pesky rules."

"No rules?" One corner of his mouth rose up mischievously.

Simone cocked her head. "Our own rules. Truth is, we don't get many people moving in or out of New York. You're born a New Yorker, you stay one. Some people move in, but they tend to leave one way or another after they got what they came for or realize they never will."

"One way or another?"

"Over the water or under it," Simone said, using her coffee cup to hide her inadvertent frown.

"And what is it they come for?"

"Money," Simone shrugged. "Power, fame." She stared at deCostas over his coffee, and he took a long sip. "But New Yorkers don't like leaving."

"You say that with pride."

"Yeah." Simone drained her coffee and leaned back in her chair. "So what's the EU like?"

"Nice. Liberal, obviously, by America's standards."

"What isn't?"

"Not too different from here, socially, but we have more . . ."

"Buildings?"

He laughed. "Yes, and we have an older culture. A relaxed one. One that knows it is in its golden years and so tries to enjoy the time it has left, with music and art, sunsets and sex. In the north we have great dykes and walls, like the one you have on the Chicago coast, but they feel natural. And in the south we have pumps and canals—more like here, but different somehow. Like old photos of Venice from before it sank. America is still like the adult who just realized he will not live forever and so is trying to hide himself from danger. It has been this way since before the flood . . . but the flood lengthened it. A very long midlife crisis, decades past its prime, trying to recapture its elusive youth. Europe is past this. We enjoy ourselves and the beauty of the world, even as the waters threaten to cover us."

"Sunsets and sex?"

"It's a line from a movie," deCostas said, pushing his hair back from his face, "but an accurate one. You should visit sometime and see."

"We have sunsets and sex here."

"Really? Perhaps I shall find out for myself," he said, raising an eyebrow.

"Do these lines work on European women?"

"Some."

"Now I know you're lying." Simone stood, and deCostas squinted up at her. She was enjoying his company, but she wasn't dumb enough to enjoy it for very long, and it was getting late. She thought about inviting him back with her. She was probably going to fuck him eventually, after all. He was hot and willing, and she didn't turn down easy sex if she thought the guy wouldn't try for anything more; and in this case she didn't think it would interfere with the work she was doing for him. The sun was behind her, and it felt warm on her back. But something distracted her. She was facing the Mission, and the door was opening. Out stepped The Blonde. The legs in the waiting room—no wonder they'd seemed familiar. Simone had tailed them the other night. "I should go," she said. "Send me some more buildings. I'll set up some more viewings."

"Why the rush?"

"Other cases." He looked over to where she was staring. The Blonde had put on a pair of sunglasses and was walking away.

"Can I come?"

"What?" Simone glanced down at deCostas for a moment, annoyed. "No."

"I'm not even sure where we are. I need you to show me how to get home. It's what I'm paying for, isn't it?" Simone pursed her lips. The Blonde was hurrying out of sight. She grabbed some cash from her wallet and put it down on the table.

"Fine, stay behind me, do exactly what I say. This shouldn't be dangerous, but . . ." she started walking quickly after The Blonde. Behind her, she heard deCostas scramble up from his chair and follow her.

"Can you tell me what the case is about?" he asked.

"No. And shut up."

She darted quickly through the crowds. The sun was getting lower, and the sunset fog was starting to rise, giving the city a gauzy orange look. She was impressed by how deCostas managed to weave behind her, but she still had to put her arm up to block him once or twice. She didn't like where this was going. Bringing de-Costas was bad, of course, but she didn't want to lose the client. She also didn't want to lose this lead she'd gained by luck. This was why she didn't like working two cases at once.

The Blonde was heading along the far-western reaches of the city, edging along the bad areas if not quite entering them. It was less pop-ulated here, with too many empty buildings and worn-out bridges. Simone didn't like it. The Blonde walked around a corner and into a large, crumbling building that Simone knew to be abandoned. After sunset, it was a spot to score drugs, but now, with the sun still setting, it would just be an abandoned room with a door to another bridge.

"Stay here," she whispered to deCostas.

"Why?"

"Just stay here." Simone walked ahead and into the building. It had been an office once. Three fluorescent lights flickered on the ceiling; the others had burned out. The carpet was torn and moldy, and whatever color it had been was now gray. Discarded newspages stuck to the floor here and there, old and peeling like dry skin. There were a few cubicles scattered around and shoulder-high, white walls lined with trash, but there was a path through them to the other side of the building where another window had been made into a door like the one she'd just come through. Between her and that door stood The Blonde, waiting. She was backlit by the sun, and the little light from the ceiling that shone on her face flickered, as if afraid to rest there. She held her hands in front of her, clutching a small strapless purse, relaxed. Amused maybe.

"Hello," she said to Simone. "Oh, and you brought a friend." Simone looked behind her. DeCostas had followed her. Shit. Simone reached for the gun in her boot and pulled it out slowly. "Oh, we don't need to do that, do we?" The Blonde raised an eyebrow. Simone looked her up and down. The Blonde had a gun, too. Simone could feel it—an instinct for firearms honed over the years. Maybe she was holding it behind her clutch and could shoot her through it. Probably. She'd had time to prepare. The pose with the one hand clasping the clutch, the other hand just behind it, looking like it was clasping the purse, too. It was too staged.

"Why were you meeting with Henry St. Michel the other night?" Simone asked. She kept her gun lowered but walked a few steps closer to The Blonde, trying to block deCostas.

"That's my business. But I do like having my picture taken. Makes me feel famous."

"I tried to get your good side."

The Blonde gave Simone a look like she'd tried to tell a joke and no one had laughed. "They're all good sides." She tilted her head, her perfect hair swaying with the motion. An earring sparkled.

"I don't know why you were taking those photos, but whoever hired you, whatever you think you're on to, you should stop."

"Why's that?"

"Because it's not whatever you think it is. I'm not a prostitute or a mistress. Do I look like one?" Simone didn't answer. "Oh, now you're just being mean."

"So why were you meeting St. Michel?"

"Like I said, that's my business."

"Did you shoot him last night?"

The Blonde raised an eyebrow at Simone.

"No. I didn't realize he'd been shot."

"Maybe," Simone said. "Maybe he shot someone. Maybe he lived."

The Blonde shrugged. "It doesn't matter. The point is, you should leave me alone. I have things to do, and they don't involve you. I don't need a fangirl right now."

"Are you threatening me?"

"Maybe." The Blonde smiled, took out the small gun Simone had known she was holding, and pointed it at Simone. She felt the prickle of adrenaline down her spine, and her brain calculated the way she could handle this if it became a gunfight: Which cubicle was the closest to dive behind? Could The Blonde shoot twice before she could fire back? She felt her heart speed up slightly, and blood rushed to her fingertips, which twitched in anticipation. Then she realized the gun wasn't aimed at her, it was aimed behind her and a little to her right. Fuck. "But it looks like I have lots of people to threaten today." She half shrugged, half giggled, her hair and earrings shimmering again. "I like options." Simone couldn't tackle deCostas before the bullet hit him, and if she was implicated in the death of a foreign student, she wasn't sure Caroline could clean that up for her.

The Blonde dropped the gun into her purse as though it were lipstick. "But I've made my point. Go away." She flashed Simone a wide grin and then turned her back on her, walking into the setting sun. Simone turned on deCostas, furious. He was pushing hair out of his face but smiling, as though it had been fun.

"What the fuck were you thinking? I told you to stay."

"I was curious," he said, turning away slightly, as if unprepared for a scolding.

"You're an idiot. You could have gotten shot."

"I didn't think you cared." He smiled again, trying to be charming.

"You're not disturbed by the fact that the little blonde woman just pointed a gun at you?"

He shrugged. "She didn't shoot." Simone took a deep breath. She put her gun back in its holster.

"You're an idiot," she repeated, walking past him out of the building.

"Can you take me home?" he asked softly. "Or at least to a main bridge?"

"Follow me. Don't speak." She led him back to the large bridge people called Broadway because it was supposedly built over the street of the same name. He stayed silent, which she appreciated.

"Here," she said. "You can get home from here, right?"

"Yes," he said, looking around. "I think I can. Should I send you more buildings, or are you done with me?"

Simone pursed her lips. It was her own fault for letting him come at all. And the money was good.

"You can send them," she said. Then she walked away.

At home, the first thing she did was check the recycling site. Sure enough, posted about an hour earlier, blue and bloated from the water, was the face of Henry St. Michel. Simone frowned and put her coat back on. Time to stop by the recycling station.

FIVE

——

THE RECYCLING STATION WAS a large brown building that thrust out of the water like the fist of a bully. It was one of the most eastern buildings in the city, located in a relatively empty area of midtown, about a mile from City Hall. No one had moored boats nearby. It had one bridge leading to the entrance, and no other bridges wrapped around it. Instead, bobbing in the water, anchored all around the perimeter, were the bright red recycling boats, their long nets hanging off them like veils.

Before going in, Simone tried calling Linnea again. Still nothing. She didn't leave a message. She'd stopped after the sixteenth call. She'd begun to consider the possibility that Linnea had decided to conclude the investigation on her own terms and had fled the city. In which case, Simone wouldn't get paid. In which case, she had no reason to be here.

She pushed open the doors to the recycling station. Simone had been there enough times before to know the layout. There was a front desk and to its right a big bulletin board with photos of the found bodies. Under each photo was a room number. You went to the room, and if you recognized the body, you reported it at the desk, made arrangements, whatever. There were usually some peepers hanging around in the lobby—people who just went from room to room, looking at the dead bodies. Most dressed in black, trying to be respectful. Many were old women. Today, only a few of them stood in the corner, murmuring to one another. They looked up at her with interest and voyeuristic sympathy. She went right to the board and checked for Henry's photo. Then she headed to the marked room. The hallways were narrow and tiled, the walls painted with that plastic-y antimold stuff that always smelled like new shoes.

She opened the door to Henry's room quickly and walked straight up to the body to confirm it was him. The room was small, just a white cube with a slab in the middle. She pulled the sheet down off his face. The eyelids were gone, eaten away by sea creatures, and part of the lips, too, but it was definitely Henry. She recognized a birthmark on his neck.

"Please tell me you're here by mistake," came a voice from behind. Simone turned. Standing in the corner, where the door had hidden him when she came in, was Peter, in full uniform.

"Officer," she said with a nod. "Why should this be a mistake?"

"Because he bobbed up with a hole in him that didn't come from the fish, and Kluren wants me to bring in whoever stops by to check him out."

"She thinks they'd come to admire their handiwork?"

"Something like that."

"So pretend you didn't see me."

"Sorry, soldier, you know I can't do that. Especially now that it's pretty clear you're not in here by mistake. Who was he to you?"

"Wife thought he was seeking outside company, paid me to tail him."

"She pay you to rough him up a little?"

"You know I don't do that."

"Where is she now?" Peter took a step towards her.

"Can't get her on the phone."

"Think she decided he'd be a better sieve than husband?"

"Not sure. There are a few players."

"What is your gun shooting these days?"

"40 S&Ws, same as yours."

"Same as the holes in the guy."

"Same as a lot of people." What caliber was The Blonde's gun? It wasn't big, but it had been hard to see exactly, with her backlit.

"Still."

"Yeah."

"You want to head over to Teddy with me?"

"Thanks for making it sound like a question." She smiled slightly and followed him out the door.

The NYPD was located in a decommissioned navy cruiser called the *Theodore Roosevelt*. Everyone called it Teddy. The whole force was stationed there and on the smaller police boats tied up around it. It was a large ship, moored on the Upper East Side, and it had been cleared out of anything deemed unnecessary when the NYPD had taken it over. On deck were some guards and a parked helicopter, but inside were all metal walls and desks. Each of the bureau chiefs had his or her own office, and the commissioner held what was once the captain's room towards the top. But the current commissioner, John Boady, was seldom seen doing actual police work. Usually he operated as more of an advisor to the mayor. Simone knew that the police force itself paid him little heed. Kluren, chief of homicide and chief of departments, was the one in charge.

On deck were a bunch of uniformed officers, taking smoke or coffee breaks, chatting and laughing, but the moment they caught sight of Simone, they went quiet. They knew her, of course. She'd been dragged there enough with her dad, first when he was a cop, and then when he was in trouble with the cops. Simone could feel the heat of their silence. Kluren was a popular chief among her men and had made her dislike of the Pierce family very public. Simone was in enemy territory and they wanted her to know it.

The day Peter had applied to the Police Academy, he'd come over and told Simone. Simone hugged him and, when he left, went to the application server and started filling it out. Her dad came home when she was up to the psychological profile section. He leaned over her shoulder, smelling of cigarettes and gin, and looked at what she was doing. Then he slammed the touchdesk off so forcefully the screen cracked.

"You don't need to do that crap," he said. "Police are all about rules. That's where corruption comes from. If you have an officer so tied up with regulations he can't move, he's going to ease free of them. You work for me. You're a private eye. We don't worry about rules, we worry about finding the truth. That's what police work should be. Trust me, you'll be better off this way." He laid his hand on her head and looked down into her eyes and smiled. "You'll be better than me," he said. She smiled back. She hadn't really wanted to be a police officer anyway.

Peter opened the door on deck and took her into Teddy. More cops were there working, but they all paused to stare at Simone, like a wall of razor blades and ice. Simone wondered how it was Peter hadn't become like these men, or turned bad like her dad said they all did eventually.

"C'mon," Peter said, resting his hand on her shoulder. She pulled back slightly, like she was sighing, removing herself from his touch. Peter led her down two flights and across the length of the ship into Tara Kluren's office. Kluren wore her hair like a helmet, her pant-suits too loose and her face in a perpetual scowl, at least whenever Simone was around. Her dad and Kluren had come up through the force together, were even partners briefly, and she'd hated him, too. Maybe it was a bad joke gone wrong, or competition between them. Simone's dad had never told her, and he'd died before she could ask.

Kluren had offered Simone a job on the force once, right after her dad died. Simone was never sure why. Kluren had never seemed to even notice her before then. Simone had said no, or not said anything, and then a few months later, working one of her first solo cases, she crossed paths with the force, and Kluren threw her in the brig for a night. She never offered Simone a job again. Or even a friendly nod. Her hatred of Simone's father had been passed down to Simone like a delicate heirloom.

When Peter led her into the office, Kluren was smiling like a water snake. Her suit that day was pale—maybe gray, maybe tan, maybe just dirty white, like the color of her hair. The irises of her eyes were gold, the telltale sign of augmented-reality contact lenses. Those weren't usually seen in the city. On the mainland, and in other civilized nations, they were popular; people could use them for networking, to avoid getting lost, for gaming, for restaurant reviews, whatever. But in New York, the maps changed faster than satellites could keep up, and restaurants were boats that, even moored, could drift in the night. Nothing really stayed put, so overlays were usually confusingly off by a few feet, or completely wrong, unless people wanted to put up small signaling devices on their buildings and boats letting everyone know exactly what sort of place it was. Not surprisingly, no one did.

But Kluren's contacts weren't for social networking or restaurant reviews. They were the obscenely expensive, Israeli-made ForenSpecs; they provided an augmented reality that could pick out fingerprints and blood splatter; they could read names off IRID signals and display those names hovering in space over the people they belonged to. They could read facial expressions and body language to determine if someone was lying. They were incredibly advanced and seldom used except by military interrogators and investigators. And they made Kluren seem a little inhuman, her dark eyes punctuated by gold, metallic circles. Simone always tried to make herself stiff around Kluren, unreadable, but she wasn't sure if she ever succeeded.

"So you're the one who stopped by to check out the leaking body," she said, leaning back in her chair. She put her feet up and looked Simone up and down. "Unlucky, that body. Should have sunk right to the bottom with the hole it had in it, but it must have drifted a bit, snagged on the corner of a roof under the water, just twenty feet down. The nets brought him up. Real unlucky."

"Maybe so," Simone said, "but not for me. I didn't kill your guy."

"*Your* guy," Kluren corrected. "Something to do with a case?"

"His wife thought he was cheating."

"And paid you to shoot him?"

"Only photos."

"Wife got a name?"

"Linnea St. Michel. The corpse is Henry."

"Mmmm," Kluren took her feet off the desk and put her hand to her chin, trying to figure out a way to pin it on Simone. "Your caliber bullet hole."

"And a lot of people's."

"True. But I like you for this. You've got killer's eyes. Your dad's eyes."

Simone said nothing but stared at Kluren. She knew who her dad was, and he'd never killed anyone, except in self-defense. Shot them in the leg to keep them from running, maybe put a hole in their hand when they were holding a gun. But nothing worse than that. Kluren was just trying to get a rise out of her. She realized she was curling the fingers on her right hand and stopped.

"Tell you what," Kluren said, standing. "No need to arrest you now. I'm going to send Weiss here back to your office, and you're going to give him everything to do with this investigation. Photos, recordings, notes, everything. Then, we'll look it over. If we can pin it on you, we will, and you'll be sunk for a good, long time. If not . . . I'll be disappointed, but this little moment is making me happy enough I should be okay for a couple years—provided I never see you again. Which means you're staying out of this. Got it?"

Simone continued to stare.

"Like talking to a MouthFoamer," Kluren said. "Weiss, take her home. Get everything. If I find out later you missed something, you'll be on hull-scrubbing duty for the next few years. Anything you want to confess to, Pierce? I'll go easy on you if you confess now. Later, I won't be so nice." Kluren glared, waiting, but Simone kept her mouth shut. "She has two IRIDs on her. One of them must be fake. Confiscate it, issue her the usual fine."

Simone stared a bit longer, wishing she'd fixed her IRID-blocking wallet. The fine wasn't a cheap one. Hopefully someone would end up paying her. Then she took out the fake IRID and handed it to Peter, who handed it to Kluren, who by now had grown bored with them and was looking at some papers on her desk.

"I heard the murder," Simone said. Kluren looked back up. Pleasure danced on her lips.

"You heard the murder," she repeated, smiling again.

"I bugged Henry, followed him, he went into an empty building on the outskirts of town, waited for someone, but I couldn't see who. I heard a shot, ran to the scene, but the body and killer were gone."

"Run real slow, did you?"

"I had to stand far off so they couldn't see me." She didn't mention her slip. Kluren would enjoy it too much.

"So you hear gunfire but don't call the police?"

"There wasn't a body."

"Ah, well. Of course," Kluren said, her words like little teeth sinking into Simone as she paused. "But what would make more sense is for me to put you in lockup for obstructing an investigation. Weiss can go by your place alone." She looked back down at her desk and waved them off again.

"I can show you where the bloodstain is," Simone offered. "If you don't mind my swimming free a bit longer."

Kluren looked at her and leaned back in her chair again.

"Sure," she said after an achingly long moment. "Show us the crime scene, give us your notes, and stay the fuck out of my life, and you can swim free a few tides more—till we hook you for something else." She sighed as she said the last few words, then stood, her body relaxed like dangling rope. "But just for fun, I'm going to have Weiss handcuff you as you lead us to the murder scene."

"Suits me fine," Simone said, placing her hands behind her back. Peter shook his head and clicked his cuffs loosely around her wrists.

"Now, let's see this crime scene of yours," Kluren said, motioning Simone towards the door. Simone led the way out. Other cops looked up briefly at her; some snickered, and most went back to work. Kluren chose a handful to accompany them to the crime scene.

Kluren made Simone take crowded streets. People stared at her, then quickly looked away. Simone held her head up, her chin pointed high. It wasn't great for business, being paraded through town in cuffs, but it wasn't as bad as actually being arrested. She briefly wondered if Kluren might accidentally nudge her over the edge of a narrow bridge in her handcuffed state, but Kluren wasn't like that. Her dad had said that was why he couldn't work with her: She was afraid to bend the rules. Simone knew that wasn't entirely true, though. Kluren wore pants, ignoring all the bullshit federal laws everyone in the city ignored. She was clearly fine with bending some rules. Simone had never asked her dad which rules he'd meant.

Simone led them to the small building, and Kluren ordered her crime techs to start examining the place.

"Someone's taken a sample of the blood," one of the techs called. Kluren looked at Simone.

"Just blood type. It's O positive, same as the vic."

"I hope to see that in the files Weiss brings me." Kluren glared, then tapped something on her wristpiece. Her eyes began glowing a bright blue—another ForenSpec feature. She looked around the crime scene. "There are a few blood drops leading out that way," she said to the techs, pointing out the door opposite where they had come in. "Follow them." She turned to Simone as though she'd forgotten she was there. "I'm done with you here. Weiss, take her home, please. Get the files. Keep the cuffs on her."

A few blocks away, Peter took off the cuffs. Simone instinctively put her hands to her wrists to feel them, though they hadn't chafed.

"Thanks," she said.

"What the hell kinda waters you swimming in, soldier?"

"You don't need to keep calling me that."

"I like calling you that. And you dodged my question."

"Why did you always let me be the soldier when we were kids?" Simone asked. "The soldier was the best action figure. You always got stuck being artillery guy, hanging back and bringing me guns when I needed them."

"You liked being the solider."

"Didn't you?"

"I didn't care either way."

Simone smiled as they walked, but looked down so he couldn't see. "And you dodged my question again."

"What was the question?"

"What sort of trouble are you in?" Simone felt him close to her, warmth coming off him and touching her shoulder like the early sun. She stepped farther away.

"The usual kind, I guess."

"You have no idea, do you?"

"I have too many ideas."

"Well, do me and you a favor and drop them all." His voice rose in frustration.

"No promises."

"Of course not," Peter sighed. They continued downtown in silence, walking an awkward space apart, trying to maintain a buffer of air, but sometimes knocking lightly against each other when the bridge swayed or the wind came on strong. Then they would put their hands out flat as if to apologize for that soft touch, to put more space between them again. The air smelled like salt and sweat.

When Simone unlocked the door, the memories of when she would bring Peter here after a night out washed over her for a moment. She pulled her hands through her hair, tugging at the roots.

"Everything is in the office," she said. He followed her and handed her a compression card, which she laid down on her touchdesk. She pulled up the file marked 31-42-21, not minding if Peter saw it. If anyone could figure out her file-coding system, it would be him, but he wouldn't give it up, either. She dragged the file to the compression card and waited as the two linked up and everything copied over onto the card—the photos of The Blonde, Linnea's information, the recordings from Henry's office, the video of Anika. She hoped that wouldn't lose her a client. There really wasn't much, it turned out. She handed the card back to him.

"Thanks," Peter said. "Sorry you had to get mixed up in this."

"It's my job," she said, smiling at him. She was sitting behind her desk; he was standing at the door. They looked at each other a while.

"I'll let myself out," he said and left. Simone took a deep breath and let it out slowly. She still had all her own copies of the files, but she was nearly content to let the case drop. There wasn't much left to go on, and chances were Linnea wouldn't be paying her anytime soon.

Then she checked her messages.

Most of them were junk, but the one that caught her eye was from Danny. The subject was "Found her again."

There was no text, just a photo attachment. It was clearly yanked from a security camera somewhere in the city and was fuzzy, with poor color quality. Simone recognized both figures in the photo. The first was The Blonde. She was smiling, wearing a trench coat and pushing her hair from her face. The other was Caroline Khan.

SIX

—

SIMONE FOUND THE BONDS of friendship to be more akin to tightrope wires that she had no balance for. Consequently, she rarely walked them. Caroline was the exception.

Simone had met Caroline when she'd been hired to investigate whether the mayor was receiving under-the-table payments to favor certain city councilmen's bills. She quickly realized that there were discrepancies in the mayor's public itinerary, events where Caroline would stand in for him last minute, leaving his whereabouts unaccounted for. Seeing these absences as an opportunity to tail the mayor to a possible secret meeting, she tried to find the next gap by accessing Caroline's schedule, guessing that she would know about her stand-in duties ahead of time.

She had thought Caroline would be spoiled, appointed for her family connections, and an easy mark. She had used a short-range EMF blocker to cause Caroline's touchdesk to malfunction, then posed as an IT specialist. Caroline laughed as soon as Simone came in and, still laughing, waved Simone back out the door. Simone tried to get a word in, but Caroline just shook her head, still laughing. Outside, she got a text on her phone: "If you think I wouldn't know what the PI investigating the mayor looks like, you must not think very highly of me. But thanks for the laugh. CK."

Simone had tried a few more tricks, like hiring actors to stand in for her, but Caroline laughed them out of the office each time, and sent Simone a friendly text after each attempt. It wasn't until Simone held a network extender outside the office and had Danny hack into Caroline's touchdesk that she finally got what she needed. She tailed the mayor the next time he went off schedule—only to find that he was going home for a nap. She had Danny hack the network again and this time was surprised to find in Caroline's schedule a note that said "1 p.m.—Coffee with Simone Pierce, MochAfloat."

Simone decided to keep the appointment, where Caroline bought her coffee and proceeded to explain that the mayor was lazy, but not corrupt—or at least not corrupt in the way Simone thought he was. Caroline was vague about anything outside the scope of Simone's investigation, but she knew who had hired Simone and why, and explained to her the overreaching political implications of such a hire—how the investigation itself was the tool, not what it turned up. Before long, she was laughing as she complained about the odd details of her job. Simone liked her. She was smart, respectful, and sarcastic. She drank hot coffee through a straw. She ended it by telling Simone she would help her finish the investigation, if Simone wanted, because she knew she was right. Simone didn't take her up on the offer, continued investigating on her own, and turned up nothing except that the mayor was, indeed, very lazy. She reported as much to her client. The next week, the papers were all writing articles about the private investigation into the mayor's practices. When that faded away, they suddenly were reporting that the mayor took naps.

She had Danny hack into the system again and put in another coffee date for her and Caroline. Caroline showed up, and this time Simone bought. She felt she owed Caroline something—maybe an apology—and they both understood that this coffee was that apology, if not in words. They talked about the various pressures of their jobs, about not being taken seriously, about their families. Simone had thought originally she could cultivate a good contact in the mayor's office but was surprised by how naturally the friendship floated into place. It was something Simone had never had before. Sure, she was friends with Danny, but she always knew that that relationship was based on the fact that Danny owed Simone his life, and that made her feel more secure. Other friends were more like acquaintances—people she could nod at in bars or contacts in the field. And there was Peter . . . but that was different. Caroline was an equal. Her friendship was earned and genuine. Simone always valued that, and was a little afraid of it, too. It meant she had to trust Caroline, and trusting people was never her first instinct.

Simone looked hard at the photo. Caroline and The Blonde were smiling, as though they'd just shared a private joke. Simone had smiled like that with Caroline.

She closed the photo on her touchdesk screen, her hands numb and barely aware of what they were doing. She stood, not sure what was happening for a moment, her mind blank, and then walked to bed, stripped off her clothes, and went to sleep.

THE NEXT MORNING, BEFORE she had time to think about anything, Simone went to get a cup of coffee and heard whistling from her waiting room. She peeked her head out. There was a man there. Had she forgotten to lock the outer door? He was sitting patiently in the chair in front of her non-receptionist's table, reading the paper. He looked up, wicked grin on his face, when she came into the room. She was wearing a worn set of sweatpants and a tank top, and her hair was a mess. He was perfectly put together in a white shirt, gold tie, and gray herringbone suit that still glistened like diamonds where the waves had hit the hem. He was around her age, maybe a little older, with perfectly parted hair that grayed at the temples and a straight-edged smile. He had the good looks of a movie star, and the acting skills not to call too much attention to it.

"Dash Ormond," she said.

"You know, I've never been in your office before," he said, looking around as though he hadn't just cased the place while she was sleeping. "It's cute."

She went into the kitchen and poured herself a cup of coffee and one for him, which she set in front of him.

"You've never been here before because you're where I send the jobs I don't want," she said, coolly.

"Oh, now let's play nice," he said. "We're not rivals. We're . . . contemporaries."

"Then shouldn't we be writing each other letters and discussing the philosophy of private investigation?"

"I'd love to. Though I fear mine would be a short letter. You see, my philosophy is simple: Get paid."

She sat down behind the reception desk and took a sip of the coffee. She didn't entirely dislike Dash. He had a good reputation, though he was perhaps willing to go a little further than Simone. He usually specialized in "retrieval," which meant finding out who had stolen something and getting it back. Those sorts of clients had reasons for not going to the police, and Simone usually didn't deal with them. She had heard rumors about Dash—that he could torture you, smiling the whole time, until you told him where you'd hidden whatever it was he was looking for—but he had always been polite to her, and she to him, and she didn't know if the rumors were true. He was hard to read. There had been several cases of his that ended in dead bodies—whether he or his employer was responsible, Simone never knew.

Sometimes, if they found themselves staking out the same hotel bar, they'd send each other drinks. He had magnetism, there was no denying that. Even here in her office, the way he crossed his legs had a distinctly sensual elegance: part wild animal, part fine tailoring. He was a good flirt, too, but Simone was smart enough to never let it go further than that.

"What can I do for you, Dash?"

"You can help me find Linnea St. Michel."

Simone took another long sip of coffee to cover the frown she was trying to hide, then tried to force a disdainful smile.

"Don't know where she is, Dash. Sorry. But feel free to finish the coffee."

"Aw, don't be like that, Simone. We can help each other out. My client wants something from Ms. St. Michel. You, I assume, want to get paid. We find her together, we both get what we want. It's a beautiful thing."

"Who's your client?"

"You know I can't tell you that."

"What do they want with Linnea?"

He shrugged slowly. "C'mon, Red, make a handsome man happy."

"I'll think about it."

"Fair enough. But think quick. I'll be looking for her myself, and if I find her without you, then it'll be you coming to my office. And I don't wear pajamas."

"What do you wear?"

He smiled and eased out of the chair.

"Nothing, of course."

"I thought you were trying to discourage me."

She raised her eyebrow and sipped her coffee, keeping her eyes on his. He grinned.

"Your teasing wounds my heart," he said, and tapped himself on the chest. He took a card from his inside pocket and laid it on the desk in front of her. "In case you've lost my number. Call anytime. Day or night. I'll be looking forward to hearing your voice."

"I'll bet."

He winked, plucking his fedora from the coatrack and donning it, left the office, hands in his pockets, probably aware that he looked like a dancer doing it. She thought she could hear him whistling down the hallway. Simone let herself smile a bit more before heading into her office. She sat down at her touchdesk, booted it up, and looked at the photo again. Danny had sent over a few more during the night: Caroline and The Blonde smiling, Caroline and The Blonde laughing, Caroline handing The Blonde a small envelope, which she put in her purse without opening. Simone pulled up Danny's message from last night and wrote back, "Where was this photo taken?"

She knew she was stuck in this now. Even if Dash hadn't shown up, she had to find out what was going on. One of her few friends was involved, and someone was dead. That meant Caroline could be the next victim. Or, said the tiny voice in the back of her mind, a killer. Maybe. Maybe Caroline and The Blonde's meeting had nothing to do with anything. But she had to know. And she couldn't ask Caroline, because if she lied, it would be like being out at sea without a piece of driftwood to float on. Until she drowned. Until Caroline pushed her under.

People lied, people cheated, people were never what they seemed, never simple, and rarely good. These were things her father had taught her every day. Why had she forgotten when it came to Caroline?

The response came back almost immediately, since Danny was always hooked to his messaging: "Outside the Four Seasons. I was going through the security camera footage from a pho shop across the bridge to check if a certain someone met a certain someone else there, and I stumbled on your girl. I zoomed in for you and cleaned it up. But this is great, right? Now you can just ask Caroline who she is."

Simone smiled at his innocence.

"No," she wrote back, "I can't. And neither can you. I need to find out what her involvement with all this is before I confront her with anything. If she's part of this in some way, I have to figure out exactly how. Otherwise, it could be a trap. She might want to use me to find my client or some other reason. So don't you dare mention to her that we've seen this photo. I'm serious."

Another response came back a moment later: "Anyone ever tell you you have trust issues?"

Simone lit a cigarette. She wouldn't be responding. But now she felt fairly sure that The Blonde was staying at the Four Seasons and, more importantly, that she was meeting people there. Maybe clients? Was Caroline a client? Anika had said she was selling something—peddling bullshit. But what would Anika, Caroline, and Henry all be in the market for? And why would that lead to Henry's death? He didn't have whatever The Blonde was selling—not if she was still going around selling it.

Simone clenched her jaw and looked at the photos again, willing them to stop making her body feel creaking and slimy. Willing their significance away. She knew the staff of the Four Seasons well enough to know they were hard to crack. Their only security cameras were in the lobby, and she still didn't know The Blonde's name, so the best she could do would be to go to the front desk, present a photo, and ask what room she was in. And Simone knew that she would be shut down right then and asked to leave, and that The Blonde would be warned. Better to be less direct until she was desperate. She would stake the Four Seasons out and, if she was lucky, The Blonde would show up and maybe meet with someone. Then Simone could start getting some information.

She stubbed out what was left of her cigarette, then showered and dressed, bought a newspage and a fresh pack of cigarettes on her way to the Four Seasons, and settled in. There was a café on a small boat just down the bridge from the hotel, so she sat there, and ordered a coffee. She read the news first swipe to last. She used the dicta feature on her earpiece to send out a few messages and listened to others—an automated job offer from a corporate espionage company, Henry

St. Michel's finances from Danny, and then, curiously, a message from Pastor Sorenson: "Dear Miss Pierce, I have the papers I would like your client to sign. If you could stop by in person on Sunday night to retrieve them, without your client, I would be most appreciative."

Interesting. Simone blew smoke out of her mouth and sipped from her third coffee. deCostas didn't really need to sign any release forms—he'd already dropped his marble. But Sorenson had said without her client. He wanted something.

She spent the next few hours watching the hotel while going over Henry St. Michel's finances. The holo-projection from her earpiece could only create a small, flickering screen, so that took a while and gave her very little information. He'd taken out a lot of cash recently, but before then, his accounts were steady. He clearly wasn't rich, and the business wasn't thriving, but he was surviving in the city, which was more than a lot of people could say. Linnea's finances were separate; Danny had tried to access them, but they were behind a heavily encrypted server that would take a while to crack. Simone told him not to bother. There was nothing here.

She'd been watching the hotel, camera at the ready, for nearly four hours. The Blonde hadn't showed, and she had other things to investigate. And now a private meeting with Sorenson to wonder about. Maybe The Blonde had already checked out, or maybe Simone had been spotted and The Blonde had cancelled her plans to avoid being seen. Waiting and patience were part of a good detective's job, but so was adaptability. There were other alleys of investigation to go down. Simone stubbed out her cigarette and left the newspage behind.

HENRY AND LOU'S BUSINESS didn't look different from the outside. Henry's name hadn't been removed; there wasn't a sign that said

"Closed due to death of a partner." Simone knocked and went in without waiting for an answer.

Inside didn't show the signs of a hasty exodus that Simone had half-expected. No frantic Lou packing up goods in messy balls of plastic wrap and cardboard. It was the same as before. Lou sat at the same desk, a cigarette drooping from her mouth. It smelled good—real tobacco. Simone wondered how she could afford it. Wondered if she'd share. She looked up when Simone came in.

"Oh, it's you."

Simone walked closer to Lou.

"The cops said I shouldn't talk to you," Lou said, standing. "Said you weren't whoever you said, from Canada. Said you're a shamus and you helped Henry take his last drink."

"That last one is a lie," Simone said. "I want to find out who killed Henry."

"That's nice." Lou took the cigarette from her mouth. She blew smoke out through her nose.

"You don't seem too broken up over the death of your partner." Simone sat down in the chair across from Lou.

"That's a dumb line," Lou leaned back in her chair. Simone stared until she looked away and started talking again. "Henry was a good guy. He worked for my husband, before he died. I liked the kid, but he wasn't family. He was always closer with my husband." She didn't talk about Henry as though he were her son, Simone thought. More like he was a family pet.

"So who would have killed him? Was he working on anything big?"

"I told you the cops told me not to talk to you."

"If you really cared what the cops thought you would have called them the moment I came in."

Lou barked a laugh. "Fair enough."

"So was he working on anything?"

"Nothing abnormal. You can look at his desk calendar if you want. The cops took his touchdesk server, but he kept everything on paper, too—people get old-fashioned in our business." She gestured with her cigarette towards Henry's desk. "Why are you even on this, anyway?"

"Linnea hired me," Simone said, standing and walking over to Henry's desk. "She thought he was cheating."

Lou laughed again. "Cheating? They may not have cared much for each other anymore, but he wasn't fool enough to cheat. Linnea was the one with the money."

"What makes you think they didn't care for each other?" Simone flipped through the calendar, finding the night he was shot. Usual business stuff was written down, but at the bottom of the page was the name Misty and "7 p.m." No address. No last name. Simone took out her camera and shot a photo.

"Oh, nothing specific. He didn't talk about her much; sometimes he sounded tense on the phone with her. But he didn't confide in me. You should ask his mother."

"His mother?"

"Trixie. She's uptown, on the *Paradise*—you know, the cruise ship they made into an old-age home? Tasteless name. When I was younger I thought it was so tasteless it was funny. Now, just tasteless."

"I know it."

"It's like a prison for people like me. I wouldn't be caught dead on one of those. I'm still in the same apartment my husband and I bought before the water started rising."

"You were there when it was retrofitted?"

"Oh yes. It was one of the late ones, built ten years before the water, so it was ready for it. Lots of neighbors moved out anyway. Cowards. Now I have a younger sort of neighbors. Noisier. I don't mind it, really, but . . . Howard used to ask them to quiet down, and they would listen to him. I don't bother." Lou sighed and took a long drag on her cigarette. "Anything interesting on his calendar?"

"Do you know this Misty he was supposed to meet with the other night?" Lou shrugged, then turned to her touchdesk and pressed a few keys. "I don't know the name, and we don't have anything on record." Simone filed the name away—maybe it was The Blonde.

"Don't suppose you know where Linnea is?"

"Linnea? I hardly ever see her. Is she missing?"

"Not picking up her phone, anyway."

"Isn't that the sort of thing you'd call suspicious?"

"My dad always taught me to view everything as suspicious." Lou cocked her head, half a nod of agreement. "Do you recognize this woman?" Simone found a photo of The Blonde on her camera and handed it to Lou. Lou held it away from her face, and lowered her glasses to the tip of her nose.

"No. Should I?"

"She had dinner with Henry the night before he died," Simone said.

"She have a name?" Lou asked. Simone shook her head. "Well, I could see why Linnea might be jealous. But no. I don't know her."

"If you do see her, or she shows up asking questions, or Linnea pops up, would you mind calling me?" Simone took out one of her cards and put it on the desk.

"I'll consider it."

"That's the best I can hope for." Simone headed for the door but turned around as she opened it. Lou was staring at the card Simone had left on the desk, unmoving. "And thanks."

"Police are idiots," Lou said, not looking up. "But you seem like you might be smart. Don't disappoint me. He might not have been family, but he was home. Part of . . . this." She threw her arm out, gesturing at the empty room, then looked down at her desk, as if ashamed to have shown a flicker of sadness. Simone stared at Lou a moment longer and saw the wrinkles around her face slowly falling, like a wave in slow motion. She looked sad. Tired. Alone. Simone

nodded and left. This wasn't a moment she was invited to partici-
pate in. And she'd gotten enough.

LINNEA AND HENRY'S PLACE was just a half-hour walk uptown,
around NYU. Once outside, Simone lit a cigarette and started walking. Her phone buzzed, announcing a new message. She tapped her
earpiece as she walked away from the shipping company. The message was from deCostas.

"Simone," her phone read to her, "I hope we're still on for more
exploration. I have selected more buildings, specifically One Wall
Street, Clinton Tower, and 590 Madison Avenue. I hope you're up
for it. I promise to be a good boy this time and follow your every
command."

Simone took a drag off her cigarette as she walked. She didn't
really have time for babysitting deCostas anymore. But . . . he was
still easy money and easy on the eyes. She could handle both cases.
deCostas would just have to stay on the back burner. A lot depended
on what she could get out of Caroline on Saturday, what she found
at the St. Michel house, and what she learned from Henry's mother.
She had tomorrow open. She wrote him back that she'd meet him
at his hotel and take him to One Wall Street. Best to do that one
earliest, considering what it became at night. But for now she needed
to figure out what was going on with The Blonde before she saw
Caroline, and that meant finding Linnea, if she could. She finished
her cigarette and tossed it into the water, then stared up at the St.
Michel townhouse. If Linnea really had run off, she might have left
behind some evidence of where she was going.

It was a simple-looking building: faded slate, glossy with Glassteel;
probably the top of some residential building that went up in the
1950s or '60s. Only three stories rose above the ocean, the first of
them slightly higher than usual. It was one of a series of identical
homes in the same building, and they all shared a wide, solid bridge,

white polished steps descending from their doors to the walkway lined with waist-high lamps in the shape of old lanterns. It was a quiet part of town. A few bridges away were the buildings and boats where what was left of NYU operated, but these bridges felt private, like a gated community. A little ways away, Simone saw a woman pushing a stroller. She felt the gel in her coat warm up in response to an involuntary shiver.

She walked up the steps to the door of the townhouse and rang the bell. No answer. So the servants had cleared out, too—if they had had any. Simone had assumed a woman like Linnea had a score of attendants, but there was no real reason to think that. She rang the bell again, but still no answer, and then tried the door. Locked, which wasn't surprising. No alarm panel visible, and it looked like a run-of-the-mill electronic lock.

Simone looked around, searching for the usual spots people hid their spare key. There was no doormat. There were small decorative sconces on the wall on either side of the door, sort of scallop-shaped, but no key tucked into either of them. She walked back down the steps to the bridge. She looked at the closest of the lanterns built into the bridge. It was a simple thing, with a metal-cone top and a tube of fogged glass. Simone glanced around to make sure no one was looking, then lifted the top off the lantern. There was no key inside the glass part, but when she looked inside the actual metal top, there was a slim, plastic card, taped so it wouldn't fall down. Simone smiled. She took the card and replaced the metal top, then hurried back up the steps and slid it into the lock, which opened with a click.

Inside it already had the stillness of a place abandoned. Simone recognized it in the way she could hear the waves outside, or how the air smelled overly cool. She called out "Hello" just in case, but no one responded, so she began her search.

None of the lights was on, and Simone didn't feel a need to change that. Silvery light came in through silk shades and a skylight on the roof. It was a nice house. It had been completely remodeled recently, by the look of it. There was no stairway to the flooded parts of the building, but a large spiral stairway went up. The color scheme was seashell pink and white, and a large tapestry of some Mediterranean city with a vibrant blue ocean dominated the living room.

Next, she searched the kitchen and then the bedrooms upstairs. Linnea and Henry seemed to have separate bedrooms—his plain with a touchdesk; hers white and pink with oversized sheets and a vanity with a few photos tucked in the sides of the mirror. Some makeup was missing, and her closet was empty. Nothing under the bed, no stray notes or clues. Even the wastebasket was empty. Linnea had definitely taken off. Simone sat down at the vanity and opened the drawers, one by one, rifling through perfume samples and hairbrushes for some real sign of where Linnea could have gone, but there was nothing. She stared at the photos stuck into the vanity mirror. Why hadn't these been taken? She tugged at one, but it was sealed to the frame. If she pulled any harder, she'd tear it. So Linnea had cleared out, fast enough she couldn't bring this mirror.

There were three photos. One of Henry and Linnea, but much younger. This one was on the right side of the frame, probably more for show than genuine sentiment. On the left were two older photos: one of a couple and a little girl, about forty years ago, judging by the clothes. Simone bent it slightly to look at the back. "Me, Mom & Dad," it said in elegant cursive. The other photo was of a young Linnea, holding a small toddler in her lap. Simone furrowed her brow. Linnea had never mentioned a kid, and when Simone had done the usual background check on her and Henry, nothing about kids had come up. She bent this photo forward, too, and looked at the back. "Me & baby M," it said. Simone shrugged. A niece or nephew, maybe?

She let the photo go, now with a slight crease in it, and sighed. There were no obvious signs of where Linnea had gone. But there was still more to explore. She went back to Henry's room and rifled through his touchdesk but didn't find anything useful there. The bathrooms were all squeaky clean, and there were no notes in the pockets of any of Henry's jackets or pants in the laundry room. There was a study another flight up, but the touchdesk was clean, except for some notes comparing the costs of tickets to the mainland by ferry and a few planes. Passage to the mainland wasn't too difficult; there was one ferry that came in every morning and left every night. It was a long voyage—just over a day—but the ferry wasn't cheap and didn't hold more than a hundred, so it took some planning. It was why the mainland government couldn't keep a steady grip on the city for more than a day or two. If you wanted to get away on the fly, you needed to hire a small airplane out of the *Ohio*, a decommissioned aircraft carrier that served as the city's one airport, or a private boat sturdy enough to make it to the mainland and with radar up-to-date enough not to hit anything getting there. There were huge storms that rolled between the city and the mainland, tearing up any small boats or planes stupid enough to be in their way. And there were other, smaller cities between New York and the mainland, empty of even ghosts, with buildings that rose up to just below the water like hands eager to pull down anything they could grab.

The next flight up was an immaculate guest bedroom and what seemed to be a large storage room. It was the one room in the house where Simone needed to turn on the lights, but it was mostly just shelves lined with plastic boxes labeled "clothes," "blankets," and the like. Simone looked at the dust on them to see if any had been gone through recently, but they had all clearly been closed for at least a month or two. Except one. It was a plastic box on the floor, in the far corner of the room. It was empty, but there were handprints in the dust on top. Simone picked it up and turned it around, looking for impressions of what had been inside. There was a peculiar smell, like chlorine and smoke. And in one corner a whitish residue. Foam?

Linnea and Henry hadn't seemed like drug users at all, much less MouthFoamers. But the box had definitely held Foam. The smell of it was unmistakable and brought back the memory of the one time she'd tried it, after her dad died and she found an old photo of her mom in his stuff. It had made her feel not numb, and not happy, either, but content. Like she'd transcended regular emotions and found some sort of Zen, Nirvana, inner-peace crap, and the ocean was a lake and the city was an opening flower, wilting as it floated. Then, a day later, she'd woken up in her dad's bed, his old clothes woven around her like a nest, and the weird, sticky drool that the drug got its name from sticking her face to a jacket. And she felt not at all at peace. Not at all enlightened. Like she'd forgotten something important, like she'd forgotten how to be happy, had forgotten if it was even really possible to be happy. She knew then she couldn't do it again. It was too good, too easy, and she knew she would just slip away like a stone into the water, and she was half terrified and half thrilled at how that idea made her feel. For a year, she'd avoided anywhere they bought and sold the stuff.

And if Linnea and Henry had had this big a box of it . . . Foam was a fine powder, smoked, and a box this big would have been a year's supply and probably obscenely expensive. Or stolen. Could all this be some sort of drug-dealer trouble? Neither of them had had any of the signs of being MouthFoamers—dazed look, the white in the corners of their mouths. Nor had anything she'd seen suggested it was a drug deal. Unless The Blonde was their distributor, and they were chemists. But that didn't make sense either. Making the stuff was a complicated affair that took constant supervision. They had lives. They didn't run a Foam Lab.

Simone put the box back where she'd found it. She sent a note to a few of her contacts who knew the Foam business and asked them to keep an eye out for a woman of Linnea's description. Maybe if they heard the name Misty, too. But it didn't make much sense. She didn't have any leads on Linnea or who killed Henry. She'd have to try Henry's mother next.

Paradise was uptown, moored somewhere over where Central Park used to be, so Simone hired a cab to take her. She lay back in the taxi boat, feeling the spray from the waves it left as it rocketed over the water, dodging building tops and other boats. It was a nice day. Strong winds, less fog, cool air.

She tried to collect the facts of the case as she cruised through the city. Henry was dead, Linnea missing. Drugs—a lot of them—recently in their home, also missing. Someone had met Henry unexpectedly. And then there was Dash, looking for Linnea. And The Blonde, whose name was possibly Misty, who had met with Henry and Anika, and had been in Sorenson's mission—for a meeting with him? And she'd met with Caroline.

What connected them? Or was everyone more innocent than they appeared? Did Caroline even know what The Blonde was up to? Simone remembered the way The Blonde had leveled the gun at her and then so easily pointed it at deCostas, as though his life—more innocent than Simone's, surely—was completely unimportant to her. The Blonde was a whirlpool of trouble, and anyone around her was getting dragged in, or already drowning.

Simone shook her head and took a deep breath. What was Caroline into?

What was Simone into?

The taxi pulled up by a stand next to *Paradise,* and Simone paid and got out. *Paradise* was an old cruise ship, at least twenty stories tall, with tennis courts and two pools. The gangplank up to the boat was unguarded, but Simone didn't know what room Henry's mother was in, so she sought an attendant, who wore white scrubs with military pockets and epaulettes—half nurse, half sailor.

"I'm looking for Mrs. St. Michel," Simone told her. The woman looked her up and down, her frozen smile melting to suspicion as she dealt with someone who wasn't a resident.

"You're a relative?" she asked.

"Her son's lawyer," Simone said.

The nurse nodded, understanding, and checked her tablet. "Room 423." Simone thanked her and walked past the senior citizens playing shuffleboard, past the wave pool, empty except for one old woman in a swimsuit, sunglasses, and bathing cap, resting in an inner tube. She took the stairs up to the fourth deck, then followed the room numbers to 423.

Simone took a deep breath. She wasn't good with mothers. She liked to think it was because hers had taken off, so she didn't know how to act around them, but it was more that she didn't trust them. Her mom had left when she was still a little girl—no two-sentence note on the dresser saying she loved Simone but had to go; she just wasn't there one day. Her dad had told her the news softly, while Simone was still in her pajamas: "Your mom is gone. She's not coming back."

Simone had only vague memories of her now. Long red hair. Lots of freckles. A giant smile. She used to sing, too. And she had that mainland accent. Simone remembered imitating it sometimes and how both her parents would laugh at the way she drew out her vowels and tilted her head to the side to achieve the effect.

Mom had read to her every night and told Simone how she loved her. And then she'd gone. Which made Simone doubt there'd been any love there to begin with. She knew there were plenty of mothers who didn't take off, who really loved their kids, but Simone suspected that more than admitted it would like to vanish, just like hers had.

She knocked on the door, which was answered by a short woman, perhaps in her seventies, with small, burgundy curls and a drink in her hand. She smelled strongly of vodka.

"Oh," the woman said. "The police said you might show up." She turned around and walked back into her room, leaving the door open. Simone followed. Inside was a simple cabin with a bed, sofa, and side table. A dresser was doubling as a bar, covered in bottles and glasses. On the sofa was some knitting in bright-red yarn.

"Did they?" Simone asked.

"Oh yes," the words caught in her throat, but Simone wasn't sure if it was the beginning of a laugh or sob. "They said you were a detective and the prime suspect."

"Mrs. St. Michel—" Simone began.

"Trixie," she interrupted. "Call me Trixie. Stupid name. Like you'd give a dog." She sat down and put her drink on the side table. She picked up the red swath of knitting and began to pick at it.

"If the police told you I'm a prime suspect, why let me in?" Simone asked.

"You didn't do it," Trixie said, exasperated as she struggled with the knitting. "I'm trying to take this apart. It was going to be a sweater. For Henry. But now . . ." She pulled at the yarn, and some of it gave, leaving her holding a long red loop out from the rest of the fabric. She smiled and looped the yarn around her wrist, pulling it and pulling it, trying to unravel the knitting. It snagged. "Do you want something to drink?" she asked.

"No, thank you," Simone said. Trixie shrugged, plucking at the knitting again. This was sad. Even Simone could feel that. The smell of alcohol was as thick as the salt in the air outside. "So how do you know I didn't do it?"

"Their theory is stupid. If Linnea wanted Henry dead she would have done it herself. She's a hands-on type. Maybe she did kill him. I don't know. Wouldn't surprise me." Trixie didn't look up but kept picking at the knitting, her fingers like pecking birds. "But she wouldn't have someone else do it. That would be . . . too messy for her. All that money. She could have hired so many maids and cooks, but she couldn't stand watching people do things wrong.

She never let me help when I came over for dinner. Not even set the table. She'd kill Henry herself. And not until after they'd sold the art, anyway. Henry was going to run off with the money by himself. Wasn't even going to take me. He said he'd write. Who runs away from his mother?"

"A lot of people," Simone said. Trixie snorted a laugh, then put down the knitting and picked up her drink again. "What art were they going to sell?"

Trixie took a long drink before answering and put the glass back down on the table. "Some old piece of art Henry dredged up from storage. Linnea said it was worth millions, and she had some idea . . . Henry didn't tell me much. He just said it was going to make him a fortune, and he was going to run away with it and leave Linnea. Called it his *Mona Lisa*. He said he'd send me a message when he was safe, that he'd set up a bank account for me." She picked up the knitting again and tried pulling out another strand of yarn. With a yank, part of it became unknitted and several bright red lines twisted away from her hands. "But I guess Linnea had the same thing planned, and she was better prepared. Linnea was always well prepared."

Simone nodded. "Do you recognize this woman?" she asked, showing Trixie a photo of The Blonde. "Maybe her name is Misty?"

Trixie shook her head. "No. Who is she?"

"I saw her with your son, the night before he died."

"She's not his type. He likes dark hair. And he never mentioned anyone named Misty. I'd remember. Worse than Trixie." She finished her drink and got up and poured herself another.

"Is there anything else you can think of?" Simone asked. "Anyone who'd want to hurt him besides Linnea?"

Trixie turned around, her glass refilled, and locked eyes with Simone as she downed the alcohol in one long drink. Simone watched the soft skin of her neck and chin bob as she swallowed.

Then she put her glass down and refilled it, and sat down again. She picked up the red yarn and began pulling at it again.

"Well, thank you for your help," Simone said, and made for the door.

"Are you going to find Linnea?" Trixie asked, still picking at her knitting.

"I hope so."

"I hope when you do you'll gut her for me. Gut her from neck to cunt and throw her overboard for the fish to eat."

OUTSIDE, THE SUN WAS lowering towards the horizon. Simone started walking home. It was a long walk downtown, but she was in the mood for a long walk. The smell of the booze in Trixie's room clung to her hair, and she kept imagining the red yarn in her hands and her mother's red hair. Trixie seemed to be right about Linnea's betrayal, but then why hire Simone? Was Simone just the fall guy? And who was The Blonde?

She had a message from Caroline asking if she wanted to get drinks, but Simone didn't respond to it. She didn't want to think about Caroline or about Caroline talking with the woman who had pointed a gun at her. She pushed that to the side and thought about deCostas instead. Much sweeter thoughts to be had there. Back on that case, she sent off a message to Mr. Ryan, who owned the next building on the list, telling him about deCostas and his request to see the stairwell. Mr. Ryan wrote back promptly, as he always did, saying he would be there to greet them at 9 a.m., sharp. You weren't late when Mr. Ryan was doing you a favor.

When she got home, someone was waiting in her office. She could see the shadow through the glass in the door. Simone sighed. It had been a long day with a lot of questions and not many answers, and all she wanted was to get into the bath. She took out her gun and held it at her side. Just in case.

She found Peter sitting in front of the empty receptionist's desk, dressed in uniform, his hat in his lap. There was a package on the desk in front of him.

"Oh," Simone said when she recognized him, and holstered her gun. She turned away and took her hat off to hang on the coatrack.

"Expecting someone else?" Peter asked, standing behind her. Simone looked down at her hat, still holding it. It felt *off* somehow. Peter was stepping closer to her. She quickly felt around the brim, and tucked inside found a small tracker. *Dash.* She was annoyed with herself for not noticing it earlier. She pocketed the tracker and hung up her hat and coat, turning just as Peter had gotten in arm's reach of her.

"You my mailman now?" Simone asked, nodding at the package on the desk.

"No," Peter said. "Some messenger dropped it off. I just signed for it. I figured that was okay. I've done it before."

Before when he spent most nights here. Before she asked for his key back.

"If you're here to arrest me, can I take a bath first?" she asked.

"No," Peter said, looking down. "I just wanted to let you know that Kluren knows you've been poking around, interviewing Mrs. Freth and Mrs. St. Michel. She's not happy. If there were enough evidence, she would lock you up right now." He looked down at the space between them.

"Lucky me." Simone stepped to the side and sat behind the nonexistent receptionist's desk.

"So you must know by now that everything points to murder for hire."

"And I'm the hire. I know. But I don't do that, Peter, you know that."

"Yeah, and so does Kluren, I think. It's why she's so angry. She's a good cop, normally. Even a nice one. But with you . . . She'll pin it to you if she can make it stick."

"Which I knew already." Simone tucked her hair behind her ears. Her neck hurt, and she wanted to rub it or crack it, but not in front of him. "So why are you here?"

"I . . ." Peter walked around the desk to her side and looked down at her. "Look, I have a boat. A good sturdy one. You can take it. Get out of town for a while."

"A while?"

"Until this blows over."

"I'm not doing that." Simone felt her spine straighten, her hands clench for a moment. "Did someone put you up to this? This Kluren or Linnea?"

"What? No, soldier, just me. Promise. I thought we could go to-gether, if you . . ."

"Sorry," Simone interrupted before he could finish. She stood, awkwardly close to him. "But no. I'm not going. Thanks, Peter." She waved her hand at the door and turned away, but he caught her hand and pulled her back, forcefully. For a moment, she thought he was pulling her into him for a kiss, the way he used to, but he let go be-fore she got close enough.

"Take the boat, Simone."

Simone turned away again, wanting this conversation to be over. She took a few steps away but could still feel Peter behind her, the way he tensed up when he got upset.

"Damn it," he said finally, his words half sigh, half explosion. "I'm trying to help you."

Simone turned back around. "I know," she said, studying him, the angle of his jaw as it clenched, the deep brown of his eyes. "But I just can't, Peter. That's not me."

"Fine," he said, his eyes flickering away from hers for a mo-ment. He stepped closer to her and took her hand in his, carefully, and then squeezed it. She couldn't tell if it was because he was an-gry or protective or both, but it was a firm squeeze, strong enough she could feel the bones in her fingers pressing together. "But be careful."

"I always am," she said. He let her hand drop and left, closing the door behind him. Simone locked it and turned back to the package on the receptionist's desk. She sliced it open with a knife from the drawer. Inside was a 3D printer cartridge from Belleau Cosmetics—the fall sampler, capable of printing out "any two lipsticks, any two blushes, and any two eye shadows from the entire collection—hundreds of possibilities!" and a note:

> Cops have been asking about you and about that meeting you were asking about. You should definitely try the sunset pearl. It'll really make your mug shot pop. Good luck.
>
> —Anika

Simone sighed and knocked the package into the trash, then picked it out again and brought it to her office, where she put it on top of her 3D printer. Makeup was good for disguises sometimes. She remembered what Anika had told her—that The Blonde was peddling bullshit. And Anika was a smart woman; Simone trusted her judgment, usually—though she could have been lying, too, to throw Simone off the trail. No one else seemed to think it was bullshit. Not even Caroline.

At least Anika wasn't holding her responsible for the cops' questioning her. If Simone made it through all this, she didn't want to lose a client.

She went to the bathroom and ran a bath. She shouldn't have snapped at Peter or gotten so suspicious. She wasn't sure who she could trust right now—not when even Caroline was hiding something.

Maybe Caroline didn't know, Simone told herself, stepping into the water and sinking beneath it. Maybe she was just friends with a dangerous woman. Maybe she was in danger herself. But Simone couldn't believe that. Caroline was the best judge of character Simone had ever seen; she saw through people and knew exactly what they were. She knew who she was dealing with. And that meant that she was as dangerous as The Blonde.

Simone held her breath under the water for as long as she could before coming up for air. It was always good to practice holding your breath. You never knew when you might end up going under.

SEVEN

—

DECOSTAS' HOTEL WAS ONE of the cheap tourist places, moored with a big, flashy chain to one of the towers of the Brooklyn Bridge. The towers were a few stories over the water, the suspension cables still coming off them, like stage curtains sloping down into the water. At one point, someone had proposed using the bridge towers as the base for a new bridge, but there had been protests that it would ruin the view. Instead there were boats secured all along the side with bridges running between them, usually lined in tourists, taking photos of the headstone-like masonry.

When Simone showed up, deCostas was already on deck staring at the cables, which dripped with rust and seaweed. Simone glanced up at them but quickly looked away. She'd never liked the rusted cords; they reminded her too much of bloody rope. Instead, she let her eyes run down deCostas' back to his ass and linger there for a moment before tapping him on the shoulder. He turned around, his face surprised for a moment, harder than Simone had seen it, but then it quickly melted into the usual flirtatious smile as he handed her one of the cups of coffee he was holding, still hot.

"You taking the price of that out of my fee?" Simone asked.

"It's a gift," deCostas said. "A thank-you for still being my guide after I stuck my nose where it did not belong."

"Yeah," Simone said, taking the coffee, "but if you think you can buy me back with a six-dollar coffee, you haven't been paying attention to my fees." She wasn't really angry with him anymore. She'd known he was senseless when she took him along trailing The Blonde; what he'd hired her for had already proven that.

"I know. You saved my life." He blew on his coffee, more slowly than necessary.

"She wasn't going to shoot you."

"How do you know?"

"She was making a point. If she'd shot you, I would have shot her, and maybe she would have dodged it, maybe not, but it wasn't worth the risk for her."

deCostas nodded and sipped his coffee. "Can I ask what you were talking about?"

"You can ask, but I won't answer. Another case. Confidential."

"I think you like keeping secrets."

"Only the ones you're curious about." Simone smiled as she sipped her coffee. "But we can walk and flirt. We shouldn't be late." She turned and walked away, leaving him to catch up.

"What is this place? I thought One Wall Street was just a rental building."

"It is . . . of a sort. It's all run by Mr. Ryan. He rents the space to a lot of people."

"A lot of people?"

"Yes." deCostas had caught up to her, so she walked a little faster. "The floors have all been emptied out, nonbearing walls torn down— but historical embellishments preserved, like the marble floors. It's a beautiful space—clean, open, well lit, totally protected. Mr. Ryan employs some serious muscle to keep it safe."

"Why?"

"At night, various renters gather there and sell their wares in a . . . nonjudgmental environment."

"You mean stolen goods?"

"Stolen, laundered, illegal. It's a bazaar, a real black market. It's where everyone goes to sell. People from all over the world come here because Mr. Ryan keeps it safe and organizes auctions for the more . . . unique items. He auctions them off personally, hiding the owner's identity, issues invitations to those he knows can afford it and would want it, and he takes only a small cut of the profits. There are a million places in the city to buy illegal whatever. But if you want the good stuff, you go to One Wall Street."

"And he's going to let me throw something down the stairwell?"

"Mr. Ryan is powerful enough to be a generally nice guy. No one is going to mess with him, and if someone does, he'll find out about it before anything bad happens, and then that person . . . well, he hires people for that. And he knows me. I've shown up as a representative for a buyer a few times, and he's hired me as an extra pair of eyes in the auction room. He trusts me. Or at least, he's unconcerned by me. And you." Simone took a long drink of her coffee, but it was cold, so she threw it in the nearest trash can.

"You know a lot of people."

"It's my job. This city is a web of important people and favors and secrets. I need to know those people, be owed those favors, and keep those secrets. Otherwise I'm not worth what you're paying me."

"Do you charge more than most detectives in the city?"

"Yeah, but I'm worth it, aren't I?" She shot him a sidelong glance. He was grinning. Simone did charge more than most, but there weren't many to compare her to. In the whole city, there were maybe a dozen private detectives. And they were all good. There were always a couple more who opened up shop every other month, but they were gone within a week or two—found by the recycling boats or, if they were lucky, making waves back to the mainland when they realized they were in over their heads. Simone had been around a long time, and she had inherited her father's business, so she thought she was probably one of the best. Her and Dash. And neither of them could find Linnea. She couldn't still be in the city, could she?

Mr. Ryan had preserved the outside of One Wall Street like a picture postcard. It was a perfect monolith. Straight angles, evenly spaced windows, rising fifty stories high from the bottom of the ocean, twenty-nine above water. Deco designs framed every window, gold lines against the gray stone. It could have been an incredibly elegant tomb. No one went in or out during the day, and there was just one narrow steel bridge to the small doorway. It was almost invisible in the shadow of the Freedom Tower complex, with its condos and fancy barge-parks where the wealthy walked their dogs.

Simone walked down the bridge, motioning deCostas to stay behind her. There was a small buzzer next to the closed door, surrounded by more gold lines. Simone rang it once. The door opened to a woman who filled the frame completely. She was tall, broad, and not smiling.

"We don't open until after sunset," she said.

"My name is Simone Pierce, this is Alejandro deCostas. Mr. Ryan is expecting us."

The woman nodded, apparently unsurprised, and stepped aside to let them pass. Inside was a wide hallway. The whole area was tiled in pink-and-black marble. She closed the door behind them.

"You're ten minutes early," she said.

"I know how Mr. Ryan hates people to be late," Simone said. "We'll wait for him." The woman didn't say anything but stepped in front of the closed door. Motioning deCostas to follow her, Simone walked down the hallway, which led to a large room. It was spotlight-bright, sun pouring in through huge windows, reflecting off marble tiles and bouncing everywhere like an insect trapped in a jar. Simone could hear the soft patter of the waves against the windows. The room was entirely empty except for the elevators and two stairwell doors. A single painting hung opposite the elevators.

Simone walked over to get a closer look. She had never been in One Wall Street during the day. Usually it was so crowded with people, she'd never even noticed the painting.

"I thought there would be stalls or shops or something," deCostas said.

"Everyone brings their own setup. They clean up their own problems that way," Simone said, looking at the painting. It wasn't particularly large—perhaps three-and-a-half feet tall and four-and-a-half wide—and was framed in the same gilded color as the window adornments. It was a subtle sort of painting. Simone understood why she had passed over it before, but now it drew her in.

It was yellow, golden really, and showed an ancient port at sunset. There were ships coming in, moored right next to the stone docks that cropped out of great columns. Not really docks, actually. Just . . . a courtyard. Framed by the sea on one side. Across from that were more columns, like the walls of a building emerging from the ocean. People were everywhere, not minding the ships parked around them.

"Claude Lorrain," came a voice, echoing across the empty room. Simone turned. Mr. Ryan was a narrow, elegantly dressed man, with a shaved head and a thin line of a mustache. She had never seen him wearing anything besides a tailored suit, complete with pocket square, and today was no different. He had a faint accent—something European, maybe, or pretending to be European. He smiled at Simone. "Please, keep admiring it. That is what it is there for. But I am afraid people get so caught up in the goings-on that they never even notice."

Simone turned around again, staring at the painting. Mr. Ryan stepped up next to her, and they looked at it together. She could feel herself looking to where his eyes looked, trying to take in what he was seeing. "It was painted in the 1630s or '40s. Lorrain was a landscape painter—very influential. Painters copied his style for generations. He painted many seaports, but this one is my favorite, so I took pains to acquire it. I love the light, the liveliness of it. It's like a city on water. Perhaps it makes me happy to know that we are not the first." He sighed happily as though this were a private joke between Simone and him. "It has two titles. Some call it *The Return of Odysseus*, and some call it *Odysseus Returns Chryseis to Her Father*. In the former case, it would be after the Trojan War, at the end of *The Odyssey*, when Odysseus finally returns home to his ever-faithful wife, Penelope, strings his bow, and slays her suitors. . . . In the case of the latter, it would be one of the first acts of contrition during the Trojan War, as Agamemnon has Odysseus deliver the captured Chryseis to her father to end a plague. But it just makes the war longer and bloodier. It could be about a man giving in to the gods, or it could be about one returning home after triumphing over them. I like that about it, too."

"I'm sorry I never noticed it before," Simone said. "It's beautiful."

"I'm glad you've noticed it now."

"It looks like New York would, if things were simpler."

"It is either the beginning or end of a war, Ms. Pierce. Surely that is just as complex as now?"

"In war, you're given orders," Simone said. "Here, you just make them up for yourself."

Mr. Ryan ran his thumb over his chin, considering. "Maybe so, but we are not here for art history lessons or philosophical debates. This is your Mr. deCostas?" deCostas had been standing back and away from them, as if wary.

"It is. He just wants to see the stairwell and drop one of his devices down it. Show Mr. Ryan the device."

deCostas pulled one of the small marble devices from his jacket pocket and held it up. Mr. Ryan approached and examined it without taking it.

"How do I know it isn't a bomb?"

"Because I'm sure one of your detectors in the hallway would have told you if it was. How many do you have now? Twenty-six?" Mr. Ryan smiled but waved a finger at her.

"It would be foolish for me to tell you that. But you are correct. I know the device has a wireless signal, but it does not convert audio or visual data, so I see no reason to keep it from the bottom of the ocean. Come!" He clapped his hands. "Let me show you the stairs." He walked them over to the stairwell and opened the door. It wasn't even locked. Mr. Ryan probably never had to worry about anyone getting as far as the stairs. The stairwell itself was like the rest of the building—pristine and cleanly ornate. Even the water lapping against the stairs seemed cleaner somehow. deCostas stepped forward and knelt down to examine the water while Simone and Mr. Ryan hung back in the doorway.

"Was there something else you wanted, Ms. Pierce?" Mr. Ryan asked, sotto voce. Simone shook her head. "I have heard that you are Linnea St. Michel's assistant these days."

"Some people seem to think so," Simone answered carefully. What did the St. Michel case have to do with Mr. Ryan?

"And are you?"

"Do you think I'd answer that?"

Mr. Ryan murmured a small laugh. "A good point. Well, if you happen to run into her, please let Ms. St. Michel know that if she is in need of funds and is willing to sell the object she once approached me about, I could put an auction together within a day. It would fetch a hefty price."

Simone watched deCostas carefully take a water sample.

"Would it?"

"Yes, it would. But I'm not giving you another art history lesson, Ms. Pierce. Either you know the object's worth or you don't. I begin to suspect you don't."

deCostas dropped the small marble into the water and watched it fall away. Then he took out his notebook and began making notes.

"Linnea doesn't tell me everything. I didn't know she had approached you about the object at all."

"Once. But then she changed her mind. Very disappointing. But if you should run into her . . ."

"I'll give her the message. Thank you, Mr. Ryan."

deCostas put the notebook away and stood back up, turning around to face them.

"All done," he said. "Thank you."

"I am a friend of education and archeology, Mr. deCostas. I hope you will remember me if you uncover anything."

"Of course," deCostas said. "Thank you again."

Mr. Ryan nodded and gestured that they should go out of the stairwell ahead of him. He followed them and closed the door. This time he locked it.

"It has been a pleasure as always, Ms. Pierce. And charming meeting you, Mr. deCostas. I hope your expedition to our City on the Sea is fruitful." He bowed slightly, but did not shake hands. "Ms. Antiphates will show you out."

The large woman who had opened the door for them appeared and gestured that they should follow her.

"I'm hoping for another art history lesson sometime soon, Mr. Ryan," Simone said as she followed the woman.

"As am I, Ms. Pierce," Mr. Ryan said. Simone turned around and flashed him a grin. He was standing exactly where they had left him, watching them walk down the hallway. Simone imagined him staying there, watching, until they were out the door and Ms. Antiphates locked it behind him again.

"That was pretty easy," deCostas said.

"Yeah. The next one is easier. 590 Madison is residential, no doorman. We should be able to walk in and check out the stairwell. Clinton Tower is the same as the Broecker Building, just not as fancy. I have an appointment for four p.m. We'll take the elevator, cancel, hop into the stairwell, and then run."

"I didn't think I'd be skirting so many security guards. I thought this was a lawless city on the water, with no authority."

"There's plenty of authority: security guards, personal enforcers, and the police do an all right job because they have an arrangement with all the private security in town to turn criminals over to them. No one enforces the mainland laws—we're supposed to, but no one does. But the big stuff? Murder, big robberies? The cops will try to hook anyone who pulls that. The truth is, there's authority because of who we are. New York is a combination of self-selection and natural selection. People have to be brave, stupid, or some combination of the two to come here. They have to be dangerous—whether with a gun, or money or something else—to survive. And those of us who were born here . . . we have a special sort of education. You try to mug someone, there's a good chance you'll be the one who ends up in the water. Criminals are careful. And it's easier to get a gun here than almost anywhere else in the world." She shrugged. "In case you want a souvenir."

"I don't think I'd know how to use it."

"Just point and pull the trigger. Easy as anything."

AT 4:16 P.M., THEY were running out of the Clinton Tower; 590 Madison had gone off without a hitch, and the Clinton Tower seemed to be going fine until an unexpected pair of security men stepped into the stairwell and walked down to the bottom floor, lighting cigarettes for a quick smoke break. All four of them had frozen for a moment, security men on the stairs, Simone and deCostas standing by the water's edge. Then one of the guards had remembered his job and shouted, "Hey!" which sent Simone and deCostas running out the door, into the crowded lobby. The guards chased after them but quickly gave up and Simone and deCostas were soon out of the building. They stopped running a few bridges away and Simone raised her eyebrows at deCostas, who was bent over, catching his breath.

"You drop your marble?" Simone asked.

"Yeah," deCostas said, taking a deep breath.

"We didn't run that far. You shouldn't be so out of breath. Or is your stamina lacking?"

"My stamina is legendary," he said, standing up and grinning at her. He pushed some hair out of his face. "I was scared, perhaps. After Mr. Ryan thinking it was a bomb, I didn't want to be locked away for terrorism or something."

"Aw, I could have protected you from that."

"My hero."

"Don't mock it, I've got a rep as an excellent hero."

"Oh? Rescuing fair lads such as myself, holding us in your strong arms?"

"Legs, more often." Simone smirked. They looked at each other in silence for a moment.

"So, is this where we part ways?" he asked. "Have that other case to worry about?"

"Unless you had something else in mind," Simone smiled.

"We could always go back to my hotel," deCostas suggested with a wiggle of his eyebrows.

Simone stared at him for long enough to watch a new sheen of sweat develop at his hairline. "Okay."

SIMONE STRETCHED NAKED IN the foggy light from the window. The room smelled like smoke and salt. deCostas was asleep, face down on the bed naked, the sheets all on the floor. He held his pillow to his face and curved his body around the imprint where Simone's body had been. His ass was nice to stare at, but Simone only gazed at it a minute. That had been exactly what she needed. She felt looser again, as though whatever had been stifling her brain and body had melted away. His stamina was almost as legendary as he'd promised.

But now she was ready to get back to the case. She pulled on her clothes and left without waking deCostas. He'd call. Outside it was dark already, just a bare sliver of sun peeking out over the horizon, blocked by buildings, diffused by fog, neon red. Algae generators glowed green under the water's surface, and the city smelled like salt and mold. Simone loved the nighttime. The world was black and red and green and wet. All these trips with deCostas had had her out during the day; she felt better now, prowling the fog and shadows.

First, she stopped by the Four Seasons. She waltzed by the doorman as if she belonged there and headed to the reception desk. She still looked rough from her tumble with deCostas and did her best to look worried, too.

"I'm supposed to meet my cousin here," she told the receptionist at the desk. "Short, blonde, really pretty? I'm totally late, though."

"Is she a guest here?"

"I think so," Simone said, trying to sound young and innocent.

"And her name?"

Simone pursed her lips, then forced her face to stay cheerful.

"Misty," she tried. The receptionist blinked, then looked down at his touchdesk and typed on it.

"No one named Misty is staying with us."

"She checks in under fake names, usually," Simone said, trying to keep her voice sweet and naïve, "but . . . oh, here, I have a photo!" Simone took out the photo of The Blonde. She doubted this would work, but it was worth the risk. She had to get to The Blonde—had to figure this case out. The receptionist looked her up and down, an oily smile on his face.

"I don't think I can help you," he said. Simone gave up the act. She wasn't getting any information without a name.

"Not even if I give you a nice tip?" she asked. The man lifted his nose and turned away from her slightly. She sighed. "Can you at least tell me if I should stake this place out or if she's in for the night?" she asked in her normal voice.

"I don't think loitering would be a very good use of your time, do you?" The receptionist continued to smile. He was almost unreadable, but Simone could tell he was one question away from calling security.

"Thanks," she said, and left. That was a bust.

Next she headed a few blocks east to the Khan townhouse. It was dark now. The ocean was calm the way it was just after sunset. The fog was so heavy she couldn't see clear outlines more than five feet ahead of her. Neon lights diffused in the mist, their advertisements unreadable, the color like the last moments of a dying fireworks display, mingling with the light from the algae and the darkness of the water. Simone took out a cigarette and lit it, pausing far enough away from the townhouse that she could see the light through the windows as inverted inkblots against the night. She smoked and leaned on a railing, staring at the mix of dark and light. The water below her was like a black mirror, reflecting back bits of her: a slice of face, a cutting of hair, the corner of a trench coat.

What the fuck was Caroline into? She'd met with The Blonde, who'd also met with the now-dead Henry, with Anika, and maybe with Pastor Sorenson. She'd pointed a gun at Simone. Linnea had vanished. Linnea and Henry had been about to make a score, were trying to auction off a piece, but then changed their minds. Maybe it was a sales deal; instead of auctioning it with Mr. Ryan, they had The Blonde act as seller. That made sense. She was meeting with rich, connected people. So it must be valuable art. Although Anika had said it wasn't.

And Henry and Linnea had enough Foam to last an addict a good year. Was the art a cover for drugs? Was everyone just saying art when they meant the Foam? Mr. Ryan wouldn't be that interested if it were just drugs, though. She knew he found drugs distasteful. So did Anika. And Caroline never touched the stuff. Simone couldn't figure out what the connections were. And it bothered her that one of the few people she trusted was somehow involved. *Bothered* wasn't a strong enough word. It disturbed her. She tried to tell herself it was just a minor meeting, two people bumping into each other on the street, but she'd seen those photos of Caroline and The Blonde. It was more than that. They were friendly, they were involved. It made her wonder who Caroline was, and if Simone didn't know that, then who was *she*? The detective who had always prided herself on knowing a person's character ten seconds into a conversation—had Caroline been laughing at her this whole time, playing the role of privileged but brilliant, ambitious but careful, lawful but . . . ? Simone didn't know. She turned away from her broken reflection on the water and leaned back on the railing.

Simone acknowledged that, objectively, she was a cold person. Not cruel, but distant from her emotions. Her father had taught her that. Simone had refused to speak to him or anyone else for a week after her mother left. Her father had tucked her in every night and told her to think about why she was angry, or sad, about what she missed. One night, Simone had finally opened her mouth and told him she had figured it out: She was upset because she had never expected her mother to leave.

"Well, from now on, don't try to expect or not expect anything," her father had told her. "Then there won't be any surprises, and you'll never be sad."

Simone had tried to follow that advice, but as a detective, she had to make guesses, assumptions, figure people out—what they would do and why. He had taught her that, too, but he told her that making a guess and expecting to be right were two different things. It was a clear distinction: mind and heart. Your heart wanted to believe a guess would be right. The mind just wondered if it would be. A mind was never disappointed, always curious. It was what made a good detective: no expectations, no surprises, the ability to guess without getting so caught up in one guess that she didn't see any other options. Open mind, closed everything else.

It's why she'd never had many friends, it's why she tended to stop seeing a guy after they'd had sex, it's why she'd left Peter after he'd told her he thought maybe they should get married. She thought she had been doing a good job. She hadn't realized how she'd come to assume so much about Caroline—that she would always have Simone's back, that she kept her nose clean, and that her hands were only dirty from cleaning up other people's messes.

Simone let the cigarette fall into the water. Her earpiece buzzed, telling her there was an incoming call from deCostas. She ignored it. Instead she walked closer to the Khan townhouse. She walked slowly, her hands in her pockets, not quite creeping. The fog was a little thinner here, and she could see farther. All the lights on the top floor were on, and she could see someone's shadow walking back and forth. After a moment, the figure stopped and leaned out the window. Simone stared up at her, at Caroline, wearing only a white bra, her hair streaming around her like shadows. She looked out the window at the city, not below at Simone. She took a deep breath. Was she worried? Satisfied?

Simone walked farther away, out of earshot but where she could still see Caroline, leaning out the window. She told her phone to call Caroline. It rang twice, and Caroline left the window, then came back to it and touched her ear.

"Hey," Caroline said. "It has been a long week."

"Yeah. Look, Caroline—"

"You're not going to cancel on me for tomorrow, are you? 'Cause I really need to blow off some steam." In the window, Caroline rolled her shoulders, and her hair shimmered with the motion. She sounded tired.

"No," Simone said. "Still on. I told you I invited Danny too, right?"

"Oh? Okay. I gotta grill him about what he's been telling the mayor's wife, anyway."

"No ambushes," Simone said, forcing a chuckle. "He's airtight." She marveled at how easy it was to talk to Caroline as though everything were normal, at how quickly she forgot and trusted her again.

"Fine, fine. But I can make sly insinuations that make him nervous, can't I?"

"I would never take that away from you."

Caroline laughed, then took a deep breath. In the window, Simone saw her stretch.

"Everything okay by you? I've been reading some stuff in the police reports that have me a little worried."

"I can handle it. Just the usual nonsense, plus Kluren and all the delights that come with her."

"Okay. But if you feel a drop, I'm your umbrella, right?"

"Right." Simone smiled.

"Good. I'm going to bed. I'll see you tomorrow. And be prepared to lose, 'cause I am going to strike those motherfucking pins every time."

"Keep telling yourself that."

"Don't need to remind myself of something I know is true. 'Night. Sweet dreams."

"Good night."

Simone clicked her phone off and watched Caroline stare out the window a moment longer, then relax her body over the windowsill, head down, hair pouring off her like water. Then she straightened up and went back into the house. The lights went out. Simone stayed, watching the house for a while longer. The water under her got choppier as the moon rose, and soon there was the feeling of spray hitting her in the face and the sound of waves crashing around her.

EIGHT

——

DRIFTER'S ALLEY OPERATED OUT of an old building so far down-town that Simone was pretty sure it had been in Brooklyn, back when there were boroughs. It used to be a product-testing facility and still looked like it; the hallways branched off into small rooms that had once been used for focus groups and now contained private lanes. The lobby was small and worn looking, with walls painted a rough black and a vinyl floor. Besides the desk, the only decoration was a neon sign of a bowling ball knocking down pins, the pins returning upright, and then the ball knocking them down again, over and over. The man behind the desk was tall, scruffy, and tired. He looked up at Simone with undisguised boredom. Simone hesitated. She could walk out, come up with an excuse to cancel. She didn't want to see Caroline, didn't want to have to smile to her face while wondering if Caroline was faking her smile, too. But how could she ask if her friend was mixed up in this trouble without making it sound like an accusation?

"I have a lane reservation under the name Pierce," she said. He looked down at the tablet in his hand, typed in the name Pierce, and nodded.

"Lane twenty-six. Gloves are in the room. You need me to show you how to use it?" He asked this in a way that made it clear he hoped she would say no.

"We'll be able to figure it out," she said. He handed her a key-card and looked back at the tablet, done with her.

"My friends will show up soon," she said. The man didn't look up, and Simone glanced down the hallway. It was poorly lit and marked with bright yellow signs showing lane numbers. The doors themselves were blank, except for the occasional no-smoking sign. From behind the doors, she could hear the sounds of pins striking and people cheering. Lane twenty-six was a small, windowless black room with a pile of gloves on a shelf next to the door. Simone flipped a switch, thinking it was the lights, and there was a sudden humming as the room changed. One wall zoomed backwards into a long lane, pins all set up, and another wall became an empty scoreboard. A panel next to the switch glowed, asking her to choose from a variety of lane options. She scrolled through them, from "Arctic," where the pins were penguins that shuffled around and the room became chilly and windy, to "Blackout," where the room was totally dark and the pins just neon outlines. She settled on "Classic," which was clean nostalgia with red-and-white pins and Elvis playing from a jukebox that materialized on the far wall.

She was looking for a mute button when Danny came in. He smiled at her, his eyes not quite focused, his head cocked to one side. She waited a few seconds more for his hello.

"Hello to you, too," Simone said. "This lane okay for you?"

Danny shrugged. "Old, but cute. Sure. Do you know how this works?"

Simone motioned at the row of gloves. "I think we put those on." She picked one up and pulled it over her right hand, almost to the elbow. It was comfortable, despite being coated in something like white plastic, and her fingers flexed easily. The scoreboard flashed, "Player One." The glove flashed on the forearm, turning into a screen.

She entered her name, and "Pierce" appeared on the scoreboard over the lanes. "Danny-Boy" quickly popped up below it as Danny got the hang of his glove. Next it asked her to choose a ball, and suddenly her hand was so heavy that she let it fall. It actually felt like she was holding a bowling ball. She looked down. It looked like she was holding a bowling ball. The screen on the now downward-facing forearm asked her to adjust her ball's weight and color. She lightened it slightly but kept it black. Danny's ball was changing color from neon green to pink to purple to blue and back again. It seemed decidedly out of place in the vintage lane.

"Maybe I should rig my crystal ball to do this," Danny said, staring at it.

"Are you high?"

"No. I'm just trying to keep my mouth shut unless it's about the bowling."

"Why?"

"Because otherwise I'll ask you if you've asked Caroline about The Blonde yet." Simone glared, but Danny just grinned at her. "You really aren't going to, are you? Come on! She's your friend. Just ask her. Be like—" he cleared his throat and then began speaking in a low monotone: "Hey, I was tailing this petite and viciously attractive blonde and saw her meeting with you and I was wondering if you'd be willing to tell me her name?"

"Okay . . . ," Simone said, her free hand on her hip, "then she says, 'Why would you want to know that? Is she connected to a case?' "

"Why, yes she is." Danny was doing what, Simone now realized with horror, was supposed to be an imitation of her. "But I can't tell you much about it. Confidentiality and all."

Simone played along, but didn't even attempt to imitate Caroline's voice. "But she's my best pal, and anything that involves her must involve me. You need to tell me what this is about, or else I can't trust you."

"Well, it's just that I saw a man pay her some money."

"And she waved a gun at me," Simone said. Danny raised his eyebrows.

"Then you should definitely ask," he said, dropping his imitation.

"I'll figure it out. Maybe I can ask without asking . . ." Simone shook her head. It was an awful idea. "Was that voice supposed to be me?"

"Too femme?"

Before Simone could give him the finger, the door swung open, and Caroline came in, dressed all in black like a coated blade. "I am so ready to kick both your asses," Caroline told them.

"Long week?" Simone asked.

"Yeah, but that thing for my parents is nearly settled, and the other thing with the guy who sailed into town is done, so I am free and I am on a winning streak and I am going to use said streak to beat both of you into mindless bloody piles. Metaphorically speaking, of course."

"You spend too much time around politicians," Danny said.

"You spend too much time with their wives," Caroline responded, turning her eyes on Danny for the first time. Danny laughed nervously.

"Business is business," he said. "Why don't you put on a glove?"

"I don't mind you peddling your faux-voyance to Ms. Seward," Caroline said, gingerly taking a glove and putting it on. "But when it becomes a news item, it lands on my desk, and then I start to get ever so annoyed. You kept me in the office, Danny. Later than I needed to be."

"Hey, some reporter spotted her coming out of my studio. That's not my fault."

"You gave him a comment!" Caroline barked, choosing a bowling ball. She went for blood red. "You said your consultations are confidential, and you'd never betray the confidence of a woman just looking for some answers."

"So?"

"So you confirmed she was seeing you."

"Well, yeah. It's good for business."

"Not mine. They even have a photo of her waiting in your parlor or whatever you call it—with all the bullshit magic symbols and crap. Not great press. Can't you invest in some Privilux or something?"

Danny glanced over at Simone. Privilux was a spray made for windows, filled with invisible nanochips that gave off a signal to blur any attempt to digitally record past them; it was the ultimate in privacy screening for a window. Of course, it was insanely expensive, and you could always get mirrored glass, so few people in New York used the stuff. Simone had sprayed every window in her apartment with it, and when Danny visited, he always complained it made the inside of his head itch. Explaining that to Caroline would be difficult, as she didn't know about Danny's unique relationship with the wireless world.

"Can we bowl?" Simone asked. She glanced up at the scoreboard. Caroline had entered her name as Genghis. She was clearly feeling punchy; definitely not the time to ask about The Blonde.

"Yeah," Caroline said, "let's bowl."

Simone threw first, the VR ball rolling smoothly from her hand and into the wall, where it continued to travel down the lane. If she hadn't been there when she'd turned on the room, it would have been believable bowling. A whole lane in a small room. Even the jukebox was operational, as Caroline started tapping it while Danny threw. Elvis was replaced by Peggy Lee singing "Fever."

The first round went to Caroline, who did a victory dance when she rolled strikes.

"This would be better with beer," Simone said.

"There's a vending machine outside," Danny said. "I saw it when I got lost coming here. Want me to get us something to drink?"

"Make it dark," Simone said.

"Two each!" Caroline called as Danny left. The door closed behind him, and Simone stepped up for her next turn. The ball appeared in her hand again. "Why did you invite him?" Caroline asked. "Was it just so I could yell at him? That would be very thoughtful of you."

"He's a good guy," Simone said. She bowled a strike. "And he was helping me out on this case."

"I don't like his line of work."

"You don't mind mine." Simone threw again, only knocking down half the pins.

"It's different. Yours is honest. He dresses things up in lies."

"To make people happy," Simone said, turning around.

"Screw happy. I want people honest."

Danny came back in, holding a six-pack of beer.

"The machine sold you that?" Caroline asked.

"Modified," Danny said with a nod. "Only distributes six-packs."

"Smart," Caroline said, taking a beer from Danny. "You're up."

Caroline popped open her beer and knocked it back. Simone did likewise as Danny stepped up to the lane. Simone saw Caroline narrowing her eyes at him, shark-like, but bit her lip. Hopefully Danny could handle Caroline's psych-outs.

"Simone says you helped her with a case," Caroline said just as Danny swung his arm down to release the ball. He rocked slightly from the question, and the ball went right to the gutter. Caroline snickered.

"Uh, yeah," Danny said, throwing a questioning look at Simone. She shook her head, signaling him to stay quiet. Danny looked at Caroline, who gave him nothing but a wicked little smile. He turned back, and pulled his arm back to throw the ball again.

"What's it about?" Caroline asked this time. The ball moved slowly and unevenly, knocking over one pin. Danny watched it the whole time before turning back around.

"I don't think I can say," he said. Caroline put down her beer and strode up to the alley, patting him on the head as she walked.

"That's okay," she said, and with one fluid movement bowled another strike. Simone took a drink from her beer and handed a fresh one to Danny, who looked confused.

"She's just trying to psych you out," Simone explained. Caroline wiggled her eyebrows at them and rolled the ball again, knocking down all but one of the pins. She sighed, putting her hands on her hips.

"It doesn't work on Simone, usually," Caroline said, walking back to her beer. "But sometimes . . ." She winked at Simone as Simone approached the lane. Simone raised her arm as if to swing and tensed, waiting for Caroline to say something; she didn't, so Simone rolled the ball. "What's the case about?" Caroline asked just as Simone was letting go of the ball. Simone ignored the question as best she could, and the ball rocketed forward, into a seven-ten split. She turned to glare at Caroline, who was just polite enough to not laugh. Simone managed to knock down one of the pins on her next roll. She turned around and walked back over to Caroline while Danny took the lane. He glanced over his shoulder nervously, as if expecting Caroline to leap at him. Simone finished what was left of her beer in one swallow.

"Be nice," Simone said softly to Caroline, as Danny swung his arm way back, apparently determined to throw the ball so forcefully not even Caroline could disrupt his stride. The ball curved wildly and took out half the pins.

"When am I nice?" Caroline asked. Danny went to take his second turn, seemingly more confident now. "Does it involve guns?" Caroline asked. The ball veered and took out only two pins. Caroline smiled at Danny as he walked back from the lane, and handed him her empty beer bottle. Danny glared but took it. Caroline stepped up to the lane and stretched her arms before the ball appeared in her hand.

"You know what's funny?" Danny asked in a vaguely aggressive tone that didn't quite work, like a kitten playing tiger. Simone stared at him. Was he trying to psych Caroline out? He couldn't be dumb enough to think he could do that. "I'm a brunet, Simone is a red-head, you're a raven-haired vixen . . ." He stopped to drink his beer. Simone was now staring intently at him. He wasn't going to do what it sounded like, she hoped. She liked him, he was a good kid, and she didn't want to have to smack him to keep him from talking. Caroline rolled the ball, and just as she did so, Danny added, "All we need is a blonde."

The sound effect of crashing pins that Caroline's strike generated was incredibly loud to Simone. She clenched her hands, resisting the urge to grab his hair and drag him out of the room. He pointedly avoided her gaze.

"I think you're psyching out the wrong person," Caroline said, with a look of amusement. Simone realized she must look very angry. "He took my beer," she lied, trying to relax her face. Caroline shrugged and turned back to the lane. Danny turned to Simone, smiling. He looked happy, as though he'd come up with a good idea. Simone desperately shook her head, but he nodded back just as emphatically. This wasn't just him getting back at Caroline. He thought he was helping.

"Do you know any blondes?" Danny asked loudly as Caroline swung back her arm. "Maybe you met one at the Four Seasons?" Simone reached out but wasn't fast enough to clamp his mouth shut. Her hand was heavy from the glove, and she ended up just patting his face. He looked at her confused, but before she could say anything, she realized something else was wrong. There was no sound of a strike. Simone looked over at the lane. Caroline was silhouetted by it, her gutter ball rolling slowly out of sight.

"Met with a blonde at the Four Seasons?" Caroline turned around, looking unhappy. She crossed her arms. "Is this a setup? Am I involved in your case?" She took a step closer to Simone and pointed at her chest. Simone said nothing. Caroline's eyes widened, and for a brief moment, she had an expression Simone had never seen on her before: She looked hurt. Then her face hardened to a Glassteel sheen. "Am I a suspect?"

"The woman you were meeting with—" Simone started to explain.

"Marina. She's an art dealer. I'm buying a Reinel for my parents. Remember? I told you I had crap to do for them?" Caroline was angry now. She threw up her arms and walked away from Simone, then back again. "Why couldn't you just ask me like a normal person? And do you really think I'm involved? You think I wouldn't tell you if I was involved in some sort of . . . what? Conspiracy?" She stared Simone down, and Simone glanced downward. Her voice got lower, colder. "That *is* what you think, isn't it? One meeting with some woman involved in your case and you think I'm conspiring against you. You think I'm that crap of a friend, don't you?"

"She pointed a gun at me," Simone said. Caroline didn't say anything—just stared at Simone and crossed her arms, waiting for something else. Simone didn't have anything else.

"And you didn't think I'd want to know that?" Simone didn't say anything. "You thought I knew? You thought . . . what, that I was in on it?" Simone wanted to say something; she could feel words bubbling under the surface, but they just crept up into her mind and went back down again, half-syllables and lost protests drowning somewhere inside her. She opened her mouth, hoping they might come together, create some excuse, some explanation, some apology, but yes, she didn't trust Caroline, she was afraid to, and not just Caroline, but . . . she sighed. Her mouth closed.

"Fuck you," Caroline said, throwing off her glove and storming out of the room.

"Thanks," Simone said to Danny after a minute. Danny still hadn't lifted his head.

"Sorry," he said. "I'm really sorry. I'm shit for secrets. I could tell you about how I'm trained to share everything I know, or how I thought I was helping, but . . . I fucked up. Sorry."

Simone shook her head. She'd been ready to hit him hard enough to dislodge the computer in his head, but all that drained out of her when she saw the expression of regret on his face. She knew she should be furious with him, but she just felt sorry for him. She was angrier with herself.

"I shouldn't have tried to keep it from her. It was stupid."

"And kinda mean," Danny added.

Simone glared. "Be quiet unless you're apologizing." Simone took a deep breath and sat down on the floor. She felt cold. "Fuck," she said to no one in particular. She reached to her side but remembered she wasn't wearing her coat. "Give me my trench," she said to Danny. Wordlessly, he complied. She took off her glove so she could fish her cigarettes out of the pocket. She lit one, leaned back against the wall, and pulled herself into a cross-legged position. When she'd had a good inhale she held her cigarette up next to her cheek.

"You should go apologize," Danny said after a minute, taking his glove off.

"It could have been an act," Simone said.

"You don't really believe that, do you?"

"No, I don't." She inhaled again. She wanted to believe it, though. What did that say about her? She didn't ask the question aloud. Danny wasn't good at lying.

Suddenly the door flew open, and Simone looked up, her mouth already curving into a smile in hopes it was Caroline, but it was the lane attendant.

"What the hell do you think you're doing?" he yelled. "No smoking!" He pointed at the sign on the door he was still holding open. Simone quickly stubbed the cigarette out on the floor next to her. "Don't do that!" he said.

"Sorry," Simone said. Then an alarm went off, a loud piercing thing, and the room turned a dull red color, shutting the VR interface off.

"You set off the alarms!" the attendant shouted. "Oh fuck." He ran out the way he came, just as sprinklers started spraying down thick pelts of freezing water on them. Danny began to laugh. He tried to cover his mouth and hide it, but he was bad at that, too. Simone stared at him as the water poured down on her, until he gave up and just let the laughter pour out of him.

"Sorry," he said, between laughs, "sorry." Simone got up and put on her coat, which was also soaked. The floor was covered with water and filling up fast. They needed to leave. Simone pushed the door open and waved for Danny to come along.

Outside the lobby was chaos as people ran from their lanes to the front door. Simone and Danny joined them, running out the front door and into New York, where waves were crashing, but at least it wasn't raining. She and Danny walked a few blocks without saying anything, Danny still giggling.

Simone lit another cigarette.

"You really should apologize," Danny said finally. "She trusted you." He shrugged at her. She didn't say anything, didn't even look at him, but through him at the city. "Okay," he said after a moment. "I'll call ya." Then he walked away, dripping wet, but with his shoulders back and his chest puffed out like he was the luckiest kid on the ocean. Simone watched him go and finished her cigarette. She lit another and finished that one too. The cigarettes weren't doing anything for her, or maybe they were just giving her that sour sensation in her stomach. She needed something else to make her feel . . . different.

She pulled her hair back and wrung out what water was left, then put it in a ponytail so it wouldn't stick to her. She dried her face on her sleeves. Her trench coat was already dry, her pants and shirt less so, but she didn't care. She headed for deCostas' hotel. She hadn't answered that message from him—hadn't even read it. She tapped her earpiece and told it to dictate his latest message to her as she walked.

"Simone, I just wanted to say how much I enjoyed our time together tonight, and that I was perfectly prepared to be a gentleman and order us dinner, or take us out for dinner—I'm not sure if my hotel does room service—had you only been there when I woke up. I hope your sudden departure didn't indicate regret or, worse, disappointment with our activities. It was the most fun I've had since coming to this city. I also hope this doesn't mean our partnership is over. I have many more buildings to inspect, and I look forward to your company—in the buildings or elsewhere. Let me know if you'd like me to send you more addresses."

Simone smirked at the message. It was *careful*, she thought with a bit of disdain. But he had been fun, and the money was still good. She'd keep up with him. She might need the money for a lawyer soon, anyway. She hadn't heard from Peter or Kluren; she didn't know if they were building a case against her, if they were waiting at her office to arrest her, or if this would just be another mark in her file. They had just as much evidence as she did. Less now. She knew The Blonde's name. Marina. No surname, though. She could ask Danny to figure it out, check the guest list at the Four Seasons, but she didn't want to talk to Danny right now. Or anybody else.

The sun was setting when she rounded a building and got a view of deCostas' hotel. A small car rolled past Simone, making the wooden slats of the bridge she was crossing shudder. Below, the water was getting anxious, splashing up in anticipation of something. Simone studied the horizon. There were some dark clouds, maybe a storm. She couldn't tell how far away. She could always get a room in the hotel when she was done with deCostas. She didn't want to spend the night, give him the wrong idea.

deCostas stepped out of his hotel onto the bridge and looked around. Simone rolled her head and stayed where she was. He didn't see her. He checked his wristpiece and walked off, away from Simone. Simone followed him.

The whole city was dark, and the water was black, except for the bright spots of green beneath the streetlights. Simone wasn't sure if it was odd that deCostas was wandering without her. Wasn't she his tour guide? It was a silly thought, of course—he could go wherever he wanted. But it felt strange. Where was he going? She followed him for several blocks, keeping her eyes on the horizon now and then, hanging back so he didn't see her stalking—no, that was Caroline's word for it—*following* him. It felt good to be doing this, to be hanging back and watching, to be analyzing the way his head turned so she could duck out of sight in time.

They ended up in front of the Four Seasons. deCostas stopped to look at his wristpiece again, and, as he did so, The Blonde—Marina—came down the steps and shook hands with him. He said something, and she laughed. She smiled and said something. It was freezing cold, like the bottom of the ocean, but they didn't seem to mind. As they walked off together, she linked her arm into his. He looked down at this gesture, as if surprised, or curious, but did not unlink it. Simone watched them walk away until they were tiny specks that vanished in the rising fog.

NINE

—

SHE WAS AN IDIOT. This was a truth which she could no longer call crystal clear, because it had been crystal clear from the start, but over the past few hours of drinking, that crystal had faded, so there was nothing left between Simone and the truth. She didn't see it, she breathed it. She lived it. She was an idiot.

Trust. That's not what it was, of course. She hadn't *trusted* deCostas. But she'd trusted herself—her judgment of him as ambitious but harmless. She'd even liked him a little—enough that she'd sought him out when she needed distraction, or comfort maybe. And he was just another pawn of The Blonde. Maybe Caroline hadn't been used in quite the way Simone had thought, but you didn't have to *know* you were being used to be someone else's piece on the board. The Blonde had a web around Simone, had wrapped it up quietly and tight, and Simone hadn't seen it coming because she'd been too distracted by a nice ass. She wondered if The Blonde had somehow been responsible for sending deCostas to Simone. Perhaps she told him to go to Caroline, knowing she'd send him to Simone. Maybe Caroline was in on the plan from the beginning.

She swayed slightly as she walked down the hall to her home. She'd drunk a lot. The smell of tobacco—real tobacco—hit her like a bullet. A cigarette. That's what she needed.

Lou Freth was leaning against the wall outside her office, smoking. The smoke hung in the air, thick under the yellow lights. It seemed to form eyes, looking at her.

"What are you doing here?" Simone asked. Lou held out the pack of cigarettes, and Simone took one. She was suspicious but wouldn't turn down real tobacco.

"I wanted to see you," Lou said.

"You could've waited inside, you know," Simone said, opening the door to the outer office. She stuck the cigarette in her mouth and fumbled through her pockets for a lighter. She lit the cigarette and inhaled deeply. Lou walked past her into the still-dark office, right up to the windows, and looked out.

"I don't like invading people's homes without their permission."

Simone smirked. "How'd you know my apartment and office were connected?"

"I didn't. I just assumed you lived in your office." She glanced back over her shoulder. "I can't be the first to think so."

Simone lay down on one of the sofas near Lou, stretching her legs out. "I used to have a separate apartment. It was where I grew up. My dad and I lived there, and my mom, too, before she bailed. But I sold it." Simone took a deep breath. She must be really drunk if she was talking about her parents, she thought.

"Why?" Lou asked. Simone took a long drag on her cigarette. There was the sound of a motorboat going by outside, the waves it left in its wake rising up and falling in whispers.

"Why are you here?"

"I wanted to see how the case was going." Lou turned around and sat down on the sofa diagonal from Simone's. She tapped her cigarette over the glass ashtray on the table between them.

Simone turned her eyes to Lou, studying her. "Did that blonde woman send you? Marina?"

"That photo you showed me? I don't know her. I told you that." Simone studied her but was too drunk to tell if she was lying. She turned back towards the ceiling.

"You're probably lying. Everyone knows her." She stuck the cigarette in her mouth and lifted her leg, bending it towards her and gripping it with one hand. With the other hand, she took out her gun and laid it on the table, next to the ashtray.

"Is that supposed to be threatening?"

"Not really."

"I don't mind dying, you know." Lou crossed her legs. She wore knee-high black boots over gray slacks, and the movement was like the wince of a bruised eye. "My husband is dead, and the only thing I have left of him is our home. Henry is dead, and all I have left of him is the business. Did you ever find Linnea?"

"No. But her body hasn't turned up either."

"I'll pay you to find her. I feel like I should do that. No one is paying you anymore, and you're still investigating. Why?"

"Because people keep telling me not to, I guess. Because there's a chance the chief of police will try to frame me for Henry's murder if she gets bored trying to solve it for real. Because I probably just lost my only friend over it, so I better see it through, otherwise what has all this . . ." Simone gestured at the room, and then let her hand fall. Her cigarette was almost gone. She sucked down the last of it and stubbed it out in the ashtray. Lou was still smoking hers. Simone didn't know how Lou did it so leisurely, how she could let the inhale linger and not just keep trying to get all of it inside her. "You got another?" Lou wordlessly took the pack out of her pocket and laid it on the table next to the gun. Simone sat up, fished out another and lit it, then lay back again.

Outside, another boat went past—this one quieter, but its light shone directly into the window, through the venetian blinds, lighting

Lou from behind, so she was only a dark silhouette, and making lines of shadow over Simone's face and the smoke that was now circling her. It started to rain, drops tapping on the glass like musical notes.

"How'd you lose your friend?" Lou asked quietly.

"I should've just asked her . . ." Simone started. "I don't trust people. Or I didn't, but now I do, but it's the wrong ones."

"Most people betray you at some point." Lou took a drag on her cigarette and let it out slowly, smoke covering her face. "Maybe it's something stupid, they don't realize what they're doing, but they do it, and it hurts because you thought they knew you, thought they knew better and would somehow know that doing whatever it was they did . . . but no one is a mind reader." Lou lifted her hand up as if to take another drag of her cigarette, but let it fall back down before it reached her face. Her shoulders slumped backwards like old buildings, worn away and finally falling.

"My dad was," Simone laughed, then coughed. "He could read guilt on a perp from a mile away."

"No one ever betrayed him?"

Simone was quiet.

"Everyone gets betrayed at some point," Lou said. "And we respond . . . well, we don't always think. So we ask forgiveness. That's all we can do."

"Yeah," Simone said.

"I didn't know how these sorts of things were done," Lou said, reaching into her purse, "so I got cash. It was hard to come by, so I hope it's something you can use." She took out and laid a stack of bills on the table. "That should cover it. Find Linnea. Find who killed Henry." Lou stood up and straightened out her clothes.

"I'll do what I can," Simone said, without looking at her.

"Do the *best* you can," Lou corrected. She didn't look at Simone. She looked at the door and, without a goodbye, began to walk towards it, dignified, and Simone was suddenly struck by the memory of an old movie she'd seen with her parents, and a scene where a woman marched to the firing squad, blindfolded, proud, and not afraid.

"It's raining," Simone said, sitting up. "I can call you a cab." But Lou was already gone, the door closed behind her, the room dark.

Simone finished her cigarette in the dark, the only sound her own breath and the rain on the window, like something trying to get in.

"YOU HAVE TO LEARN how to swim, Simone," her mom said. "Especially out here." Her mom gestured around them—but they were on a cruise liner with tall railings, and the ocean could be heard, but not seen. She was five and was sitting on the edge of the pool her mother was in, wearing floaties on her arms. Her mom stood in the shallow end, water up to her knees, red hair streaming out in the breeze. She had on a floppy sun hat and huge sunglasses. She'd brought Simone to this public pool to teach her to swim, but Simone didn't like the look of the water.

"Come on, baby," her mom said. When she grinned, her nose wrinkled up, and her freckles danced on her face. "Just jump in. I'll catch you." Simone hooked a finger into her mouth, sucking on it, and looked at the water her feet were dangling in. It wasn't like ocean water. It was clear, and the pool was painted blue. Her feet looked bone white. This water wasn't safe, she knew. No water was safe. Here it seemed like an old dog that couldn't bite anymore, but it was still water.

Her mom came to the edge of the pool and, in one swoop, lifted Simone up and put her in the water before she could protest. She bobbed there a moment, the floaties keeping her up, the water luke-warm.

"See? See how easy that is?" her mom asked, crouching down so she was eye-level with Simone. Simone paddled her hands so she was up against her mother and clung to her, as best as the floaties would allow. "Nothin' to be afraid of," her mom said. "Just water."

THE SOUND DIDN'T JUST wake her; it made her whole body convulse. Simone used the blanket to cover her ears, but it didn't help. She knew she had been dreaming, and she remembered the smell of chlorine and feeling safe. That was gone now. Instead, there was the sound, the horrible sound that burrowed into her skull like a drill and wouldn't go away. She opened her eyes. The room, thankfully, was dim, her blinds down, the lights off. She lay on the sofa, still fully clothed and smelling of stale smoke. And still the horrible sound persisted: her phone. It was on the floor, where it had fallen out of her ear. A weak holoprojection shone out of it, the name too blurry to make out. She hit it. Sensing no ear, it went into speaker mode.

"Hey soldier."

"What do you want, Peter?" Simone rubbed her temples, and stayed on the sofa, eyes closed. It was an awful hangover, but a survivable one.

"Thought you'd want to know, a snitch fingered Linnea St. Michel sometime last night. I didn't get the call, or else I would've told you."

"Where was she?"

"Trying to score some Foam over on the West Side." Simone furrowed her brow. Drugs again. Why would she need more?

"That doesn't make sense," she said.

"Snitch swears on his mother it was her. They sent some blues over, but she was long gone. Thing is, I know this snitch. We're not the only ones he talks to."

"And there are plenty of people looking for Linnea right now," Simone said, thinking of Dash.

"Yep."

"Fuck. Thanks for telling me." Simone tried opening her eyes again but gasped as the light sliced her eyes, julienning them like soft grapes.

"You sailing smooth, there, soldier?"

"Just need a shower," Simone said, rubbing her face.

Peter paused. "Guess you better take one, then," he said.

"Yeah. Thanks again." She hung up on Peter and made her way to the bathroom, where she shook out a handful of painkillers and took them without bothering to count. She tried Linnea's number again but hung up when she heard the outgoing message. Then she took a shower. She'd screwed things up with Caroline; Linnea had briefly appeared, but was still missing; deCostas was meeting with Marina—The Blonde—and somehow this was all about drugs and art. Simone didn't know anything about art.

She toweled herself off, feeling a little better, and drank several glasses of water. Then she got dressed and went to her touchdesk. When she turned it on, a screen was already up. Memories came back to her, hazy, sea-glass-stained from last night. She'd been searching the web for Reinel, the name of the artist Caroline had mentioned. Paul Reinel, born in 2063, died 2170. He went to art school in Chicago, then dabbled in painting for a while. But he was most known as a coral sculptor—one of the early ones. When the waters were rising, one of the bits of technology that was quickly born out of desperation was accelerated coral growing for making reefs to keep particularly nasty tides at bay, like breakers. They worked okay for a little while; New York probably still had some sort of reef somewhere around it, though no doubt dead from pollution by now, just a wall of bone. But the technology also led to a fad in the art world, where artists would grow coral, almost like bonsai, into the shapes of animals, plants, humans, or other, less definable forms. Reinel's work was noted but not actively sought after or especially valuable.

She stared at some images of his art: eerie human forms bending backwards or laying down, arms stretched out as though they were reaching for something. Their outlines rippled because of the coral, so they seemed like they were underwater, drowning. Simone wasn't an art collector, but she could tell they were good—just not good enough to kill for. And certainly not *valuable* enough to kill for, judging by recent recorded sales. He was just a sculptor who sold some work and taught college art classes. He wasn't even dead that long. Simone shook her head. She had fucked up things with Caroline getting Reinel's name, and still hadn't learned anything new about the case.

She could *try* to fix it at least, she thought. She went online and found a place that sold straws—neon, bendy ones, Caroline's favorite kind. Simone smiled thinking about Caroline and her straws. Simone had asked her once about it, and Caroline had said she thought it made life a little more fun. Simone shipped a carton of them—enough for a small restaurant—to Caroline's address. No note. She didn't know what to say.

The touchdesk beeped, and a reminder popped up. She had a meeting with Pastor Sorenson tonight. Simone leaned back and folded her hands together. That was for the deCostas case—except it wasn't, really. Sorenson had told her to come alone. It was an excuse to meet with her privately, to talk to her about something else, which is why she decided to go. If it had just been about deCostas . . . Simone wasn't sure what to do about that. She still hadn't responded to the message from him. But he'd met with Marina. That meant everything he'd told her could have been a lie, that that little routine where she pointed a gun at him was staged. deCostas didn't seem like the type to try to play her. Didn't seem smart enough. Was he that good an actor?

Simone rolled her head. She'd meet with Sorenson, find out what she could about Marina, figure out where the fuck Linnea was, solve this case, and make good with Caroline somehow. After that, she was taking a nice long vacation—and only working cases involving missing pets.

She'd stop by the West Side to ask the junkies about Linnea on her way to the Hearst Building, where Sorenson would be waiting. But before that, she needed to walk, to breathe in the brine of the ocean, and think. She got up, made herself eat some toast, then threw on her trench and hat and headed out.

The day was a damp one, the sea beneath her particularly active, the sky gray, the fog thick. She lit a cigarette as she walked and took a long drag. So that art Trixie had mentioned—this Reinel—was somehow valuable, even though valuable Reinels didn't exist. The package she had seen Henry pass Marina must have been payment for her services as a broker. And Marina was going around offering up the Reinel sculpture to various people who could afford it—the Khans, Anika, Sorenson. Was deCostas on that list? He was only a student, but he had some funding.

But what coral sculpture could catch the fancy of all of them? The sculpture couldn't even be that old—no more than a century, which wasn't much these days. And Reinel wasn't much more than a footnote in an art history class.

Simone thought of heading to Undertow, but her head still felt soft from the drinking last night. Instead, she turned uptown and walked towards the ferry docks near City Hall. She used to go there when she was little, with her mom. Mom would talk about the mainland, where she'd grown up, and about going back some day. Simone never realized it would be without her. The docks were made of solid wood and stretched out for the mainland so far that if you stood on the end you might think you could see the shoreline. The ferry had already left that morning, so the platform was deserted. Simone sat down on a bench and looked at the water. White froth swirled around the dock legs, all white lines and bubbles, like excited children around a clown. They kept the water clean there, the bridges and buildings, too. When the tourists got off the ferry, they saw a dream of New York, not the real thing. If they were lucky, that's all they ever saw. The air felt cool on her face as she leaned back, squinting into the sunlight. She took her hat off and put it on her lap, letting the wind blow out her hair. Salt singed her scalp, burning away the toxins from last night, boiling her bad choices out of her.

It felt like she had all the pieces to the puzzle, but they just weren't fitting together. Why didn't Linnea just resurface, sell the sculpture, and leave? Maybe Marina had double-crossed her—had murdered Henry, and Linnea had gone into hiding, fearing she'd be next. But then Marina wouldn't still be shopping the Reinel around. And who had hired Dash? She reached into her pocket and felt for the tracker she'd taken from her hat. She hoped he'd been following her around. At least then she wouldn't have been the only one wasting her time. But now she knew something, and she didn't know what she might stumble on next, and didn't want him to follow her to that, so it was time to return the thing. She stood up and put her hat back on, looking out at the clean water one more time. Then she threw what was left of her cigarette into it and walked away.

DASH'S OFFICE WAS IN one of the newer buildings in East Midtown, all sleek, black lines and open expanses of glass daring the ocean to puncture it like a balloon. He kept his apartment and office in the same building, like she did, but his office was downstairs, connected to the apartment by a glass spiral staircase suspended by wires.

It wasn't very early—she'd gotten a late start—so she was surprised to find the door still locked. Dash sometimes had a secretary; more often, though, one had just quit after he'd slept with her, then her best friend. Or so Simone had heard. She'd only been to his office once before, when they'd been asked to bid on some security work. Dash had probably thought home-court advantage would help him, but Simone had won the job anyway.

It was a plain door with a simple gold plaque on it announcing "The Ormond Agency." The lock was more complex, with an electronic keypad. Luckily, it was a screen, so Simone leaned over and breathed on it. The 2, 3, 4, and 7 keys all bore fingerprints. Simone rolled her eyes, typed in the numerical equivalent of DASH, and went inside.

It looked like it had last time she was here: black leather sofa in the waiting area, black desk for the receptionist, white walls with chrome detailing. Light poured in through the huge picture windows. The floor was a pale wood. The spiral staircase was the focal point, ethereal and arresting. Simone had never been up it. She knew she shouldn't snoop too much—Dash hadn't done that much, he'd only bugged her, and there was a code among private investigators. It was a murky, nebulous code, but rifling through his files would have been a violation. Still, she could poke around.

The staircase made low, hollow notes that sounded like sighs as she walked up. Upstairs was a small balcony with three doors. One was probably his private office, the others his living space and maybe a bathroom. Simone opened the door on the left to find black-and-white tile, a black sink, and a black toilet. She rolled her eyes again and closed the door. The next room was his office, in which there was a black-and-chrome touchdesk—the latest model. She stared at the office a moment. Dash seemed to know why people were after Linnea, and while the code was foggy, she felt she could probably get away with looking through his things, provided she was only looking for something that would help her on her case. Besides, she would gladly trade in the relationship she had with Dash to get back the one she had with Caroline.

She stepped into the room. It was unseasonably warm with all the light coming in through the window. She tried turning on the touchdesk, but it asked for fingerprint validation. Simone pursed her lips. She thought of taking some tape and removing a fingerprint from the keypad, but she didn't have tape on her and Dash didn't seem to have any in his office. No filing cabinets either. Everything seemed to be on the touchdesk.

Simone stepped back out onto the balcony and opened the last door, which led to his bedroom. Clothing and rumpled white silk sheets at the foot of the bed. No underwear, Simone noticed.

She headed back downstairs to check the receptionist's desk for tape. She sat behind it, opening drawers and closing them again, until she heard the click of the lock in the front door. She quickly sat up, leaning back in the chair, her feet up on the desk, as though she'd been waiting.

When Dash opened the door and spotted her, Simone was pleased to see a look of shock on his face before he covered it with a mask of humor and an arched eyebrow.

"Hello, Simone," he oozed, closing the door behind him. "To what do I owe this pleasure?"

"Well, you said you'd be naked, so I thought I'd take a peek."

"I'm sorry to disappoint," Dash said, walking closer to her. "But I am happy to oblige, if you'll just let me wash up first." Simone cocked her head as if considering.

"I have some time," she said.

"Lucky for both of us." He went upstairs and into the bathroom, where Simone could hear the water running, then came back down, his hat, gloves, overcoat, and jacket all gone. He wore a patterned button-down shirt—gray check on white—a red tie, and black slacks. He loosened, then undid the tie as he walked back towards the desk. He slipped the tie off his collar like a whip crack and put it down on the desk in front of Simone, then smiled at her. Then he began to undo the buttons of his shirt, keeping eye contact with Simone the whole time, a perpetual smirk on his face that she mirrored. He finished unbuttoning his shirt entirely and let it hang open as he took off his belt. His bronze stomach muscles looked somehow polished. When he undid the first button of his fly, Simone put up her hand to stop him.

"As much fun as this show is," she said, "I'm really here to return this." She reached into her pocket and took out the bug she'd found in her hat. "I think you must have dropped it at my place."

"Ah," Dash said, not rebuttoning anything and taking the tracker. "Thank you. These things are expensive."

"You don't use the dissolving kind?" Simone asked.

"Not in cases when it's just a hunch and I don't know how long I'll need to follow. It was really just a backup plan. I always have a backup plan."

"I don't know where Linnea is," Simone said.

"I gathered that," Dash said. "I've been watching your movements. You seem as confused as I am."

"I am," Simone said. It came out as more of a threat than a confession. "So what do you know?" She didn't want to team up, exactly, but she didn't mind sharing a little information, as long as it was on her terms.

"Linnea was selling something. My client wants it."

"The Reinel," Simone replied. "And I'm assuming your client, having hired you, is the sort who would prefer to get the Reinel for under the asking price?"

"*Au contraire*," Dash said, walking over towards the windows. "My client just wants to be sure that they get what's coming to them." Dash slipped off his shirt. His back was to Simone, but Simone was appreciating the view. He threw himself onto the sofa, stretching out on it, face to the ceiling.

"You mean because The Blonde—Marina—is auctioning it off? Your client is afraid of being outbid?"

"Precisely. Or of the goods not being delivered. Or of the Reinel not being what everyone seems to think it is."

Simone stood and walked over to the sofa, looming over Dash. "And what does everyone seem to think it is?"

Dash looked up at her, appraising. His body was damp with the first pinpricks of sweat, his muscles highlighted, his skin honey gold. "That they haven't told me. Just that it's not about the art, but what's in the art. I keep picturing a chocolate egg with a prize inside. I was hoping you'd know."

"Nope," Simone said. "All I know is there shouldn't be any piece by Reinel that's worth this much trouble."

"Everything is trouble to somebody," Dash said, reaching out and taking her wrist. "I was hoping we might cause a little trouble for each other." Simone considered it, could feel Dash tugging her onto him, and could imagine that it would be fun to just fall. To forget for a while. Even with Dash. But she didn't trust him— didn't even think he was a good person. But she could get around that, she thought, looking at the curves of muscle on his stomach, his shoulders, his hips. But there was too much happening. She needed to stay afloat right now. Solve the thing. Then she could relax.

"Tempting," Simone said, pulling her hand away. "But let's wait till the case is closed. Then we'll celebrate."

"Tease," Dash said. Simone smiled and started walking for the door. "So where did you plant your tracker?" he called after her. "Tit for tat, right? One of my belts?" Simone turned and waved over her shoulder, then walked out the door.

Outside, Simone stretched and let her body cool down in the open air. She didn't know everything yet. But she finally felt like she knew enough to start putting the pieces together. She needed to know more about the Reinel, and what could be hidden inside. There was only one other person she knew who had seen it. She hoped he'd see her without an appointment. She told her earpiece to call Mr. Ryan's line. He picked up after four rings.

"Ms. Pierce," he said. He sounded primped and prepared as always, as though her calling was no surprise at all. "What can I do for you today?"

"I was hoping for another art history lesson. On Paul Reinel."

On the other end of the line, Mr. Ryan paused. Simone could hear the sound of a glass being clinked down on marble. "And when were you hoping for this lesson?" he asked, his tone exactly the same.

"Today," Simone said. "If you're available."

"Come by at five."

"Thank you, Mr. Ryan."

"And, Ms. Pierce, let me be frank: I don't give away anything for free *except* art history lessons. Are we clear?"

"Absolutely."

"Excellent. I look forward to our meeting, then. See you at five." He hung up without waiting for a reply. Simone checked the time on her earpiece holoscreen. She still had a few hours, and there were a few more places where she could fish for information.

First she headed west, to where the junkies and bums lived. The buildings there, the high rises of what was once Chelsea and Hell's Kitchen, had been some of the first coated in Glassteel, before the formula was perfected, and so they stood, but they were crumbling faster than everywhere else. They were also usually the first to get hit by storms. The buildings had probably been nice once—large buildings filled with spacious family condos—but now they were rotting and always smelled like mold. People who were down on their luck, who were still determined to rise up and live as good a life as New York could offer, had the old penthouses. There it didn't smell so bad, and no one else bothered them. They just had to deal with walking up dozens of flights of stairs and the knowledge that when a storm hit, they were the most likely to get blown away.

Everyone else in the area lived on the lower floors, where whole apartments had been cleared out, with cheap plaster walls or curtains for privacy. People shared molding mattresses and threw plastic tarps on the floor to keep it dry. A lot of these people were Foam addicts, and they stuck together, forming dens and packs; the rest had just given up and stared out their windows all day. Their view wasn't of the city, just of the huge expanse of ocean, and Simone thought that to them it probably looked tempting, like a future they were waiting for because they were too tired or scared to go outside and claim it themselves. Simone understood that. The edges of the city—the flat foreverness of the ocean—appealed to her. These places were quiet and peaceful. When the sun cast long lines of light on them they looked like a good place to die.

Simone knew some junkies and dealers and walked around the neighborhood looking for them. It was chilly, and the water seemed especially black. The bridges here were thin, reedy things that creaked underfoot and groaned like old instruments. The smell was worse than in the rest of the city—from rotten wood and rust, and the damp smell of people who hadn't bathed. Simone stuffed her hands in her pockets and kept her feet firm.

Her few contacts didn't have any new information for her. Neither did the junkies she found lying in the corners of bridges, their mouths white, their eyes vacant, almost looking drowned, breathing heavily. Yeah, they said, a woman who looked like Linnea had been around. She'd scored some Foam, pocketed it, and vanished downtown. No one had seen her today, though. That was it. Maybe Linnea was a former MouthFoamer, falling back on old habits because of the stress. But Simone didn't think so. That stuff left permanent damage—a glazed look, like only being half awake—and Linnea hadn't shown any signs of that.

Next stop was back downtown, to Above Water Exports/Imports. It was open, despite it being Sunday. Lou was inside, going through some large crates that now filled the room. She had her back to the door and didn't turn around when Simone shut the door behind her.

"We're not really open today," she said, "I just had to be here to accept this shipment."

"I'm not here to buy, Lou," Simone said, walking towards her.

"Oh," Lou said, turning around, "the shamus. Sober by now, I hope?" She raised an eyebrow as Simone sauntered forward, nodding.

"You can help me get this lamp out, then." She jabbed at the crate with her thumb, then stepped away from it, took a cigarette out of her pocket, and lit it. Simone looked over the top of the crate—about the same height as Lou—and saw that the lamp was stuck under a rocking chair. It was a heavy desk lamp, curving around like a spring or an ancient staircase overrun with trees. Simone managed to unhook it and hand it to Lou, who was by now haloed in smoke.

"Thanks," Lou said, taking the lamp under one arm, cigarette still in hand. She walked over to her desk and put the lamp down, evaluating it. "What are you doing here?"

"I think Henry was killed because of a sculpture he found in your inventory."

"Why would Linnea kill him for a sculpture?" Lou asked, blowing smoke out her mouth. She folded an arm over her chest, looking unimpressed.

"If it *was* Linnea, it was because they were trying to sell it. For a lot. The art is by Reinel. You have anything in storage?"

Lou raised her eyebrows, then started to laugh. "Reinel? Who would kill for a Reinel? The man was nobody special."

Simone shrugged. "I know. But that's where the evidence is pointing, and beauty is in the eye of the beholder. Maybe someone thought this art was worth killing for."

Lou shook her head and went to her touchdesk, where she typed a few things with the hand that wasn't holding the cigarette. The smoke was making Simone want a cigarette, too, so she fished one out of her pocket.

"No smoking in here," Lou said, glancing up from her table screen. "At least not that crap. Here, take one of mine." She tossed Simone her pack.

"Thanks," Simone said. She took one and lit it. It tasted like burnt earth and melting sugar.

"We had a Reinel a few years back, but we sold it to a small museum in Brazil. Nothing since then."

Simone walked closer and handed the cigarettes back to Lou, still breathing deeply, enjoying the beautiful filth of the tobacco.

"And you don't know why a Reinel would be valuable?" Simone asked. Lou shook her head.

"They're nice sculptures, and they're early coral work, but he never made a big splash. Only an insanely rabid collector would kill for one. Only someone stupid would pay more than . . . maybe twenty grand for one of his really big pieces, or a bust of someone famous, maybe. But those are all in museums." She shrugged, rippling the cloud of smoke around her.

"That's what I thought. This whole thing makes no sense."

"Sorry I couldn't be more help."

"That's fine. Thanks for the cigarette. I gotta get to an art history lesson."

Lou snorted a laugh. "And I was just starting to like you." Lou headed back towards the crates, not turning back around. Simone looked after her, wanting to bum another cigarette for later, but instead turned around and left. It was almost five.

TEN

——

ONE WALL STREET HAD an edge of anticipation about it early in the evening, especially on an overcast one like this. The lights were on, glowing an angry yellow through the windows and fog, and people milled around nearby, waiting for the doors to open but trying to look like they weren't. They cast occasional glances at the door and then at each other. Their faces varied from angry to ashamed, but none of them looked friendly. Simone could feel their stares as she walked down the bridge to the door and pressed the buzzer.

Ms. Antiphates opened the door quickly and, seeing Simone, stepped aside. Once Simone was inside, she slammed the door closed.

"Mr. Ryan is waiting on the twenty-fifth floor," Ms. Antiphates said, walking down the hall to the main room. Inside, the room was midway transformed: merchants' stalls, only halfway set up, looked like skeletons, just metal poles suggesting frames. Soon there would be walls made of curtains, draped over and around, and signs listing vendor names and available goods. Most of the merchandise was still in locked trunks, though a few merchants were laying things out in clear cases. Simone saw guns and jewelry, exotic spices and foods, and plenty of alcohol. Some of what was sold there was legal in the mainland but taxed to the point where it was only affordable to the obscenely rich; the jewelry especially—the "vanity tax," they called it. Women couldn't wear pants without getting fined, but they were allowed to wear jewelry, if they could afford it.

"This way," Ms. Antiphates said, summoning an elevator. Simone turned away from the stalls and followed her into the elevator. Simone had only been to the upper floors of One Wall Street once before, for her initial interview with Mr. Ryan when he was deciding if he could hire her for anything. It hadn't just been her, then. It was her father, too. She was the junior, the apprentice, but Ryan had interviewed them both as though they were partners, and Simone's dad didn't correct him. Simone felt tougher after that. Today she didn't feel tougher. The elevator moved quickly, and for a few seconds she felt seasick.

The doors opened onto a hallway lined in red-and-gold mosaics. Standing in the center of the hall, waiting as though the walls were spreading out from him like fiery wings, was Mr. Ryan, in a navy suit and red tie, holding a walking cane.

"The last time you were here was with your father, wasn't it?" Mr. Ryan asked before she could even step out.

"Yeah. I was just remembering that, too," Simone said, stepping into the hallway.

"I'm sorry if the memory is unpleasant," he said. "I only just remembered when the door opened. I had a memory of a young woman—you were what, eighteen?" Simone nodded. "Eighteen and already a detective. Your father was nervous, I remember, but you just stared at me with that quiet smile you have, like you were never going to be defeated. You didn't wear a hat back then. Your hair blended with the walls . . ." Mr. Ryan motioned at them with his walking cane. "They were originally on the first floor, these mosaics. They were removed when the waters rose. It took me nearly a year to get them back once I'd bought the place, and more than a little finger-breaking." Simone said nothing, the flickering shadow of her father at the edges of her vision. He was tall back then—not like when she found his body. He seemed so small then. "Well, come along. Let's get to your lesson."

Mr. Ryan nodded once at Ms. Antiphates, who disappeared behind the closing elevator doors. He turned and walked down the hall, and Simone followed.

"Thank you for doing this," she said. "I know it's short notice and an odd request."

"Ms. Pierce," Mr. Ryan said without turning around, "I am happy to tell you all I know about Paul Reinel. But I suspect you're here because you want to know about a specific piece of his, yes?"

"Yes," Simone admitted.

"Do you in fact represent Ms. St. Michel, and has she sent you here to ask me to auction off the piece in my little market?"

Simone considered lying but knew it would be a stupid lie, the kind that was sure to get her in trouble and lose her a regular client.

"No," she said. "I'm here because I know that it's a Reinel now, but I don't know what would make a Reinel important, or worth killing for. And I need to figure it out, because right now I'm suspect number one." And Caroline is suspect number two, Simone thought, with half the city lining up to join her. Ryan opened a door and led Simone into a white room with a white bar, white sofas, and a white carpet. The glasses on the bar were white, the table was white. It was all a canvas, a display for the one thing in the room that wasn't white: a large sculpture in the center of the table. It was a deep, dried-blood red, and had a texture that looked like thousands of tubes facing out, packed so closely together that it seemed soft. The sculpture was of a naked woman reclining on a low table. Her legs were stretched out to the side, bent, and a robe or shawl was draped loosely around her. In one hand, she held what looked like a branch, and around her were animals—pigs, goats, and a cat. They all looked at her, pleadingly, but she looked straight ahead, her expression an invitation.

"*Circe*," Mr. Ryan said. "One of Reinel's earlier coral pieces. The only one I have. It's made from pipe-organ coral, which was unusual. Most of the coral sculptors used something less fussy, like fan or lettuce coral—the sort of thing people expected. This is his only piece in the pipe organ. I love the texture of it and, of course, that color." Simone approached the statue, wanting to touch it. Circe's gaze was magnetic. "Would you like something to drink?" Mr. Ryan asked, going behind the bar. "I'm going to have a glass of the white Bordeaux."

"Sure, thanks," Simone said, still staring at Circe. She was beautiful, but beautiful enough to kill for? And how was it more than just a sculpture? Dash had said he thought it was like a chocolate egg, but Simone couldn't picture anything *inside* the coral. Mr. Ryan handed her a glass of wine and sat on the sofa in front of the sculpture. Simone sat next to him.

"So you want to know what makes a Reinel worth killing for. Does seeing one answer your question?"

"No," Simone shook her head. "It's beautiful, Mr. Ryan, but . . . to kill for? I expected something people could say is worth something, something concrete."

"You don't think people would kill to possess something beautiful?"

Simone was silent. She took a long drink of her wine. It tasted expensive and heavy.

"Maybe," she finally conceded. "But I've been told it's not the art that's worth killing over. It's something *in* the art. Or maybe about the art. And unless you can crack this open—and I don't think anyone would do that—I don't see what it could be."

She still had one more stop before her meeting with Sorenson. She didn't have more time for art appreciation. She had thought that with Reinel's name she would be closer to solving this, to getting herself out of Kluren's gold spotlights, to getting rid of The Blonde, and to getting her friendship with Caroline fixed. But she didn't feel closer to any of those things. She felt like she was in a white room, drinking wine, and staring at a bloodstain shaped like a person.

Mr. Ryan stood and walked around the statue, regarding it.

"His early coral work is more daring. More beautiful," he said. "After this, he becomes just another coral sculptor. Early for the technique, yes, but not exciting. Not interesting. A shame."

"What does that have to do with his art being something else?" Simone asked.

"He started as a painter, you know," Mr. Ryan continued, as though Simone hadn't said anything. "In general, I actually prefer his paintings. They weren't just paintings; they were almost mixed media."

"But—" Simone tried to interrupt, but before she could speak, Mr. Ryan brought his cane down on the floor in a loud thud.

"I promised you an art history lesson, Simone," he said quietly. "I'm giving you one because I saw in your eyes a genuine interest and appreciation when you looked at the painting downstairs. I saw you become, for just a moment, something more. I saw it again when you looked at Circe here. That's something art does to some people. Not many, unfortunately. But I saw it in you, and I want to encourage it. I'm not here to solve your problems or solve your cases or give you some vital clue." He paused, and his face softened, his voice became lighter and smooth, like the oil coating a frying pan. "Unless, of course, you'd care to give me something in return?"

"Something like what?"

"There's an item coming into the city in a month or so. I want it. Would you be willing to retrieve it for me?"

"Like an escort?" Simone asked, but she knew that wasn't what he meant. He shook his head.

"Like a thief, Ms. Pierce," he said. Simone took another sip of her wine.

"I'd like to hear more about Reinel," she said softly.

"As I was saying, I prefer Mr. Reinel's paintings. Generally. Circe is certainly more impressive than any of his early paintings, but he had a style in his brushwork: hard, glamorous. Common people he met on the street looked like movie stars. And they were fused into objects around them—hair turns into streets on a map, lips become bridges."

"Maps?" Simone asked. Mr. Ryan's lips turned up at this, but then he shook his head slightly, as if a little sad.

"His early work involved taking photos with an old-fashioned smartphone. This was just when the water was rising. He'd mark on his map the place where the photo was taken. In his studio, he would project both these images over each other, onto a canvas, and from that he would paint. He would combine the scene and the map. And then he'd spray the whole thing with Privilux, so no one could take a photo of it. He said it was about art from media; but media from art from media was one too many layers. He needed his work to be appreciated in person."

"So he painted a scene with a map, and it couldn't be photographed," Simone said, standing. "It's a treasure map."

Mr. Ryan sighed with disappointment. "Do you want an art history lesson, Ms. Pierce, or do you want to solve the case?"

Simone stared at Circe. "I want both, Mr. Ryan. That's the truth. But I need to solve the case first. Can you tell me what Linnea's Reinel was a map to?"

"Are you willing to pick up the object next month?"

Simone shook her head. "But I'll work security for you—free."

"It's my job to know the value of a thing," Mr. Ryan said, shaking his head. "This information is worth more."

"It is," Simone agreed. She needed to know what the map led to. She felt suddenly so close, as though there was merely one more wall to be scaled. "Can I get back to you?"

"You're going to go try to figure it out yourself, you mean, and if you can't, then you'll come back to me?"

"Yes." Simone saw no point in lying to him.

"I'll allow that, but you're giving me that free security no matter what. Five nights' worth."

"Two," Simone said.

"Let's just say three then," Mr. Ryan said. "And you will come back for a real art history lesson. I miss having people to share my collection with. I miss seeing that look. That look used to be like home for me."

"I promise," Simone said. She reached out and shook Mr. Ryan's hand. "And thank you."

"I hope you don't take this the wrong way, but I won't wish you luck. In fact, I hope you have to come back to me. I would very much like that object, and Mr. Ormond's rates keep going up. Besides, he's so much less pleasant than you."

"Everyone is less pleasant than me," Simone said, downing the last of her wine in one gulp. She put the glass down on the bar.

"There are degrees, though." Mr. Ryan opened his mouth as if to say something else but closed it again, then extended his arm for Simone to take. "Let's take the elevator down together, shall we?"

Simone was silent as they walked through the hallway, reminded again of her father.

"You thought my father was scared, the time we came to see you?" Simone asked as they got in the elevator.

"Oh yes. Terrified. I'm familiar with the look."

"I never thought he was afraid of anything." The elevator plummeted downward.

"That's probably how it should be with fathers and daughters," Mr. Ryan said. Simone remembered the flash of red on her father's temple when she found him, like a button oddly sewn onto the leather of his remaining skin.

"Probably," she said. The doors opened on the lobby, which was now fully alive. The people who had been waiting furtively outside prowled the hall, going from stall to stall—the empty frames now plush, silk-lined tents, like some sort of ancient bazaar. It smelled of gunpowder and spice, bitter and acidic and dusty all at once. People spoke softly, but there were enough of them so that it was like a cool murmur blending with the waves outside. When customers wanted to buy something—an antique pistol or a pound of un–genetically modified peanuts—they flashed their wristpieces and transferred money directly into the seller's account. Money was moved around, but nothing was bought on paper, so no taxes applied. The system had been put into place by the mainland to help the very wealthy manage their finances, but it worked well for the black market as well. This sort of thing couldn't exist on the mainland. All it would take was one loyal citizen calling it in, and everyone would go to prison. Too risky, there. In New York, no one cared. It was part of doing business.

"I don't suppose you're looking to buy anything tonight?" Mr. Ryan asked, dropping his arm. "We have a few art dealers in."

"I can't afford any of this, and you know it," Simone said. "And besides, I'm late. I need to get to church."

Mr. Ryan clutched at his chest as though having a heart attack. Simone almost leapt to help him before she realized he was joking.

"A pastor wants to see me. Don't worry, if he tries to reform me, it won't take."

"I should hope not."

"Thanks again, Mr. Ryan. I'll be back for the next lesson."

"And for that free security you promised. I'll send you the dates."

"Sure," Simone said, shaking his hand before taking off for the door. The crowd was getting thicker as she walked, and people pressed up against her in a surge before she could get outside.

THE SUN WAS HALFWAY into the ocean, a gold semicircle burning through the layers of gray fog. Simone still had some time. It was a good thing Sorenson had wanted this meeting at night—although that meant he wanted it after most of his parishioners and staff had cleared out. Simone walked to the end of the bridge leading away from the black market, weaving her way through the people heading in the opposite direction.

She wanted to call Caroline, to talk the case over with her while they ate at someplace awful and greasy that Caroline had chosen. She stopped at a hot-dog vendor—one of those small boats that bobbed just off a low bridge, cooking and selling all day—and bought one. It was salty, and she ate it too quickly, leaving her chest feeling burnt out. She took a taxi to City Hall, knowing Caroline would still be at work.

When the waters had risen, the old City Hall had been covered pretty quickly, and the politicians had had to find a new spot. They chose two adjacent buildings in midtown—once called the MetLife Tower and the MetLife North Building. Their Art Deco exteriors had been carefully coated in Glassteel, so each angle shone in the fading light. A large dock surrounded them and filled the space between, acting like a wooden plaza. Streetlights thrust up through the plaza on the perimeter and then again in a circle around the center. From above, Simone imagined it looked like a shooting target in bright white, the green of their algae generators winking up between the wooden slats of the platform. There were potted plants and even a small sea-water fountain that someone had rigged to pump stuff up from the ocean and shower it back down again. It was lit from underneath, so when the sun began its descent, the fountain seemed to spray liquid light. The entire area was called City Hall Plaza and was often featured on brochures put out by the city's plucky travel bureau, with the Chrysler Building glowing behind it. This was probably because it looked, in many ways, how New York used to look—that is, if you cropped out the ocean waves rising up angrily just beneath the plaza.

The mayor's offices were at the top of the tower, above the other municipal offices. That's where the balconies were, and the mayor reportedly enjoyed a nice lie-down on a hammock he had set up out-side. Caroline's office was right next to the mayor's, but anyone who knew the city knew to get an appointment first. Simone sat down on one of the benches and stared up at Caroline's office. It was too far up to see anything specific, like a person moving around, but the light was on. It glowed a lonely pearl color, the only one on the floor.

Simone tapped her earpiece, said the word "call," and almost said "Caroline," but waited long enough that her earpiece told her in soft metallic tones to repeat the command. She wondered why she was always looking up at Caroline's window. *Stalker.* She could almost hear Caroline whisper the word in her ear. Then the light went out in Caroline's office. Simone sat down at the end of the plaza farthest from the door. She wasn't in shadow—there was no shadow in the plaza, not with the streetlights and the fountain—but she thought she'd be hidden by the water bubbling up between her and the door.

So she knew that the Reinel was a map. But what could it lead to? If it were just deCostas, she'd assume it had something to do with underwater air pockets—maybe the location of a particularly well-coated building or something, but for Sorenson to be interested, or the Khans? They were too smart for all that. She knew Caroline didn't believe in that pearl-diving nonsense. Then again, Anika had called it bullshit—so that lined up. But how could the painting show the location of an airtight building? Did he paint a large sign in the back-ground that read, "Future site of Underwater Living"? Simone shook her head. The revelation that Reinel painted maps had seemed so significant, but now that she was thinking about it, she felt just as lost as before.

The door across the plaza flashed open, and Caroline walked out. Simone stood, then squatted again, but then stood entirely. Caroline didn't seem to see her. She walked past the fountain, but Simone stood where she was, then turned to follow Caroline. When she had cleared the fountain and there was nothing between them but space, Caroline stopped. She stayed there a moment before turning to look at Simone. She held a black leather briefcase in both hands. She was wearing black gloves and a dark green coat that fell down to her knees in the shape of a bell, and under that something white and high collared, like a priest.

They stared at each other for a while. Caroline once opened her mouth, as if to speak, but then closed it again. She was too far away for Simone to read her eyes. The air was cold, and the saltwater from the fountain was blowing on her with every gust of the rising wind. The salt felt like small shards of glass biting into her. Simone looked down, took a deep breath, not sure what to say, but knowing she had to speak first. But then she heard Caroline's footsteps, and when she looked up, Caroline was walking away, dissolving into the mist and darkness.

ELEVEN

——

SIMONE SMOKED THE CIGARETTE down to the very last bit of ash as she walked to her meeting with Sorenson. The night had come in on heavy sheets of gray, and the fog was weaving itself into thick knots, moments of blindness Simone had to walk through on faith. That meant soon there'd probably be rain for a couple days. Hopefully nothing too hard. She didn't want to be locked up inside her office, unable to go out without getting killed.

A few people were milling around outside the Hearst Tower when she showed up. They were dressed conservatively and speaking in low tones. They all turned to stare at Simone as she pulled open the door of the building. She winked at one of them, and he blushed a bright scarlet. Inside, the receptionist was packing up to go home and told Simone the pastor was waiting for her in his office on the top floor.

Simone took the elevator up. The doors opened onto walnut walls and big open windows that let in the damp air. Large religious paintings hung on the walls. Sorenson sat behind his desk, looking at Simone expectantly. Behind him, staring out one of the windows, was—

"Marina," Simone said before she could stop herself. The Blonde turned to her and smiled.

"You learned my name," she said. "You care. That's sweet, it really is, but we don't know each other that well. Maybe you should just call me Ms. Beck."

Simone's hand was already at the gun in her boot. "Is this some kind of setup?"

Sorenson rose, his hands extended, palms out, reassuring. "No, no, Ms. Pierce, I assure you, this is no setup. Ms. Beck and I just need your help. She told me about your . . . encounter, so I thought perhaps it would be best if I didn't mention her bein' at this meeting."

"I am sorry about that," Marina said, walking forward from the window to sit on Sorenson's desk. "You see, I'm used to transporting large sums of money and valuable artwork, so when someone is following me, I assume they're trying to take it from me. I didn't know who you were. That you were working for Linnea. Like I am." She smiled pleasantly, an obvious mask, but a good one, as Simone couldn't read anything but insincerity in her tone. She couldn't tell if Marina was lying or not.

"You're working for Linnea?"

"Well, it was Henry and Linnea. But turns out you were right about Henry being dead." She raised her eyebrows, as if amused by a titillating scandal of some sort. She was good. Everything about her dripped with false friendliness, but *only* false friendliness. She didn't have a single tell. Simone had a sudden itch to play poker with her.

"Ms. Beck was hired by the St. Michels," Sorenson said.

"To sell a Reinel painting, I know," Simone said.

"I guess I'm not the only one who's been doing her homework," Marina said.

"I bought the painting," Sorenson said. "But with Linnea hidin' away somewhere, I have yet to receive it."

Simone narrowed her eyes. "If you bought it, why was she meeting with deCostas last night?"

"Oooh," Marina said, smiling. "Very good. I'm impressed, really. Keeping tabs on your clients like that. Does he know?" Simone kept staring. "Well, as the painting still hasn't surfaced, I'm still taking bids on it. Pastor Sorenson here has outbid every competitor so far, but if I can get a higher number out of him, well, he won't blame me for trying. I work on a retainer *and* a percentage, after all."

"You can see why I'm anxious to get the paintin'," Sorenson said. "With Ms. Beck here handling the sale, the price just keeps goin' up."

"You haven't answered my question. Why deCostas? He's just a student."

"With some serious investors. When I was finding out about you, I found out about him. He seemed like a potential buyer, so I approached him."

"He didn't mind, after you'd pointed a gun at him?"

"Said having the gun pointed at him was the second most exciting thing he's done since he got here." Marina paused to let her statement sink in. Her smile was cool as a bullet. "But he couldn't afford it."

Simone crossed her arms.

"We just want to know where Linnea is," Sorenson. "So I can get my paintin'."

"The thing I don't get," Simone said, pausing, considering how much to pretend to know, "is what the fuss over this painting is. Reinel shouldn't sell for more than ten grand, tops. I imagine you're paying quite a bit more, Pastor?" Sorenson straightened his back and nodded after a moment.

"You don't know, then," Marina said, getting off the desk. "Well, I guess that's the thing we've kept the most secret. It's a Reinel, sure. But it's not about the art. You know what he did, right, in his paintings?"

"Maps and photos sprayed with Privilux, yeah."

"Right. This particular piece is a portrait of a couple, one of the last Reinel did before he got into the whole coral thing." She waved her hand, as if discounting his entire body of work—Circe included. For a moment, Simone wanted to slap her. "The waters were just rising. People were still thinking it wasn't going to be a big deal—just lay down those floating plastic platforms, and the city would be fine. But the couple isn't important. The trucks are. In the background." She took a step forward and Simone raised an eyebrow. "Big trucks," Marina continued, "marked with the C-Rail Corporation's logo. It's an ugly logo; all yellow and blue. You know it?" Simone shook her head, and Marina looked disappointed in her. "Anyway, there are C-Rail trucks, and they're unloading huge parts of . . . a tunnel, I guess, or a tube—a big one; large enough for a train to drive through. And they're unloading them into a building."

"Seriously?" Simone asked, closing her eyes.

"And," Marina continued, though she didn't need to, "the location of the building is marked on the map part of the painting." Marina stared at Simone. "One would need to compare it to old maps and do some research, of course. But you could figure out where the painting was painted." Simone held her breath, then expelled it. She was disappointed in them right now, in the entire city. It felt like she was tied to a pole with rough rope while around her everyone jumped into the water and drowned, while she screamed at them to stop. Instead, she forced herself to smile.

"I can't—" She pinched the bridge of her nose, trying to hold back her anger. This was the only theory she'd actually had, but she'd dismissed it as too absurd. And here it was, alive in front of her. "A pipeline? You think this painting shows the location of a pipeline between here and the mainland—a magical, waterproof one that would stand up to any pressure?" Simone relaxed and looked up, made herself chuckle. Marina chuckled with her, which answered that question—Marina didn't believe, but she had no problem selling fantasies. Sorenson did not look amused.

"It's real," Sorenson said forcefully. "Or one of them is. The government tunnel was never finished—they didn't have the budget, they were too busy airliftin' monuments from DC to Salt Lake City. But private corporations—several of them—all tried to take advantage of New York's soon-to-be offshore status. Private companies funded by millionaires and defense contractors, like C-Rail. I've seen the records: These tunnels were all built, or at least started. But the waters rose faster than they thought. None of the tunnels were made really ready. But some are just waitin' under the waves. Almost ready. And the American government ain't the only one lookin'." Sorenson took this moment to gesture fiercely at his chest with one hand, as though he were being martyred. "There are more unsavory sorts who would love to get their hands on a passage like that, finish it up, use it for the black market. That Mr. Ryan for one. Can you imagine? Or this deCostas fellow, making it an EU property? Or even the Khans—then it would be a private, family-owned tunnel. You may be friends with Caroline, but do you know her parents?" Simone shrugged. She'd shaken their hands once or twice. Sorenson furrowed his eyebrows. "Vicious, greedy, power-hungry. And others that are worse. We all know each other, and we're all lookin' for a workin' tunnel. There were over a dozen started. I think at least one of them is in near-workin' condition. We could finish it and connect the drowned city to the mainland. No more day trips to the Appalachian Islands, hopin' your ship doesn't snag on a building, and then another day by maglev train to the mainland proper. No more rickety planes that can't hold cargo. No more storms makin' shipping unsafe and a bad investment. The mainland could extend its reach—we could get building supplies out here within days. Extra military could be sent to control a crisis and not get here a week too late. We could set up more missionaries, re-build the city, make it part of the mainland. Think of how good that would be for the city."

Simone pursed her lips. She and Sorenson had very different ideas of what "good for the city" meant. She didn't want New York to be-come like the mainland, with its decency laws and dress codes. And if they were easily connected, that's exactly what would happen.

"I don't know if it's real or not," Marina said, sounding bored. "But that's what the painting shows. So if it is real, I could understand its value. We can't use traditional imaging techniques to just map the ocean floor around the city. Too much debris—cameras, sensors, and even echo-devices all get clogged and useless within moments. But a map? A map is easy."

Simone shook her head, looking down.

"Someone killed Henry for a fairy tale," she said.

"Not a fairy tale," Marina said. "A dream. People are always killing for dreams."

"Linnea killed Henry," Sorenson said. "She double-crossed him so she wouldn't have to split the money."

"Everyone keeps telling me that," Simone said.

"You don't believe it?" Sorenson asked. Simone shrugged.

"Lot of people want this painting, like you said. Even more than I knew about, it sounds like. Why haven't people been searching for it before now?"

"No one knew it existed," Marina said, rolling her eyes. "Reinel gave the painting to the couple he painted. That was what he always did. Usually they sold it, or their kids did, but this one was never in a museum. It was in someone's home, for decades. They probably didn't realize what they had." She looked down, splayed out her hand, and glanced over her nails. "You think Henry had the painting and it was stolen. But I don't think so. It's not a small painting."

"He didn't have it with him," Simone said. "But maybe a key."

Marina shrugged and walked back to the window. Sorenson sat down.

"I pray for Henry," Sorenson said after a moment, "and his murder was an awful thing. But I'm not askin' you to find out who killed him. I just want you to find Linnea. I'll pay you well if you can get me my paintin'."

"You want me to make sure you get the painting and Linnea doesn't run off with it, you mean."

"That's exactly what I mean," Sorenson said in a near growl.

"Fine. I'm already looking for her anyway."

"Good. My receptionist has those release forms for deCostas. You can bring him by again whenever you want. She also has the code for the stairs now. I don't expect to see you again until you have the paintin'. I've wasted enough time and money on this."

"Fine by me, preacher man," Simone said, turning to go.

"Nice meeting you, Simone," Marina called out musically. Simone didn't turn around, but she could feel Marina waggling her fingers at her in a wave goodbye. She took the elevator down, ignoring the people still gathered outside the Mission. Her mind was elsewhere. There was someone else she wanted to see.

SHE FOUND TRIXIE OUTSIDE *Paradise* on the bridge in front of the gangplank. She was standing in front of a large metal barrel with a fire in it. She had on an oversized knitted sweater, and her arms were crossed tightly around her chest, like she was cold. Around her, the fog was thick, and she looked alone in the world. Simone walked up to her slowly, respectfully. Trixie looked up at her, then back at the flames.

"They wouldn't let me burn it on the ship," she said, half explaining the fire, half complaining. Simone looked closely at the barrel. It was filled with trash, but on top was a heap of bright red yarn, burning down into black, ashy strands. "I thought I should burn it. That seems like the right thing to do, right?" She looked anxiously at Simone. Simone nodded. Trixie looked back at the flames. "Right. We buried him yesterday. Well, we poured what was left of him into the ocean. That's what burial is here, I guess."

"You're not from here?"

"No, I was born on the mainland. I married young. My first husband, he used to hit me. A lot." Trixie rubbed her hands up and down her shoulders as if trying to warm up. "And then I met Frank. We fell in love, but divorce is illegal, so we just ran off. We stopped here and acted like we were married; no one questioned it. We did pretty good for a while." Trixie smiled, her eyes on the fire. "Had Henry, had a family. Frank got sick—one of those weird diseases that popped up when the Mercury ice melted. And now Henry is gone, too." She stopped rubbing her arms to tuck a stray hair behind her ear. Then she crossed her arms again, staring at the fire.

"I'm sorry."

"Don't be sorry for me," Trixie said, taking a thin glass bottle of liquor from her sweater pocket. She took a long drink from it. "I don't need pity. I don't need anything, I guess. Just a fire and a drink." She pointed her chin at the fire, looked into it, and smiled faintly. "What do *you* need?"

"I know why Henry was killed. It was for a painting. Well, the myth of the painting, really."

"I don't care," Trixie said flatly. Simone nodded. They watched the fire in silence. It popped and made sounds like crinkled cellophane, and it smelled heavy with chemicals and dust. "I wasn't totally honest, last time we talked. I didn't tell you something."

"Oh?"

"Linnea was never really rich. She had fancy things, sure. But she didn't come from money. She was a grifter. A con artist. Henry knew. He liked that about her. Said it made her exciting. And she was looking to retire, so they settled down together."

"Why are you telling me now?"

"Because I thought you should know about her past. I just didn't want you to think Henry was stupid . . . trusting someone like that. He was a good son."

"I know he was," Simone said. The yarn and trash crackled, and the fog came in thicker, like a down blanket tossed over them.

"Thank you," Trixie said. She peeked into the fire. "It's all gone. Do you know how to put out a fire?"

"Sure. Stand back, though." Trixie took several steps back, and Simone used her feet to scoot the flaming barrel towards the edge of the bridge, near an empty taxi stand. It was hot but didn't burn through the soles of her boots. Finally she got it to the edge and kicked it over.

"Oh!" Trixie said as it fell into the water, taking a few steps forward. Then she stopped. The barrel turned sideways in the water, bobbing half above the surface for a moment, then began to sink. Trixie began to laugh. Simone turned to look at her, and she looked genuinely happy, her eyes fixed on the barrel as it went under. A small stream of bubbles popped on the surface, quickly at first, then slowly, then not at all. Trixie kept laughing, and Simone smiled. But the laughter went on and on, longer than it should have, and still Trixie watched the spot where the last bubble had come up. Quietly, Simone turned and walked away.

When she got home, the fog was thick, and the air sliced past her ears like the sound of a sharpening blade. There would definitely be a storm tomorrow, probably a bad one. Simone frowned as she walked up the stairs to her office. She knew almost everything now, and she still didn't really know anything.

Simone ducked the moment she opened the door to her office. The smell of blood was clear and sharp in the darkness. She took her gun out and stayed crouched by the door, listening for an intruder. She stayed that way for what seemed an eternity but could have only been a few minutes, but there was no sound—just the smell, rusty and floral. She cautiously raised a hand up and flipped on the lights but stayed crouched, her gun ready. There was just one figure in the waiting room, slumped over in the chair in front of the receptionist's desk, as if waiting for an appointment, but clearly dead. Blood sparkled on her fur coat like rubies. It was Linnea.

TWELVE

LINNEA HAD BEEN TORTURED before she was killed and deposited in Simone's waiting room. Simone did a quick search of the office and her apartment. There was no one else there—just Linnea's body, wrapped in her coat, topped with a hat and veil. The coat hung open, and under it she was naked, with cuts and bruises on her face and stomach, a few puncture marks in her arm, and several red cigarette burns crawling up her leg to a single, blackened cigar burn on her inner thigh like a smudged thumbprint. No obvious sign of how she'd died. The ends of her hair were matted with dried blood, and stuck to her chest. It was a thorough going-over.

Simone turned away from the body. There was something too easy about it, too natural, and it chilled her. She could almost imagine Linnea was merely asleep in her coat, wearing red stockings and waiting up late in bed for the husband who never came home. Well, they were together now, whether they liked it or not. Simone pressed her hands down on the desk for the secretary who would never exist. She bent her head. Linnea wasn't her friend, but Simone hadn't disliked her, which was more than she could say for a lot of people.

Normally she'd call Caroline now to tell her a case had come to a body in her office and she was going to call the cops; she'd ask

Caroline to come over, smooth things out, maybe let her lean on her shoulder a little. It wasn't the dead body. Simone had seen bodies. And it wasn't the sense of invasion. It was something else. She found herself thinking of Trixie, and the way she'd looked when Simone kicked the trash-can pyre into the sea.

"Phone," she said, and her earpiece beeped, ready to be given an order. "Call Peter."

"Hey, soldier," he said when he picked up. He said it with a creak in his voice that she recognized, the way he talked as he was sitting up in bed and stretching, like he had after sex, asking her if she wanted something to drink. Then he'd walk to his kitchen naked and bring back a few beers. They'd lay in bed and drink, the sweat from the bottles slowly dripping down their arms and onto their bodies.

"Hi," Simone said, realizing she'd let the pause linger.

"You called me." He was smiling; she could tell.

"Did I wake you?"

"Don't worry about it. I had to work late, I was just grabbing a few hours where I could."

"If you need to sleep, I can call back—"

"What's wrong, Simone?"

"Can you . . ." she trailed off. "Can you meet me at the battle-field? I don't want to talk about this over the phone."

"Yeah, I'll be there in ten minutes." She could hear him moving, putting on clothes.

"Thanks." She hung up before he could reply. She turned around again and leaned back on the desk, taking a long look at the body. She memorized the way the body fell, one arm over the back of the chair, head leaning. Natural, but not. Just the wrong side of alive. She stared at the burns again, circles of different sizes, like a map of the solar system, and the lines of dried blood like empty riverbeds. Then she tightened her coat around her, turned out the lights, and left, locking the door behind her.

Outside, it was colder than it had been when she'd gone inside. How long had she been staring at the body? It hadn't felt long, but it must have been an hour, at least. The night was brittle, and the fog rose up like steel walls.

She went over suspects who would put the body in her office. This wasn't about someone trying to frame her; it wasn't calculated enough for that. It was a warning. Whoever had done this was telling her they were willing to kill—and worse—for the painting, and leaving Linnea in her office meant, "find the painting, or you're next." But find it for whom?

Simone sighed as she realized who had done this. No one else made sense; it had to be him. Charming Dash Ormond. Linnea was just another of those dead bodies that always seemed to end his cases. But Simone didn't know who'd hired him. She could call and ask, but Dash would just deny the whole thing. And there wouldn't be a shred of evidence on the body pointing to him, either. Cold, beautiful Dash would be clean about it. He must have been cleaning off the blood when he went to "wash up" during her visit. She must have really scared him, waiting like that when he'd just gotten back from leaving a body in her office. She wouldn't be sending him any more drinks at the bar, she thought. Maybe she'd send him a bottle of something wherever he ended up, though.

She got to the battlefield first. It wasn't too far from the office. It wasn't really a battlefield, either. That was just what Simone and Peter had called the Douglass Farm Building as kids, when they played with their army figures, laying out strategies and maps for taking over hostile territory. The corn was usually the hostile territory. They attacked from the potatoes.

There were a lot of farms around the city. Most produce was grown in the ocean as algae before being turned into paste for 3D printers, or in the crystal floating houses that bobbed on light plastic, hovering on the waves, built for this environment. But there were a couple of farm boats and a few dozen farm buildings. Not all buildings broke the water's surface at the twenty-first floor. That was just a gen-eralization. New York had had an upward slope once. The Douglass Farm was a building that, because of the height of the floors, had a partially submerged top story—a foot or two of water at the bottom and nothing to stand on above. No one had known exactly what to do with buildings like this—rooftops on the ocean, with nothing liv-able beneath them. Then someone got the bright idea to open up the rooftop, leaving the rest of the building in place. They coated the inside with thick, insulating layers of desalination filters, and then covered the rest up with soil: a seaside farm with constant freshwa-ter underneath, and if the waves started looking high, just put up a big tent for a while. The vegetables grown on them always tasted salt-ier and windier, somehow, but they were cheap compared to the stuff from the mainland or other countries.

The farms were strangely beautiful, too. The desalination filters—so many of them together—resulted in the walls of the buildings being crusted over in salt, making them look like the tip of an ice-berg sticking out of the sea, leveled into a plateau and patterned in rows of plants. When she was little and they'd scaled the fences to sneak in, like she did now, Simone had thought it something from a fairy tale. Tonight it looked like a mountain of bone. Beyond the fence, the farm was still laid out as it had been back then. She headed for the borderline, where the potatoes met the corn, and squatted down to touch the dirt. Then she stood, lit a cigarette, and waited.

Peter showed up when the cigarette was half gone, eleven min-utes after they'd hung up, even though he lived much farther away.

"Hey," he said, when he was still far enough away to just be a shadow in the fog.

"Hey," she said back. He came closer. He was wearing a plaid shirt, open more than he would normally wear it. She stared at the gap in the fabric where his skin and chest hair showed through. He glanced down at where she was looking and buttoned the extra but-ton. She took another drag on her cigarette.

"What did you want to meet about?" She looked up into his eyes. "You sounded upset."

"There's a dead body in my office," she said. He narrowed his eyes. "I didn't put it there."

"I didn't say you did," he said, taking a step back.

"I just didn't want you to have to ask. It's Linnea St. Michel. She's been beat up pretty bad. Cuts, burns . . . someone wanted something from her."

"And then they left her for you?" Simone shrugged. "Kluren isn't going to like this. That's why you called me, right? To report it. You didn't want me to . . . help you hide it, did you? Pitch her in the water?"

"No," Simone said. "She deserves better than that. But Kluren is going to lock me up as soon as she sees the body."

"Yeah, but you'll get out. Caroline can help with that."

"The body is a warning. Someone wants me to . . ." She turned around. She didn't know how much Peter knew.

"You kept digging, didn't you?"

Simone took a long drag on the cigarette. She could vaguely feel him stepping closer, a faint heat on her shoulders. "Yeah."

"So who is the body a warning from?"

"Don't know. I mean, I know the delivery man, but not the guy who sent it."

"Who's the delivery man?"

"You're not going to find him, and if you do, he's going to be cleaner than a bar of soap."

"So you're not going to tell me."

"It'll make things more complicated if he thinks cops are sniffing around him."

"You're going to have to tell Kluren something."

"I'll tell her the body was there when I came in. I don't need to tell her my guess as to who put it there." Peter was silent at that, but she heard him kicking the dirt behind her. She turned around and found him closer than she'd thought, almost face to face, except that he was looking down at the ground. She reached a hand out, half the distance between then, but then pulled it back. When he looked up, she focused on his eyes, and how they seemed almost colorless in the dark.

"Okay, soldier. Show me this body."

HER OFFICE WAS A forensic circus within twenty minutes. Peter had walked back with her, both of them silent. When she unlocked the door and opened it for him, he didn't say anything but laid a hand on her shoulder and tapped his earpiece. His hand stayed there, almost locking her in place as he talked to other officers on duty. The forensic team showed up with two uniforms who spoke directly to Peter, ignoring Simone, except to occasionally glare at her, as though the dead body was her fault. They took the place over pretty quickly, dusting and shining lights and examining the body while Peter and Simone waited in the hallway outside.

When Kluren showed up, she had two more uniforms with her and was barking orders at them. Simone hoped for a moment she might not even see her, but after Kluren glanced in the room, she came back out, that same water-snake smile on her face.

"Some fish you throw back, but they just don't learn. They swim right onto the hook again." She stared at Simone, the gold in her irises twinkling. "I was having a nice dinner, you know."

"You still could be," Simone said. "I'm sure the restaurant is saving your table."

"I'm pretty sure I told you to drop this case."

"Sometimes, you throw something behind you, you find it on the bottom of your boot later."

"That would explain the smell." Kluren looked back into the room. "We have a cause of death?" she called at the sea of blue around her.

"Chief," said one of the techs, deliberately putting himself with his back to Simone. "She didn't die from the cuts. It was a heart attack, probably from stress and the drugs in her system. I'll have to run some tests to confirm, but I'm fairly sure."

"We know what drugs?" Kluren asked.

"Barb of some kind. We already did a quick blood test. I'm guessing one of the more upmarket truth serums. I'll know more at the lab."

"Okay," Kluren said with a nod. She looked back up, as if suddenly remembering Simone was there. "Weiss, cuff her, take her to Teddy. I'll do the interview myself."

"Cuffs?" Simone asked. "You can't think I did this."

"You're a person of interest in two murders now. I don't think you're dumb enough to kill her and then keep the body in your office, but you know a hell of a lot more than you're telling, and for some reason you seem to think that's your right. It isn't. I told you you were off the case, you didn't listen. Now you get the cuffs. If I can make it stick, you'll get some prison time, too, maybe a year if I'm lucky, and then maybe, just maybe, you'll realize that we're the professionals and you're just the daughter of a dropout cop who left the force when things got tough. You don't know better, Pierce. We do."

Simone bit her lower lip and inhaled. She put her hands behind her back and let Peter cuff her. Kluren stared at her, squinting for a moment. Simone wondered what her lenses told her.

"You can take the cuffs off her once she's in Teddy," Kluren said, waving them off like they were children.

Peter led Simone out of the building and took the cuffs off her. Simone nodded her thanks.

"That went better than I thought it would," he said.

"Yeah?" Simone rubbed her wrists.

"I thought she'd be a lot louder, maybe order all your stuff taken away for testing." Peter walked next to her, his hands in his pockets. He was still out of uniform, and he smelled like leather.

"She could still do that."

"Nah. She would've done it in front of you, hoping you'd throw a fit."

"I throw fits?"

"I guess not."

It was a quiet night. The fog seemed to muffle other people's footsteps and hide their shadows. Simone walked slowly beside Peter. They'd gone a few more blocks before he spoke again.

"You know, you could escape."

"And do what? That won't help my case."

"I have that boat."

"No, Peter." She said it firmly enough that he just nodded and kept walking.

"So what are you going to tell Kluren?"

"I walked in, found a body, called you."

"And when she asks why it was left on your doorstep?"

"I don't know. I guess she hasn't solved that case she said she was going to solve yet." The words came out with a tang of nastiness that seemed to vibrate the fog. She took a deep breath. She had to keep cool.

"That jab about your dad stung?" He asked. Simone fished out a cigarette and lit it, then inhaled deeply. "Your dad was a great cop. My dad always said so."

"Dad didn't talk about life as a policeman," Simone said, her voice low in the fog. "Or why he left the force. Just . . . work. How to think, investigate." From the time her mom left, he was a detective, and she was his protégée. All he talked about was work. Never Mom, never their life before she was gone, never even what was right or wrong. Just how to be a detective, how to solve the case. She had a sudden memory of him, showing her how to load a gun when she was eight years old, pushing each bullet neatly into the row of the clip.

"Good . . . carefully, though, don't crowd them." He'd had a low, gruff voice, and large, rough hands that cradled hers. "Then we push it into the gun here, till it clicks." He had moved her hands so that she loaded the clip of the gun. "Good. Then we just point and shoot, like this." He had knelt behind her and moved her arms forward. "Both hands . . . brace yourself, it's going to knock you back pretty hard when you fire it. Remember, shoot them before they shoot you."

"How will I know if they're going to shoot me?" Simone had asked.

"You'll know. And if you're wrong, it won't matter, as long as you shoot first."

"Well, he was a good cop," Peter said, bringing her back to the present. "And he didn't quit when it got tough. He and Kluren solved a really tough multiple homicide; once it was wrapped up, he quit. He waited until he wasn't gonna mess anything up by leaving. A stand-up guy, my dad always said."

"Thanks."

They got to Teddy, and Peter led her onto the boat and down to the interrogation rooms. A few cops glanced up at them, but then went back to what they were doing. When the department had taken over the ship, they'd cleared out a number of small bunks to create the interrogation rooms, bolting a steel table to the floor and throwing in a few cheap tin chairs. The two-way mirrors, which took up almost an entire wall, didn't match the old bolted bulkhead. They shone too sleekly, felt too clean. Simone sat down in the chair facing the mirror.

"I'm going to need your weapons," Peter said apologetically. She nodded and unzipped her boot, pulling her gun from it and placing it on the table. She didn't zip the boot back up but instead unzipped the other, letting her legs breathe. "Thanks," he said, taking the gun. "I'll get us some coffee." He left her alone, staring at her reflection. The overhead light was strong, and from where she sat she could see how it cast shadows in the hollows of her eyes. She leaned back and took off her hat and trench coat. Peter came back in, put a paper cup of coffee down in front of her, and sat down opposite. He had his own cup of coffee and blew on it, making the steam wave out like a gray flag.

They sat in silence a long while. Simone drank all her coffee, burning her tongue on the first sip. Peter got her another, but this one she only held until it got cold. When Kluren finally showed up, she was a shadow in the doorway, looking down at both of them.

"Weiss, out." Kluren said. As he left, Peter shot Simone a look that was hard to read—pity? solidarity? Simone turned to Kluren, trying to keep her face level, unreadable. Kluren took her seat and leaned back, staring at Simone. Her gold irises seemed to twist, as if amused by Simone's attempts to shut herself down.

"Isn't it unusual for the chief to be doing the interview?" Simone asked, still holding her coffee.

Kluren put her hands behind her head, leaned back, and looked at the ceiling. "I can run my boat however I want." She took her hands down and leveled her gaze at Simone. "Now why don't you tell me about the case I told you to drop?"

"You got everything off my server."

"I'm sure you've made some progress since then."

"I dropped it, just like you told me."

"Do you really think lying is somehow going to get you out of this mess? Your client was murdered and left in your office. I know you're not dumb enough to do that, even if you act like it most of the time. And I know that whoever left it there staged it as a warning, not to frame you. I'm your life preserver, here, Simone. I'm being very nice." She leaned forward, her arms making a triangle, pointing at Simone.

"You said you wanted to throw me in prison."

"Would you prefer to end up like Linnea? 'Cause I don't see this playing out any other way."

"You think I'm gonna let myself get sliced up?"

"Let? I think you're running towards it with open arms." She leaned back, slapping the table. Simone stared at her, trying to decide if Kluren was angry that Simone was putting herself in danger, or just angry at Simone for continuing to exist.

"I'm trying to solve a case."

"One I told you to drop."

Simone put down her coffee and folded her arms. "You're not my boss."

"Which is a shame, 'cause you need a boss. You're the sort who drowns because she doesn't realize she's underwater till it's too late. Now tell me who sent you the warning."

"I don't know." Simone held eye contact with Kluren, daring her ForenSpecs to say she was lying.

"Then you're not doing a very good job investigating, are you? Did you find out what the package was for, or who the blonde was?"

Simone kept holding Kluren's gaze but said nothing.

"Cute, the silent thing. 'Cause if you answer a question, you think I can tell if you're lying. Or maybe you're hoping I'll tell you what we know about the little art deal your client was working on." Simone raised an eyebrow. "Didn't think we knew about that? We know more. So just tell us who left you the body and we can get on with solving it. You might even get to go free, depending on how I feel in the morning."

"Did you really just say that?" The door had opened halfway without either of the women noticing, and now Caroline Khan pushed it the rest of the way open and gave Kluren a questioning look. "The mayor is trying to cut down on police corruption, Kluren. Let's try not to say exciting and provocative things in front of the private detective, hm? Wouldn't look good in the press."

Kluren stared warily at Caroline, but stood. "Does the mayor have an interest in this case?"

"He will if I tell him he does," Caroline said with a smile.

"Now who's saying provocative things in front of detectives?"

Caroline folded her arms and nodded in Simone's direction without looking at her. "She might be an untrustworthy bitch, but she also knows I'm here to get her out, so I think she'll be good for a while."

"You can't take away a suspect."

"She's a person of interest, not a suspect, which means she can go if she wants. If you upgrade her to suspect then you have to arrest her, and then she gets a lawyer and you don't get to talk to her again anyway, so why not just let her go and I'll have a little chat with her and decide what's best for the city? Right now, I'm going to be a lot scarier than you think you're going to be." She leaned back on one of her heels, arms still crossed.

Simone stared hard at Caroline, but Caroline wouldn't make eye contact. Kluren, on the other hand, was staring at Simone and smiling.

"Sure, fine. Besides, if whoever killed Linnea kills her . . . my life would get easier. Go." She waved them off like insects.

Caroline strode from the room without looking back, and Simone quickly zipped her boots, grabbed her hat and coat, and followed her. Caroline still wouldn't make eye contact, but as Simone came closer to thank her, she spoke first.

"Don't say anything," Caroline said. Her voice was cold. "Come with me."

"I need my gun," Simone said. Caroline finally turned to look at her, and Simone felt like she was being prodded with a red-hot poker.

"Get it," Caroline said. Simone turned around and spotted Peter in a corner. She walked up to him and he handed her her gun back.

"I called her," Peter whispered. "She didn't sound happy. What's going on?"

"Thanks," Simone said, putting her gun back in her boot. She turned back around to find Caroline was halfway down the hall, so

Simone ran to catch up. They walked off the boat in silence. They walked a few blocks more before Caroline finally turned around.

"You're a fucking idiot," she said. Simone shrugged. "And I really don't like you right now. And if you don't trust me, I don't know why I should trust you."

"I'm sorry—" Simone started, but Caroline cut the air with her hand and Simone stopped.

"I don't want to do this right now. I don't have many friends."

"Me neither."

"I know. But I bailed you out because . . . for old times' sake. And because I know Kluren is gunning for you, and it's unfair. But I'm angry. And things aren't good between us."

"I know," Simone said, staring at the wooden bridge under her feet. "I fucked it up."

"Yeah." They stood there in silence. Simone looked up at Caroline, who was staring at her, her mouth slightly open, her face more slack than usual. But when she saw Simone looking, she clenched her jaw and turned her head, staring off.

"I'm going home now. You should find somewhere to stay. I'm guessing cops are still swarming all over your apartment."

"Yeah," Simone nodded. "Thanks, Caroline. And I really am sorry."

"Good night." Caroline turned around before the conversation could continue. As she walked away, she threw her hand up in a gesture that was half wave, half "go away." Simone stared after her until she was gone, then turned and walked in the opposite direction.

She walked for a while with no particular destination. The storm on the horizon was growing ominously closer, but she didn't care. She felt as though she ought to be thinking about something: the case, the comments Kluren made about her father, how she could make it up to Caroline—but her mind was curiously blank. She was blank all over. She was breath in a body in a city on the ocean, and that was all there was.

. . .

SHE WOUND UP AT Danny's because it was the place that made the most sense to go. She could have tried Peter . . . but that was complicated and messy, and he would have kept asking about what was going on with Caroline.

All the lights were out except the neon one that read, "The Great Yanai," and the sliding door was locked. Simone dictated a message to him over her earpiece saying she was outside, and a few moments later he waded out of the shadows behind the glass and opened the door.

"Sad," he said, looking her over.

"So are your pajamas."

He looked down at the bright yellow briefs he was wearing. They had a large cartoon octopus over the crotch. "These? I like these," he shrugged, then looked back up at her. "Come on in. What happened?"

"Client's dead body showed up at my place, police hauled me in, Caroline got me out, but told me she really didn't want to see me, so now I can't go home, I can't go to Caroline's. I was hoping I could crash here."

"Why not call up that delicious tourist of yours?" They walked forward through his office and up the back stairs to his apartment.

"deCostas?" The thought of it made her mouth bitter. "No."

"How about you give me his number, and I call him up, then?"

"I forgot to take photos of him naked for you, sorry."

"That's okay. Some things are better left to the imagination. Anyway, the couch is yours. I have some blankets and a pillow somewhere around here."

"Thanks."

"Hey, you took me in when I had nowhere to go. This is the least I can do—besides all the free help I give you." He walked into his bedroom, and Simone sat down on the couch. It was comfortable.

It would do for the night. She took off her boots and lay back. Danny came back out with a thick blanket and pillow and put them down on the sofa next to her. For a moment he stared at nothing, that vague look he got when searching the web, then he smiled down at her. "You wanna talk about it?"

"You just read the police report, didn't you?"

"A prelim report from one of the on-the-scene techs. Your apartment is still being processed, but the word *torture* stuck out."

"My client. Linnea," Simone breathed the name out softly and felt a stab of guilt in her lungs. She fished in her pocket for a cigarette and took it out. "You mind?" Danny shook his head. She lit it and inhaled deeply, filling her chest with something else. "Linnea. Tortured, left in my office. Some sort of warning."

"Who from?"

"Dash Ormond, I think. Don't know who he's working for, though."

"Dangerous Dash? I thought we liked him." Danny sat down next to her on the sofa.

"We liked him when we weren't in his crosshairs. But he's just the weapon. Someone else is pulling his strings, and that someone wants the painting Linnea had and thinks I know where it is."

"Why do they think that?"

"Because she hired me to spy on her husband, to make sure he didn't double-cross her."

"You want to go over this from the top for me?"

Simone inhaled deeply on her cigarette. She didn't usually share her cases. She didn't like asking for help.

"Can I ask you something else, first?" she said, without looking at Danny.

"Sure."

"What do you know about my dad?"

"Only what you've told me." Danny leaned back into the sofa.

"Seriously?"

"I know he ran the business before you. I know he taught you. I never looked into him. It seemed . . . You're the first person I met when I escaped, you know? You're the first person who saw me for who I was and helped me, and, yeah, we both know you did it 'cause you knew I'd come in handy, but you also did it 'cause you're a good person."

"I'm really not."

"You are. You're not *always* a good person, and you don't trust people, and you're kind of a bitch sometimes, but I don't mind that. I was raised assuming no one could trust anyone except the people we worked for. That's why I don't mind it in you. That's why you're still one of my few real friends. And I know you might not trust me completely, but it doesn't matter to me that you don't, because I know I've never dug into your past—or your family's. That's not what friends do. Or so reruns of ancient TV shows on the web tell me."

Simone smiled and inhaled deeply on her cigarette. "You're a good guy, Danny."

"I'm the product of a secret government experiment, all the information on the Internet, and what's left of New York."

Simone shrugged. "Still . . ." Her cigarette was nearly out; she had been dropping ash on the floor. "Sorry," she said, staring at it.

"I'll get it in the morning. Just put it out in the sink." Danny motioned at the kitchen, and Simone rose and walked over, throwing the butt in the sink and running the water. "Why did you ask about your dad?"

"Something Kluren said. Can you . . . will you find out what you can for me?" She shut off the water and looked at him. He was staring at her—really staring, not online.

"I can . . ." he said slowly. "But are you sure you want to know? I never had real parents, exactly, but it seems like a weird thing to go looking into. What if I find something—I wouldn't say bad, but . . . something you wouldn't want to know?"

"You won't," Simone said. "You'll get some files and some information, but you won't know what it means. I'll know."

"So?"

"So, you can't hold anything back, and anything you do tell me—I won't blame you. That's what you're looking for, right?"

"And I don't want you to be . . . hurt, I guess."

"I'll be fine, Danny."

"You want me to do it right now?"

"No," Simone said, walking back over to the sofa. "We can do it in the morning. And then I'll tell you all about the case . . . and then maybe I'll throw myself in the ocean." She smiled without meaning to.

"It worries me when people say things like that and smile." Danny stood, and Simone lay down on the sofa, pulling the blanket over her.

"Thanks, Danny."

"Anytime, boss." He shut the light and padded quietly to his bedroom. Simone closed her eyes. Outside, she could hear the ocean washing softly against the building. It was so dark in this room— nothing but waves and black.

THIRTEEN

—

A HIGH-PITCHED WHISTLE WOKE her up, and, for a moment, Simone forgot where she was. But then it all came back at her like the vibrant slashes on Linnea's arms, and she lifted herself up on the sofa so she was sitting. Danny was in the kitchen, and the whistling was from a tea kettle.

"You have coffee, too, right?" Simone said.

"I do, but only decaf," Danny said. Simone frowned. "I have the Internet in my head. It's hard enough getting to sleep as is."

Simone groaned and put her head in her hands. Her hair streamed over her face, bright red in the morning light.

"There's a coffee boat that docks right down the bridge in the mornings. If you need it, go get yourself a cup."

"I will in a minute. Can I shower first?"

"Sure—right there." Danny pointed at the bathroom and poured himself some tea. Simone showered quickly, splashing the water over her face until she felt awake. When she got back out, Danny was sitting on the sofa, drinking his tea and staring ahead vacantly.

Simone sat down next to him, toweling her hair. He glanced over at her, anxiously, then went back to staring ahead.

"What'd you find out?"

"I . . . I looked into your dad like you asked. It was just hacking NYPD files. You probably could have done it yourself . . ."

"Probably," Simone admitted. "But I don't like computers. That's why I have you."

"I do so love the way you make me feel like a complete person, after my time being raised as a tool for the government."

"You're just angry I didn't bring you those naked photos of deCostas."

He looked at her, his eyes focusing on her, his brain going offline. "You're really not good at apologizing, are you?"

Simone stopped drying her hair and raised her eyebrows. "I was just kidding."

"I know, but it was a little over the line, considering you're the only one who knows how not-human I am. But I don't mind that. I'm just making an observation. Did you apologize to Caroline?"

"I sent her a bunch of straws."

Danny laughed in a way that seemed a little cruel. "That's something, anyway." Simone stared at him in silence, and he looked away for a moment.

"What did you find out about my dad?"

"You sure you want this?"

"Yeah . . . And hey. I am sorry—you know, if I offended you with that crack. You are a person."

"Your dad and Kluren had an affair." He said it quickly, like he'd been holding it in.

Simone looked down. "How can you know that from hacking a server?"

"Kluren admitted it." Simone felt her face go warm. "They had an affair. Your dad broke it off. They figured it out when Kluren asked for a transfer, asked her flat out. They were both reprimanded, and Kluren was demoted. They were going to demote your dad, too, but he went for early retirement instead."

"And that's when my mom left, too." Danny didn't say anything. Simone felt a chuckle leave her mouth, but the rest of her was cool. "Never make assumptions," she said quietly to herself.

"What?"

"Nothing." Simone looked up at Danny and smiled.

"You okay?"

"Yeah, thanks. I'm just going to get that coffee," Simone said, heading for the door.

"Okay. And sorry about your dad."

She didn't turn around as he said it but paused before opening the door. Then she kept walking.

Outside it was bright and clear, the sort of day that makes happy people smile and inhale deeply and unhappy people go back to bed. The light glared off the water, hurting her eyes. She put her hat on and kept her face down, pacing to the end of the bridge, where a small coffee boat run by a man with a large mustache was docked. She got a hot black coffee and sat down on the edge of the bridge, her legs over the edge. There was only a cheap rope railing, barely noticeable, and she stared through it at the ocean, drinking. When the coffee was nearly done, she lit a cigarette and called Caroline at work. She picked up after three rings.

"I don't know if I want to talk to you," Caroline said.

"Fair enough. I shouldn't have, but . . . Did you know my dad had an affair with Kluren?" There was silence.

"That explains a lot," Caroline said, her voice sounding cautious.

"Yeah." More silence.

"Look, I have work to do."

"I'm sorry. I just . . . I saw you in a photo with The Blonde, Marina, and my brain went into work mode. Imagine if I tried to park a boat in the city without a permit."

"That's a crap example, Simone. I thought we were friends and then one photo and you think I'm trying to kill you. That's not friendship. That's . . . I don't know."

"I didn't want to ask you about it. I didn't want to put you in a position where you might have to lie to me." Simone stared at her cigarette, then tapped the ashy end of it into the water.

"This isn't helping your cause."

"I just was afraid that if I told you about it, you'd get angry and . . . well, we'd end up where we are."

More silence. A seagull soared over her, then dove into the ocean like a brick.

"So your plan was a failure," Caroline said.

"Big time."

"So you had Danny ask me—"

"No—that was all him," Simone interrupted. "He found the picture, and I told him to keep his mouth shut. But he's Danny."

"Did you think I had anything to do with the case, though? Did you think I'd hired Marina to threaten you?"

"No . . . Can we talk about this in person?"

"Afraid the line is tapped?"

"I'm being closed in on right now. Lot of pressure."

"I'll call you back, then. I'll use the mayor's fancy encrypted scrambler line. That good enough? Or do you think he's involved, too?"

"That's good," Simone said, and they hung up. The sun beat down on her, making her clothes cling. Her earpiece rang, the little light from under her ear projecting the incoming call from "unknown."

"Yeah?" she clicked the phone.

"Secure line. I think you were apologizing? Poorly?"

"Okay, I thought maybe you were involved. But I didn't think you'd sent Marina after me. Marina pointed the gun at me 'cause I was following her. She wasn't hired to do that. I just didn't know how you fit in. And I didn't want to ask you. So I kept investigating. Once I knew how you were involved, I would have told you." Simone tossed what was left of her cigarette into the ocean. It cartwheeled into the water, one end leaving a trail of sparks like blood splatter.

"Instead of asking."

"Yeah. That was the dumb part."

"In case I was involved in something bad."

"Yeah."

"You didn't want me to lie to you about it."

"Yeah."

Simone could hear Caroline typing something. She took a long sip of the coffee. It tasted bitter and chalky.

"I got your straws," Caroline said after a moment.

"Did you like them?"

"It's a lot of straws."

"Yeah."

"I'm still pissed."

"Yeah," Simone said, closing her eyes. She waited for Caroline to hang up. She didn't.

"So do you know where my painting is? My parents are asking."

"*Your* painting?" Simone asked. The sun felt a little brighter on her neck.

"Yeah. We won the auction. Marina said she'd get me the painting as soon as it was recovered, but I guess one of the losers didn't like being a loser and went after it themselves."

"You won the auction?" Simone said.

"That's what Marina said."

"Sorenson told me he won the painting. In front of Marina. She said he won it."

"That bitch," Caroline said.

Simone let the silence hang intentionally this time, and smiled. "I know you're not my biggest fan right now," she said.

"Yeah?"

"But maybe you want to tag along when I go visit her?"

"Are you asking me along to watch you interrogate someone I'm angry at in an attempt to repair our friendship?"

"That is exactly what I'm doing."

"Will you let me hit her?"

"If the opportunity presents itself."

"Okay. But it's going to take more than this and some straws."

"Can I swing by your office? We'll head over together?"

"Sure. I want to hear all about this case, though. Every tiny detail."

"I will. I trust you."

"No you don't."

"I'm trying."

"Try harder."

DANNY WAS IN COSTUME by the time she got back to his place.

"Thanks for letting me crash here," Simone said.

"Going somewhere?" Danny asked, adjusting his turban.

"I got a lead. Caroline and I are going to check it out."

"Caroline?"

"Yeah, and if you say the word *trust* I'm going to hit you." Simone checked her pockets and under the sofa, making sure she had everything. "Caroline is still pissed, but I got my foot in the door, and I'm going to fix this. And solve my case."

"Busy morning," Danny said, sounding impressed. "Weren't you going to tell me what this case is about?"

"Rain check—later, with beer or whatever." She stood and turned back to look at Danny in his ridiculous pajamas. The feather in his turban bobbed like a buoy. "I promise. Thanks again. I'll let you know how it turns out."

"Call me if you need me." Simone dashed out the door, her coat tight around her, and headed for City Hall.

THE FLOATING PLAZA AROUND City Hall was busier during the day: tourists from the mainland shooting photos, people on smoke breaks by the fountain, and a row of black yachts docked across from the plaza, their bows dipping like praying monks, with a line of drivers standing in front of them like guards. She walked past them into the building, flashed her IRID at the guards, and headed up. She wasn't a familiar enough face that guards and secretaries stopped to chat with her, but she visited often enough that they knew who she was and that she was allowed in the building.

Caroline's senior secretary glanced up at Simone when she stepped out of the elevator, then back down at her touchdesk, her mouth a thin line of worry at the prospect of an unscheduled appointment. "I don't have you on the calendar, but I'll let Ms. Khan know you're here. She'll be out soon, I'm sure." She picked up the phone and told Caroline that Simone was waiting, then nodded and hung up. "She's just finishing up a conference call with the mainland." The secretary leaned forward conspiratorially, clearly excited to have someone new to gossip with. "Some big project they want to do, all very secret. Do you have any guesses?" Simone raised her eyebrows, which the secretary took as a cue to continue. "I think maybe they want to start a whale farm out here. Just think how great that would be." This was more insight into the mind of Caroline's secretary than Simone wanted. Thankfully, at that moment, the office door sprang open, and Caroline beckoned wordlessly from inside. Simone shrugged at the secretary and followed Caroline into her office, closing the door behind her.

"So, before we head over to the Four Seasons, you're going to tell me everything," Caroline said, leaning back on her desk and closing her arms. She was wearing a gray suit with a white collared shirt. Her mood wasn't as good as Simone had hoped. She had thought—optimistically, apparently—that by telling Caroline about Danny's gaffe, they'd be on the road to reconciliation. She wasn't so sure now.

"Okay," Simone said. "Can I sit?"

Caroline nodded at one of the chairs in front of her desk. "And if you leave anything out or lie, I will know, and that will be it. I am offering you a do-over. I'm letting you talk to me like you should have talked to me from day one."

"Okay," Simone said again, sitting gingerly.

"And you should say 'thank you' for that."

"Thanks," Simone said, somewhat flatly. Caroline raised her eyebrows, then spun around and went to sit behind her desk.

"From the beginning."

Simone told her everything, from the case Linnea had hired her for, to the first murder, to Linnea's body showing up in her office. She found it was easy once she got started—easier than her usual routine of glossing over the truths of her work, withholding information. Caroline watched and listened, her feet up on the desk, her face rarely betraying anything besides interest.

"A map." Caroline said when Simone had finished. She stood and looked out her window. "I thought it was just some art for the foundation. I didn't know . . . My parents are nuts, you know that, right?" She turned back and looked at Simone, and for a moment, Simone felt hopeful—Caroline was talking to her. Was complaining about her parents, like she used to. But then Caroline seemed to realize this too, and her mouth became a straight line again. She sat back down at her desk, her back straight, her movements all mathematical, hard geometry. "Why stay on the case?" Caroline asked, after a moment. "When Kluren told you to quit and your client disappeared? Why keep digging?"

"Kluren was fitting me for a prison jumpsuit."

"Bullshit. Kluren may not like you, but she's a good cop, religiously by the book, and you know it. She wouldn't have locked you up without cause. Why did you keep digging?"

Simone looked down, and her hat fell off her head onto the floor. She stared at it a minute, her now loose hair partially obscuring her vision.

"You were involved," she said after a minute.

"I was involved? So what, you wanted to make sure I wasn't secretly a criminal mastermind?"

"I wanted to make sure you were okay." The hat had fallen at an angle, but with the rim up, so she could look into the hat and its black lining, where a few of her hairs had curled like red ink, words in calligraphy so fancy she couldn't read it. She heard Caroline get up from behind her desk, and looked up at her. Caroline was looking out the window.

"Okay then," Caroline said. "Let's go see Marina. You can tell me your theory on the way."

FOURTEEN

——

FORGERY. THAT WAS SIMONE'S theory. That, and Henry and Linnea were so busy looking at each other, expecting betrayal, they never counted on someone coming for the painting without paying. They'd been in over their heads before they even finished conceiving the plan.

"It's the Mona Lisa con," Simone explained as they stopped for pretzels. "They find a lost painting, maybe stolen, something, but they know it's valuable. So instead of auctioning it off to just one buyer, they get greedy: forge a whole bunch of them and sell them to all the buyers."

"Wouldn't their buyers find out, eventually?" Caroline asked. Simone bit into her pretzel and started walking towards the Four Seasons, Caroline keeping pace beside her.

"That's why you do this with a stolen painting," Simone said between bites. "No one catches on because no one wants to admit they bought a painting they know was stolen. In this case, though, people aren't really interested in the painting. They're interested in the information contained in the painting. So when they sell the painting—no one admits to buying it, because then people will try to find out where the painting is and steal it, or at least the information. Everyone keeps the painting secret."

"But won't they all just end up meeting at the location on the painting?"

"I imagine Marina and the St. Michels were betting that the location is a dud." Simone took another bite of her pretzel and swallowed before continuing. "Just some random apartment building, nothing special. That's what I'd bet on."

"So people buy the forgeries, check out the location, see it's nothing, and then go back to their lives, having lost however much money they were willing to spend."

"Which is why they hired Marina. She works people—she got you to pay exactly your maximum for the painting, didn't she?"

"The maximum my parents told me to pay, but yeah." Caroline rubbed the space between her eyebrows. "I can't believe they got me mixed up in this."

"Everyone knows the painting could be fool's gold, your parents included. Everyone has a set amount they're willing to risk and have it turn out to be worthless. And Marina works people to get to that price. It's a great scheme. No one gives a fuck about the painting once they realize it hasn't led them anywhere. And if they do find out someone else bought it, well, the St. Michels and Marina—and their forger, whoever he is—are long gone by then. Plus no one wants to admit they bought a treasure map that didn't lead anywhere." Simone swallowed the last bite of her pretzel and licked the salt from her hand.

"So who killed Henry? Was it Linnea?"

"No. Henry and Linnea were going to turn on each other, and each knew it—that's why Linnea hired me in the first place. But neither was going to try that till after the paintings were sold. For them, it was about the money. Linnea was killed by Dash, I'm almost positive. Someone hired him to get the painting. But she didn't have it, or wouldn't give it up." Simone put her hands in her pockets, remembering Linnea. "Probably wouldn't give it up. I'd say Marina has it, but then she would've just given it to the highest bidder, given everyone else their money back, and acted as though it were a normal job. It wouldn't have been as big a payday, but she wouldn't have had to split it."

"So who's left?"

"The forger."

"And who's the forger?"

"That's what we're about to ask Marina."

Simone stopped and stared up at the Four Seasons. They'd arrived, and she needed to prepare herself for what she had to do. She wasn't going to torture Marina, the way Dash had done to Linnea, but she wasn't above punching her in the jaw, either. Marina was smart, though, and her primary instinct would be survival. With Caroline there, Simone could make a compelling case for pinning the whole thing on Marina and sending her off to prison. Hopefully, Marina would talk to avoid that.

"Let me do most of the talking," Simone said as they walked up to the door. "I'm going to use you—your position—to intimidate her. Make it seem the law has her and she's about to get locked in the hull of some prison ship for the rest of her life if she doesn't cooperate. Bring out the legalese to back me up, if you need to; otherwise, stay quiet and look angry."

"I thought you said I could hit her."

"If the opportunity presents itself."

"Okay, but my interpretation of 'presents itself' may be looser than yours." Caroline walked into the elevator and hit 30. "She's in room 3003."

"You should knock. That'll be better," Simone said. She took her gun out of her boot, checked it was loaded, and put it back while Caroline watched in silence. The elevator rang, and the door opened. Caroline led the way down the hall.

"She really got to you when she pointed the gun at you, didn't she?" Caroline asked in a low voice. Simone shook her head, then nodded at room 3003. Caroline held her fist up as if to knock, then looked at Simone. Simone leaned against the wall next to the door and nodded. Caroline knocked.

The door swung open. Simone couldn't see Marina, but she could hear her.

"Caroline! Hey! You should have called, I would have put on some nice clothes." Her voice was perky, but with an edge of anxiety Simone enjoyed hearing. "What's up? Is this about the painting, 'cause I promise, I will get it to you, it's just a little complicated be-cause the sellers—" Simone stepped out from the side of the door, right behind Caroline. "Oh." The false cheerfulness slipped off Ma-rina's face like silk lingerie. She stared at them both and sighed, half resigned to her fate, half bored. She turned around and walked back into the room. Caroline and Simone followed, closing the door behind them. Marina sat down on the bed and crossed her legs. She was in one of the hotel robes and nothing else. Her hair was wet and pulled back from her face, making her seem more exposed than Simone had ever seen her. She looked up at both of them. "I knew about your relationship, of course," she said. "But everyone said how professional you were," she was staring at Simone now, "how you never betrayed your client's trust. I guess they were wrong about that. People have been wrong about a lot lately. Fuck people." She leaned back, stretching her arms behind her to hold herself up and arching her chest slightly.

"Where's the painting?" Simone asked.

"You know I don't have it."

"But you know who does."

Marina sighed again and stood up. She walked over to the desk in the room. It was a large room, with a balcony. There were a few room service trays on the desk. She was probably afraid to leave too often. Afraid she'd be the next Linnea. Simone tracked her. There was no gun in sight. Marina picked up a pack of cigarettes from the desk and lit one.

"You don't mind, right?" she asked.

"The forger, Marina?" Simone asked. "That's who has the painting, right?"

"Figured it all out, did you?" Marina asked, exhaling smoke. "Yeah. The forger has it, I think. But I don't know where the forger is. Or who."

"You don't know who the forger is?" Simone rolled her eyes.

"Don't roll your eyes at me. I'm just the saleswoman. I didn't do the hiring or even come up with the idea." Marina turned and looked out the window, away from them, one arm holding the elbow of the other. She brought the cigarette to her lips and inhaled again. She exhaled slowly, so the smoke was like a thin sheet rising from her lips.

"Caroline here is deputy mayor," Simone said, gesturing with her thumb. "You're the last known person left in an art forgery con. Caroline, can you tell Marina what she's won for that?"

"Forgery could be a good decade below deck," Caroline said matter-of-factly. "The con will probably bring it to twenty-five."

"Bring in someone like deCostas," Simone said, "some poor innocent grad student you scammed . . . maybe even higher. If you're really lucky, eighteen years with good behavior." She glanced at Caroline, who nodded authoritatively.

"I'm always on my best behavior," Marina said without turning away from the window. "And deCostas isn't poor. He's being funded by three or four governments. That's why I went to him. Don't you research your clients?"

Simone shook her head. "Why would governments fund him? It's a fool's errand."

"Who are we to know that? We may think it's bullshit. I do, you do—even Caroline here does, and she paid a lot of money for it. But what do we know? Have we researched it like he has? No. All I know is that that painting, even a copy of it, is worth a lot to a lot of people, even if we all know it's just a bunch of salt." She smiled, apparently thinking of how much money she almost had. But then her smile faded and she sucked at her cigarette again, almost desperately. "But it doesn't matter. I don't know the forger. He's someone Linnea brought in. Knew him from Europe, I guess. She had a stupid nickname for him. I think she was trying to make Henry jealous."

Simone stared Marina in the eyes, and Marina stared right back, her cigarette held at her mouth, one arm crossed across her robe. Marina was the sort you could never actually trust, but Simone didn't think she was playing a game.

"What was the nickname?" Simone asked.

"She kept saying My Little *le furgay*, or something like that. My Little Forger, My Little *le furgee*. In a silly voice, too. She had that heavy accent. I assumed it meant forger in Swedish or whatever." She shrugged and leaned against the desk.

"That's not Swedish for forger," Caroline said. "That's not Swedish for anything."

"Well, sorry," Marina said sarcastically, "I only speak Japanese, Chinese, Spanish, French, and Italian. Never took Swedish. Or Dutch, or wherever in the EU Linnea was from."

"It doesn't mean forger in anything," Caroline said.

Simone looked over at her. "You sure?"

"Yes," Caroline said, clearly offended at being asked. If it wasn't a pet name, it was another sort of name. And Simone had a first name that needed a last.

"I'm going to step into the hall to make a call," Simone said. "Keep an eye on her." Simone walked out into the hall, activated her earpiece, and told it to call Danny. Inside the hotel room she heard a noise like a loud slap and furniture moving.

"I'm about to see a client," Danny said. "What's up?"

"I need an address: Misty LeFurgay. She's somewhere in the city. Maybe a hotel."

"How do you spell that?"

"However. But I need it now, if you can."

"Okay . . ." Danny's voice trailed off. Inside the hotel room there was the sound of furniture falling and metal clattering. "M. LeFurgey. That's F-U-R-G-E-Y, by the way. She's not in a good part of town."

He gave her the address, and she thanked him before hanging up and going back into the room. The desk was on its side, room service trays spilled all over the rug. Marina was slumped against the wall where the desk used to be, still smoking, gazing up at the window, a large red mark on her face. Simone barely glanced at her.

"I got it," she said to Caroline. "Want to come?"

Caroline turned to look at her, a big smile on her face. "Sure. Nothing left to do here." She turned back to Marina, still smiling. "I expect my money back tomorrow. Early." She left without waiting for a reply.

"Now would be a good time to leave town," Simone said. Marina looked up at her wearily.

"I never really liked New York, anyway," she said. She looked as if she might smile but instead brought the cigarette to her lips. Simone left her there.

"So where are we going?" Caroline asked.

"West Side. Sort of between where Linnea was seen buying drugs and where Henry was killed. Not a nice neighborhood. Lot of MouthFoamers. You might want to hide your wristpiece."

"You have a gun," Caroline said. "Why don't you just display that?"

"I will."

CAROLINE PAID FOR A CAB, and Simone had it drop them a few bridges away, where it wasn't too seedy. It was midafternoon, and the sun pressed down, simmering the garbage that floated between the buildings and sending up a dirt and shit smell. Flies buzzed just over the waves, their paranoid hum rising up whenever the sound of the waves faded. Simone shaded her eyes with her hands and looked for the building Danny had directed her to. It was a short walk, over bridges littered with sleeping bodies and people in salt-stained clothes, their mouths white, their eyes glazed. Behind the buildings, off on the horizon, there was a massive storm cloud heading their way. They'd have to be fast.

She led the way, flashing her gun when any of the MouthFoam-ers glanced up at them. Caroline walked just behind her, eyes straight ahead, fearless. They wove around poorly finished bridges and, at one point, climbed up to the top of a building to get to a bridge that was higher up. The building they finally came to was gray stone, one of the Glassteel test cases. It was covered with the stuff so thickly it actually looked laminated, cheap and tacky, like a build-ing made of wax paper. The door was open, so they walked in and up a few flights. Danny had homed in on this location from server and cloud usage, but he couldn't find an apartment number; the clos-est he could get was that she was probably in the top northwest corner of the building.

The stairwells were metal things, crusted with salt and smelling of plastic and decay. Simone knocked on a few doors as she ap-proached the northwest part of the top floor. No one answered any of them until they reached apartment G. There, the door flew open as though someone was expecting them.

The woman who opened the door was young and wore only a blue dressing gown tied loosely around her. She didn't even look at Simone and Caroline but walked away from the door as soon as she'd opened it. The apartment was a large flat, empty of all furniture save an unmade bed, a dresser, an old leather sofa that was also being used as a bed, and a wooden chair in front of a small table. An easel stood by one of the large frosted windows that let in a cold, gray light. A few other windows were open, and wind blew around the room, wet with the ocean. The woman sat down on the wooden chair and crossed her legs, apparently waiting for Simone and

Caroline. Simone saw nowhere else to sit, so she stood across from the small table, eyeing the woman. The woman stared directly ahead of her, not looking up. She was pale, and her skin seemed loose on her pointed features. Her hair was ash blonde and fell in long, frizzy waves in all directions. Her lips were dry, and the cracks in them were white—she was clearly a longtime MouthFoamer. She reached forward, took a pack of cigarettes and a lighter off the table, and lit one. The smoke from the cigarette floated around her, blending with her hair, fanning out around her like a nebula. Her eyes were the palest blue and didn't seem to see anything.

"You're Misty?" Simone asked. Caroline hung back as Simone walked forward. The woman looked up at Simone's face as though she were trying to remember it. Suddenly, her eyes focused for a moment, and she saw Simone. Finding nothing familiar there, she just sighed and let her head drop back down, her eyes unfocused.

"Yeah," she said after a moment. "Do you know where Mom is?"

"Mom?" Caroline asked in a whisper, the question directed at Simone, not Misty. Simone frowned. The hair and eyes were different, but she could see it now, around the jaw and cheekbones. She looked around the room again, not wanting to look at Misty. She could guess what had happened.

"Your mom brings you the Foam?" Simone asked. Misty didn't move for a moment, then nodded. "Since you were little?" Again, a long pause, then a nod. Caroline stepped closer to Simone.

"Sometimes," Misty said suddenly, as though she were in the middle of a conversation already, "I wanted to do other things. But Mom always said I was too good at painting. I had to paint." She gestured sleepily with the hand that held the cigarette, then dropped it.

"So she brought you the Foam," Simone said sadly, "and you got more when you painted." Misty didn't say anything but looked up again and, for a moment, seemed to see Simone and Caroline.

"So where's my Foam? I finished the paintings." Her eyes unfocused again, and her vision dropped back to the nothingness in front of her. Simone stepped around her and headed towards the table. Caroline followed her.

"Whose daughter is she?" Caroline asked.

"Linnea's," Simone said. She didn't want to think about that now, though. She headed for the easel. It was covered. Behind it, in the shadows, leaning against the walls, was a stack of at least two dozen canvases, also covered. Simone heard a sudden scraping of a chair being pushed back and turned. Misty was looking around the room as though she'd just woken up there, taken from her bed. She was afraid.

"Where's my mommy?" she yelled. "Mommy?" Caroline looked at Simone, clearly unsure of what to do and uncomfortable with being unsure about anything. Simone walked back over to Misty and pinned her arms at her sides. She was frail and went limp quickly, but she kept staring at Simone, her eyes huge and terrified.

"Your mom isn't coming," Simone said. "But that's okay." Better than okay, she thought, considering what Linnea had done. "This lady here is going to make a call, and some people are going to come and keep you safe and get you better." She turned back around to Caroline, who was already dialing on her wristpiece. "Why don't you sit back down?" She placed Misty back in the chair, where she shook like a sick dog. Simone hovered behind her, waiting for the shaking to subside, but it didn't. She walked back over to Caroline, who was hanging up the phone.

"I called in a favor. I got a friend at the hospital to put her in their rehab program. Ambulance-boat will be here in a few." She paused and looked over Simone's shoulder at Misty, then back at Simone. "Her mother was her dealer?"

Simone nodded. "Used it to get her to focus on painting. A lot of artists use Foam for clarity. Linnea used it to make her daughter into a little forging machine. That's probably how she made all her money back in Europe."

Caroline took a deep breath and shook her head. "Sometimes I feel like we never really survived the flood, y'know? Like we're all underwater."

"Like we're all drowning."

"Yeah."

"Yeah." Simone put her hand on Caroline's shoulder for a moment, then walked back to the covered easel. In the distance was the sound of the ambulance-boat's sirens. Simone pulled the cloth off the easel and stared at the painting—the one people had killed and died for, the one that would "save" New York, if that was even possible. It wasn't much, she thought. Just lines and colors. It didn't resonate in her soul, give her an experience, bring a tear to her eye, the way *Circe* had. But it did tell her who had killed Henry.

FIFTEEN

———

OUTSIDE, THE DARK CLOUDS had reached the city, and a light rain began to patter on the windows. Caroline walked around the room, shutting the open windows. Then she came back to Simone. Simone ignored her and the EMTs who were trying to give Misty a shot of tranquilizer before taking her back to the hospital.

"You keep staring at that thing like you understand it. If you want to know where it marks, we have to find an old map and compare it to the new map to see where it is now."

"No we don't."

"Why not?"

It was a painting of a smiling young couple looking at each other lovingly. The woman proudly held out a key. Her hair spun out around her and turned into streets. His jacket did the same. Parts of their bodies were missing, replaced by map, but their expression was clear, as was the loading dock in the background with the shipping crate on it—the box clearly marked with the C-Rail logo. It wasn't a lot to go on, but, with the water at their feet, Simone could see how people could think of this painting as a treasure map. There was one other thing that was perfectly clear: his boots—old-fashioned rain boots, bright blue, with little ducks on them.

Behind her, Simone could hear Misty murmuring, "Nononon-onono."

She called Danny. He didn't pick up, but she left a message: "Can you find me the address for Louise Freth? ASAP. Thanks." She hung up and turned around. Caroline was glaring. Behind her, Misty was backing away from an EMT with a jet injector. Simone knew she should help them—help Misty—but her body felt too heavy, almost soggy with sadness. She hadn't expected much from Linnea, but it was a lot more than this. She had liked Lou, too. Maybe thought that when she was older, grayer—if she even lived that long—she'd be like her. Sad, maybe, but tough, and smoking real tobacco cigarettes.

Simone explored the room further. The dresser had some clothes in it, and a drawer with two plane tickets to the EU for Misty and Linnea Frost. Matching fake IRIDs, too. Good quality. Simone put them back and took a deep breath.

"You said you'd stop hiding things," Caroline said. Simone turned around. The EMTs were closing in on Misty.

"I know. I'm just sad is all." The EMT lunged at Misty with the injector; Misty dodged, but the other EMT grabbed her. She struggled animally, her moans primal and terrifying as the wail of a storm. Simone turned away.

"Who's Louise Freth?"

"Henry's partner. Older woman. I liked her. That's her in the painting. I think that tunnel, if it exists, is in her apartment building."

"So how does that tell you who killed Henry?" Simone made the mistake of looking back at Caroline. Behind her, the EMT with the injector pressed it to Misty's throat, and she fell back limp in the other's arms. Simone looked down to avoid watching them lift her body.

"Wait," Simone called to the EMTs after she'd heard the knock of them laying Misty's body down on a gurney. She walked towards them as they glanced up, then looked over at Caroline. They knew where the power was. "Can you put a sheet over her? And under the gurney, can you hide these?" She gestured at the forged paintings. "We need to smuggle them out."

"Why?" Caroline asked. She was getting angry again.

"Because if I were Dash, I'd be following me. And all he wants is the painting. We're going to smuggle all these out. Dash'll come in, assuming we found the paintings, and not find them—I'll take the chance to lose him. I'll call Peter and have him meet you and the EMTs at the hospital to recover the paintings. Then you can decide what to do with them. I'm going to go see Lou."

"Why?"

"Because I want to know why she did this. I want to give her a chance to turn herself in."

"She did it because Henry stole the painting from her, if it's hers," Caroline said, putting her hands on her hips.

"She's not someone who would kill over a painting," Simone said. Her earpiece buzzed, and she answered without checking the ID. Caroline crossed her arms.

"Danny?"

"Who is Danny?" came deCostas' voice. "Should I be jealous?"

Simone sighed. "I can't talk right now."

"Okay, I just want to see if you got my last message with the buildings?"

"I need to go." Simone hung up with a tap of her earpiece.

"So you're going to confront a murderer because you like her?" Caroline asked, raising an eyebrow.

"I guess so." Simone shrugged.

"Alone?"

"She's an old woman."

"She's killed once already. I'm coming, too."

"Why?"

Caroline paused, thinking of a reason, then smiled. "So that if there is an underwater tunnel, a city representative will be on hand to figure out how to deal with it." She folded her arms over her chest, chin up, proud of her reasoning.

"There's not going to be a tunnel."

"Other people seem to think there might be."

"It's dangerous."

"You said she's an old woman. And the EMTs aren't going to smuggle your paintings without my say-so." The EMTs had their eyes on Caroline, waiting for her approval. "Besides, I want to know why, too. I want to see how it ends."

"Fine," Simone said. "But we have to play this right. When we leave the building, look anxious, but don't say anything. Just follow me."

"Sure." Caroline nodded at the EMTs, and they loaded the paintings onto the gurney. They barely fit, and the EMTs had to drape a cloth over Misty like she was a corpse to obscure them, but they were hidden. They rolled the gurney out carefully, wanting to impress the deputy mayor.

Simone called Peter.

"Please tell me there isn't another dead body," he said.

"No, just one that looks it. I need you to head to the rehab facility at Mercy Hospital. There's an ambulance coming in; they have a whole lot of paintings you might be interested in."

"Damnit Simone, if you found the painting, you need to tell me where you are. This is for the police."

"I can't, Peter. I'm giving you the paintings, and I'm hoping to get a confession by the end of the day."

"Kluren is going to lock you up for tampering, you know."

"She was going to do that anyway, sooner or later."

"Tell me where you are."

"I'll see you later, Peter." Simone hung up. The phone almost immediately rang; she waited for caller ID this time, and when it displayed Peter's name, she ignored it. Then a message came in from Danny, with an address on the Lower East Side, a note that Lou owned the entire building, and a request to please stop bothering him while he was at work.

"Okay," she said to Caroline. "Let's go."

When they left the building, Simone made a show of looking around to see if she'd been followed. If Dash was there, he was too good to be spotted, but she thought maybe she saw a pinstripe cuff on the pants of a silhouette draped in rags. She didn't stare. She needed Dash to think she hadn't seen him. Then she turned to Caroline and spoke, her voice soft, but carrying.

"Okay, do you want to get the police or some hired muscle to get the painting out of there?"

Caroline's eyes widened for a moment, but she played along. "I have some family security. They'll handle it." She typed into her wristpiece for effect, to sell it. "I don't want to stay here, though. Let's go back to my place. I have some old maps there." Simone nodded and led them to the nearest taxi-boat stand. She told the driver to go towards Caroline's place but halfway there had him change direction, and head towards Lou's place. Caroline was silent the whole ride, her hair whipping wildly around her in the wind and rain. It wasn't a heavy rain yet, but the sky was dark, and it would be a real storm in a few hours. Simone hoped everything would be finished by then.

Lou was not a suspect she could have seen. She had figured it was Marina or the forger. But she'd believed Marina when she said she didn't do it, and Misty didn't have the presence of mind to kill someone. Lou had said she knew every piece in their inventory, but Trixie had said Henry found the painting in storage. So someone had lied. The painting was of Lou and her husband, so it would have *been* Lou's—Reinel gave his paintings to his subjects—and Henry had stumbled on it and figured out what it was and what it was worth. Then he tried to steal it out from under Lou, and she tried to take it back. He'd probably been going to pick up the original painting from Misty when Lou caught up to him in the abandoned building,

thinking he had the painting on him. Shot him . . . but the case
had been empty. That was the scenario that made the most sense to
Simone. But why shoot him over a painting? It was personal, clearly,
but it was just an object. Simone just couldn't see Lou pulling the
trigger. It takes hardness to do that. Lou was hard, but hard in a
way that endured, not in a way that killed. Killing was born out of
desperation or madness. It was the act of a person worn down to a
bloody shard. Lou was no shard. She was an old brick wall.

"This is it?" Caroline asked. She paid the cabbie, and they hopped
out onto the bridge surrounding the building Danny had directed
them to. It was one of the newer ones, built with Glassteel in place
but not very tall. The architects hadn't thought the water was going
to get this high. It looked like four floors of mirror, shaped like an
oval from above, flat on top. But it was in disrepair. The windows
were still mirrored but stained with salt, and moss and fungus were
creeping down from the roof, making it look older than it should
have. There was only one bridge leading up to it, thin and old. The
building was alone, overlooked, forgotten.

Simone and Caroline walked to the door. Inside was a glass-
ceilinged stairwell, with dim light glancing through. A circular,
transparent stairway rose out of the water. There was no lobby; just
landings with doors, presumably to hallways with apartments.

"Not airtight," Simone said, pointing at the waves.

"So which place is hers?" Caroline asked. Simone shrugged. They
climbed up to the third floor, and Simone exited into a narrow hallway with tiled floors and a flickering overhead light. Simone knocked
on the first door, which opened to her touch; inside was an abandoned apartment with a few pieces of broken furniture pushed into
a corner, crept over with fungus like small, dying landscapes. The
next few apartments were the same.

"No one else lives here," Caroline said. Simone shrugged. They
went back to the stairway and climbed to the top, their footsteps
echoing on the glass. Above them, the sky became even darker, and

rain began to pound heavily on the roof. Silence faded into the deep white noise of a storm.

The top floor had no hallway, only a small foyer with a door and the letters PH next to it. Simone tried the door. It was locked.

"This is it," she said, kneeling down and taking lock picks from her pocket.

"Are you breaking the law in front of me?" Caroline asked.

"Turn around." Simone picked the lock quickly, took out her gun, and pushed the door open. This apartment was furnished, if sparsely. There was a kitchen with a bowl in the sink, a bedroom with a made bed, and closets filled with clothes that looked like Lou's. Lou didn't seem to be at home, though.

"We should have tried the office, maybe," Simone said, poking her head around.

"This shouldn't be here," Caroline said, pointing at a large column in the center of the apartment. It was big enough to be a bathroom, but it had no door.

"What do you mean?"

"I mean, it's giant, and it serves no purpose. It's not holding the building up."

"So it's decoration."

"Taking up this much space? No. This is a hiding spot. Maybe a walk-in safe." She put her ear to the column and rapped it with her hand. Simone chuckled.

"What?" Caroline asked. "Isn't that how you find secret panels?"

Simone walked around the column. There were a few shallow shelves set into it, holding what looked like old glass plates. They reminded her of seashells. Behind one of them was a small indentation. Simone pressed it, and part of the column wall slid open.

Simone and Caroline looked into the space. It was empty—no floor, just a long, dark shaft.

"You don't think there's actually . . . I mean, this can't go all the way down, right?" Caroline asked.

Simone shook her head. "No way. But it is an elevator shaft—look," she said, pointing at the sides of the shaft.

"So the elevator is gone."

"Or someone rode it down to wherever it goes." Simone looked down into the shaft, but it was too dark. There was a maintenance ladder along the side and she grabbed hold of it. It shook, apparently unused for years, but held. "You coming?" she asked. Caroline nodded. Simone started climbing down. After about ten feet, the ladder stopped at an old metal walkway, which turned into a spiral staircase downwards. It was narrow and dark, lit only by a few wall sconces. Caroline joined her on the platform.

"This looks unsafe," she said.

"Yep," Simone said, starting down the stairs and clinging to the wall. She held her gun in the hand that touched the bannister, not putting too much weight on it in case the metal gave way. Caroline followed. They walked down for five minutes, placing each foot down gently on a step before giving it their whole weight.

"Okay," Caroline said. "We have to be below the surface by now. The building was only four stories above water. We're at least seven stories down. It has to be real."

"Maybe it's just an air pocket," Simone said, though she knew Caroline was right. They had to be below the surface. "That happens, right?"

"This is crazy."

Simone swallowed. She leaned against the wall, feeling as though the metal stairs were shaking. She could hear her heart beating rapidly in her chest, and she was afraid that even that small vibration could bring the walls crashing down around them.

It was real. She was below the water, and she was still breathing. "Yeah," Simone said after a long pause. "Yeah. Do you want to head back up?"

Caroline took a while to answer, and when she did, it was in a soft voice. "No."

They spiraled downward for what seemed like an hour, the only sound their footsteps and breathing and the pale noise from the storm so far above. When Simone heard the music, she thought at first it was her mind playing tricks on her. But then Caroline hissed, saying she heard a bass. Simone nodded and put her finger to her lips. They walked down more quietly now, their feet light on the metal, as the music grew louder and clearer. It was something with bass and saxophone—old music with sweeping riffs performed by brass orchestras—the sort of music that felt like the happiest moments of life before the flood. A brighter light shone on the floor where the stairs landed. There was an elevator car there, with fogged glass. The shaft opened in an archway, from which a dim light poured through. Simone stopped at the edge of the archway and motioned for Caroline to stop behind her. She poked her head around.

It was a train station. Huge, with platforms and tracks that went on for the length of a cruise ship before stopping at towering sealed metal doors. The walls of the station looked like glass, curving upwards into an arc until they met a strip of metal at the top, where a chandelier hung. Outside the glass, the light from inside spilled into the ocean a short way, and Simone could see fish swim by and, in the distance, the bright green dots of the algae generators on the surface. From here, they looked like stars. It couldn't possibly exist, but it did, and Simone was in it, under the water, looking up at the city she thought she'd known her entire life.

The station wasn't being used as a station, though. Someone had set up sofas, a large bed, a table, floor lamps, even a TV and speakers, which was where the music was coming from. One of the sofas was positioned so that anyone sitting on it could gaze through the glass at the ocean. And Lou was sitting in it, humming along with the music. Simone raised her gun and stepped out into the station.

"I know you're here," Lou said, turning around. "A bell sounds whenever anyone opens the shaft upstairs. You could have just called the elevator." Simone walked towards Lou, her gun still raised.

Caroline stepped out behind her and gasped at the sight of the station. Lou turned around and smiled at Simone. She looked different down here. Maybe it was the light or the water casting strange, moving lines on her, but she seemed softer. "Do you have it?" Lou asked. "Do you have my painting?"

"The one you killed Henry for?" Simone asked. Lou's face wavered, and she looked down.

"He stole it from me," she said. It wasn't a defense, just an explanation. "For years my husband and I had it down here." She gestured at the large metal doors, and Simone could see there was a space where it looked like a painting had been removed, its outline left in dust. "But when he died . . . I didn't want it down here anymore—not for a little while, anyway. Until it hurt less to look at. So I took it to the warehouse and hid it there, so I wouldn't have to look at it. But Henry found it, and instead of asking me what it was—and he knew it was mine, anyone could tell that—he didn't ask . . . he just took it. Can you imagine? We'd treated him like family, and he stole it from me—a painting of me and my husband—so that he could make some money telling people about this." She gestured to the ceiling, her fingers outstretched, her palms curved like a halo. She laughed. "Whoever built this place never finished it. If you open those doors, the whole place floods and it becomes just like anywhere else in the city. But we found it, after everyone else had left. We stayed, and we found this secret place. Useless, but . . . beautiful. We lived here, under the waves. It was our home. And Henry wanted to sell it." She frowned again and looked at Simone sadly. "So yes, I killed him. Do you have my painting?"

"The police have it," Simone said. Lou looked as though she'd been slapped across the face and was about to cry, but looked down instead. "I came here so I could take your confession and bring you in. They'll go easier on you that way."

"Everyone is going to know about this place now, aren't they?"

"Probably," Simone said.

"It's amazing," Caroline said. She was walking along the other glass wall, dragging her hand across it. "It's unreal." Lou looked up and nodded.

"You should take a moment," Lou said. "You should look around, and enjoy it. Then I'll come with you." She turned around and sat back down on the sofa. Simone lowered her gun.

"It's pure Glassteel," Caroline said. "Molded without a base structure underneath."

"We think it was supposed to be a showpiece," Lou said, still gazing out at the water. A family of fish swam by, then darted off into the darkness. "The chandelier, the glass walls. It was supposed to be some sort of demonstration of how the rich could weather the floods, how they could create underwater cities."

"But they never finished it," Caroline repeated. "Or something went wrong."

"When we found it, there were some plans. Apparently beyond that door there was supposed to be another station to offload large shipments, and the tunnel would go back to the mainland and to other spots in the city. There was even a station at the edge of the city marked 'to Europe.' They had big ideas."

"Do you still have the plans?" Caroline asked.

"Upstairs somewhere. We cleared them out when we made this place our home. Our private little paradise." Lou paused. "And now it's going to be destroyed. People are going to come down here, walk in and out. Make it a museum or science experiment." Simone and Caroline exchanged a glance but said nothing. They knew she was right. Whoever claimed this place might even try to make it work.

Simone walked the perimeter of the room, touching the Glassteel walls. They were chilly, almost icy. In the water, just outside the perimeter of light cast by the station, she could see the silhouettes of buildings and rubble. Grit floated in the water. By the metal doors there was a control panel with light switches, a switch for the doors, and blank monitors. She stared out at the water again and looked at the shadows of buildings and the shimmer of fish. She thought of her father's ashes, poured down here. It wasn't a bad place to end up. She was happy about that.

"Okay, Lou, I think we should get going." Simone said, turning back to Lou.

"I don't think you're leaving quite yet," came another voice. Simone spun around to find Dash, his arm around Caroline's neck, a gun to her head. She tried elbowing him, but he swerved out of the way with a chuckle.

"You didn't go in for the painting?" Simone asked, raising her gun. "You followed us?"

"I always have a backup plan. That tracker I left in your hatband was fun, but when I saw your wallet—with the hole in it—how could I resist? So I put another there. I thought you'd find that one too, eventually. Or at least get the wallet fixed. But I suppose not all of us deserve our reputations."

"What's the point now?" Simone asked, walking closer. Dash tightened the arm around Caroline's neck, and Simone stopped walking. Caroline screamed in frustration and tried pulling away and kicking, but Dash held her tight. "We already found the station. We know about it."

"Yes . . . but I don't think my employer will mind that you found it first. I'll just give him a call, and he'll send over a small army of guards. Then it'll be his—and his discovery. So I just need you to clear out and keep quiet about what we found—which I think you'll do, so long as I have your deputy here." Simone had never seen Caroline afraid before. Fierce many times, and snide and condescending and amused, but never afraid. Her face seemed oddly blank, her eyes wide. Simone tried nodding at Caroline, but Dash pulled her closer so their eyes couldn't lock.

"So, you're going to go," he repeated. "I'm going to call my client, and he's going to come and take this place over, and then I'll let the deputy free and disappear. It's so easy, you should be paying me, too."

"You have a gun to the deputy mayor's head," Simone said. "The police will hunt you down."

"With the amount of money I'm getting for this, I won't be around long. I'm thinking of buying one of those custom-made islands, from the Japanese fleet. Live somewhere warm."

"We'll still be able to take this place over," Caroline said, her voice hoarse. "The moment you let me go, I'll have this place swarmed. The police will get rid of whoever you tell about this place."

Dash laughed. "You'll stay quiet. I'm pretty sure."

"Why?" Caroline said. Dash just smirked.

"Who's paying you?" Simone asked.

Dash shook his head with a smile. "Do I seem like the sort who would kiss and tell? Now get on the elevator. Take the old woman, too."

Simone lowered her gun and started walking towards the elevator. "You killed Linnea, right? That was you who left her in my office."

"I thought leaving you flowers would be too ordinary. Plus I wanted to let you know I'd found her first. That I was a step ahead—like I always am."

"Aren't torture victims supposed to tell you what you want to know before they die?"

Dash narrowed his eyes. "Sometimes things don't work out right away. But as you can see, it's been a good day."

"Just pointing out I'm not the only one not living up to my reputation."

"Get on the elevator," Dash snarled. "And you," he said, turning his gun on Lou, who had moved from the sofa to the control panel Simone had spotted earlier. "Go with her."

"This is my home," Lou said, her voice cracking with anger, or maybe sorrow. "This is where my husband and I were happiest. I won't leave it."

"That's sweet. But then you die here. It's funny, really, you'll die under the water, but I'll still have to drag you up and throw you in to sink you."

"We all die eventually," Lou said, and with surprising quickness, she reached out and pressed a button on the control panel.

SIXTEEN

———

IMMEDIATELY THERE WAS THE loud whining of sirens, and two red lights by the large metal doors began to flash.

"What the fuck did you do?" Dash asked. Lou smiled and walked back towards the sofa she had been sitting on. The doors began to groan.

"She opened the doors," Simone said. "We have to get out of here!"

"Close it!" Dash screamed. Lou sat back down on the sofa, staring out at the water, her back to Dash and Simone. "Fuck!" He ran for the elevator, dragging Caroline with him by the neck. He got in the elevator and pushed Caroline aside as he activated it. It closed, locking them out.

Behind them, the doors had begun to open and the ocean was starting to rush in with the sound of an angry mob. It flowed over Simone's ankles, cold and black.

"Lou!" Simone called out. Lou looked back at her and smiled, then went back to staring out at the water, the ocean at her feet splashing wildly and soaking her. The elevator was moving upwards. Caroline stared at Simone, still afraid. "Fuck," Simone said, holstering her gun. The water was above their knees now, and the doors were opening wider. Simone grabbed Caroline's wrist in one hand and, as the elevator rose above them, grabbed onto one of the bars on the elevator's underside. They began to rise with the elevator, Simone and Caroline a human chain just above the water. She glanced back once at Lou, but the water had risen over her head, and all Simone could see was the ocean, taking back what it had been denied for so long, all angry froth and the smell of rot.

Caroline's hand was slippery with sweat and the moisture in the air. Simone would lose her grip soon.

"I'm going to try to lift you," Simone called down to Caroline. Below them, the water was churning up the elevator shaft, a storm in a bottle about to break free. She tightened her grip on the elevator bar and lifted up the hand Caroline clung to so that Caroline's head was at her waist. Simone's arm was getting weak and groaned against the effort, as Caroline got wetter and heavier.

"Grab my waist," Simone said. Caroline stared at her like she was insane. They were flying upwards, and falling was death. Caroline's hair streamed down behind her like smoke. "Hold onto me so you can reach the elevator, too. I can't hold you like this much longer." She could feel her arm giving way, burning with pain. Caroline was sliding away, as if the water were pulling her under without even touching her.

Caroline twisted herself, reached out with her free hand, and managed to wrap it around Simone.

"Let go!" Caroline called, her words muffled by the sound of the water below. Simone let go of Caroline's hand and she slipped away. Simone felt a shock—the sudden cold of Caroline's absence—and cried out, fearing Caroline had plunged into the water, and thinking of letting go, and joining her. But Caroline had just managed to wrap herself around Simone. Simone reached up with her free hand, grabbing the elevator more securely with both hands. The elevator rose quickly upwards for just a moment more, then stopped suddenly, jarring Simone. She felt Caroline's arms digging into her ribs and gasped, half choking on her own breath. She re-tightened her grip and looked down. The water below had stopped rising, but it was still frothing and gurgling softly. The only other sound in the elevator shaft was the creak of straining metal.

The platform that led to the stairs they had come down was just off to the side, its ladder leading back outside, where Dash was escaping.

"I'm swinging us over to the platform," Simone said, moving herself, hand over hand, to the edge of the elevator and starting to swing. "You let go first."

Simone swung her hips and Caroline let go, catching onto the metal platform's edge with her hands. It groaned at the sudden weight and bent. Simone held her breath, but the platform didn't fall. Caroline pulled herself up, and then Simone swung her way over, landing halfway on the platform, legs dangling off. It screeched again and wobbled under her but still held. Caroline, standing on the platform, pulled her up.

"She just killed herself," Caroline said, "drowned herself like that."

Simone didn't have time to think about that. Dash was getting away. She climbed the ladder and ran out of Lou's apartment to the stairwell, just in time to see Dash through the glass stairs, leaving at the bottom floor. She ran down quickly, her body aching and fiery with every step, her reserves empty of everything but adrenaline. She was damp with sweat and sea spray, and everything seemed slimy to her. Outside the building, the storm had kicked into full swing. It was pouring rain, and wind whipped frantically around, the noise like a funeral dirge.

Dash was running out of sight, just the barest outline of him visible through the heavy rain. Simone took off after him. She found herself running faster than she knew she should. Catching Dash wouldn't make up for everything that had happened, but it would be better than it all vanishing under the waves, like Lou.

Dash turned around a corner; Simone was catching up. He was headed for one of the bigger bridges, probably hoping to lose her in the crowd there, catch a taxi to a safe house, and hide out for a

while before sneaking out of town. She wasn't going to let that happen. The rain was pouring hard, and her clothes felt tight and
heavy. The bridges were empty, and she could focus on just him, on
chasing him, on catching him. She was gaining ground. She could
see more than his outline, now. She could see the panic in his face
when he looked back over his shoulder. He drew his gun and shot
behind him once or twice, but they were lazy shots, Simone didn't
even have to dodge as they went wide. He looked tired. Simone
smiled. She could do this all night.

He turned another corner and another—he wasn't heading for a
main street. They were going further downtown now. The bridges
were weak and slippery, and Simone slowed down, but then Dash
pulled ahead, leaving her no choice but to speed up again. When
she felt her foot slide at the edge of a bridge, she wondered if that
had been his plan.

Then she was flying out, weightless over the water.

The world seemed to take a breath. She fell in slow motion, noticing the details around her, like the splash of the rain hitting her
stomach as her body went parallel to the surface. She felt the spin of
her legs as they spiraled downward. She heard her lungs inhale their
last breath like a loud sigh played in reverse.

And then she was beneath it.

She felt the bubbles scatter-dance around her as she plunged into
the ocean, the surface closing above her instantaneously, like the slam-
ming of a prison door. The water was freezing, and her body sang
out with shock in the first moment, but that singing faded into a
lullaby as she sank farther into the water, propelled by the force
of her fall. She felt the undertow manacle itself to her wrists and ankles, pulling her deeper. She opened her eyes. All around her were
black shadows of a city under the waves. This would be her grave,
she knew. Maybe one day she'd be pulled up by a recycling boat,
and maybe someone would recognize her, or maybe not, but either
way she'd be turned to dust and poured back down here. This was

where she was going to end up. And it was beautiful. Living above the waves all this time, she'd assumed below was a frightening pool of inky black and all the worst, darkest thoughts of the people of the city. But when she'd been under the waves in Lou's home, it had been different. It had been like a clear night. She could fall asleep under the stars. People used to do that, didn't they? Stars were mostly invisible now, covered by smog and pollution, but the stars under the ocean—the green pinpricks of light, swirling like small nebulae—those she could fall asleep under.

The bubbles dissolved around her, and she thought about trying to claw her way back up to the surface, taking one last breath. But the waves here were strong, and pushing her all around, and she wasn't entirely sure which way the surface was anymore. Besides, why go back? She pulled her hands down and looked at them in the dark water. They seemed oddly pale and faintly green, as though life had already left her and she was a ghost, forever tossed beneath the waves. Maybe she was.

So Dash would get away. So people had died. Would it make a difference? She suddenly thought of the painting Mr. Ryan had showed her—*The Return of Odysseus*. A man trying to get home to his city on the water. She remembered other things about the myth, too—the image of Odysseus strapped to the mast of his ship as sirens sang his men into the water, and of his wife at home, waiting. Simone had no one waiting above the water. She thought of her father, and she could see now how easy it had been for him to give in. And she gave in, too. She would die here, and she would have no regrets. Still, she turned in the direction she thought was towards the air, just for one more look. The surface of the water rippled with raindrops, and above that it glowed.

FROM ABOVE, CAROLINE KHAN was a dark inkblot on the bridge. The rain had plastered her hair to the sides of her face so it looked like a cowl. She ran forward, slowing down sometimes to wipe the water from her eyes. She paused at an intersection of bridges and looked around, narrowing her eyes against the storm. She ran down one of the bridges, then stopped and ran back again, in the other direction. At the end of this bridge was a turn, wrapping around a drab gray building turned nearly black by the water. Caroline stopped there and examined the wooden railings at the edge of the bridge. They were broken and splintered, burst outward towards the ocean like two reaching arms. The wood inside the broken railings was still dry.

Caroline got down on her knees and stared at the water. It was dark as onyx and just within her reach. She could dip her hand down into it and bring it back up.

She saw the hat first—floating on the water like a paper boat. Then a flash of red on the water's surface—rust-colored and swirling like blood in the water. But it was in strands. Not blood. Hair. Caroline leaned over the edge and thrust her hand into the water, then yanked back like she was trying to catch fish in a net.

She fell backwards, a clump of red hairs in her hand. She leaned forward, took more of the hair, and this time pulled more slowly, lifting the weight of Simone's head to the surface. Water poured off her face in thick sluices, and she sputtered into the air.

"Get the fuck up here!" Caroline shouted, extending her hand for Simone to grab onto. Simone stared at her, blankly. "Grab my hand!" Caroline shouted over the storm. Simone grabbed onto Caroline's arm, and Caroline heaved her back up onto the bridge. Simone grabbed the edge of the bridge and, with Caroline's help, pulled herself up, drenched and gasping.

"He got away," Simone said when she'd caught her breath.

"Yeah."

"Fuck." Simone shook her head. She was soaked and had lost her hat. Her hair fell over her face in thick bars. She looked past them at Caroline, whose hair stuck to her face in lines like cracks in a porcelain mask. She was wet and her mouth was slack. They were both breathing heavily, and it was cold enough that she could see the little wisps of breath flying from their mouths like ghosts in the rain. "Thanks for pulling me out." The air smelled like electricity, and her mouth tasted of metal.

"Yeah. Well. You're welcome. Didn't think I could handle this city without you around." Caroline smiled as she said this. She was still on her knees, her hands clasped in her lap, but she let her body fall sideways into Simone, leaning on her, shoulder to shoulder. They stared out at the shadows of New York. It was barely visible, gray and green. Dash was long gone and Simone felt a knot of anger wrap itself around her chest, but then she breathed in and let it go. She shivered. Her coat was soaked too deeply for the warming gel to kick on.

Caroline laid a hand over Simone's. Her hand was warm, and Simone took a sudden deep breath without meaning to, and coughed a few times. She looked at Caroline, who was looking at the ocean.

"Okay," Caroline said. Simone almost couldn't hear her over the rain. But she knew what she meant.

They leaned back against the solid railings. Rain poured down around them for a while. The sound of the ocean taking in each drop like a sinking stone echoed. It was like a thousand people swallowing, not all at once, but one after another after another.

"What do you think he meant?" Caroline asked after a moment. "When he said I'd keep quiet?"

"I think he was bullshitting," Simone said. "I think he was going to get us outside, then shoot us and push us under. Easier to get two walking bodies above water than carry two dead ones."

"I guess," Caroline said. "I hope." The rain began to fall even harder. It felt like bullets, but sounded like overwhelming applause.

"Fuck," Simone said.

"What?" Caroline shouted over the rain.

"I just realized who hired Dash." She was cold and wet, and her hair was plastered to her face and neck. The wind was whipping through her like knives. She stood slowly, her body stiff and cold and burning all at once, but she stood. She held a hand out to help Caroline up. "Let's go home."

SEVENTEEN

——

SIMONE LEANED BACK IN her unused receptionist's chair, her feet up on the desk. She waited for him to knock first and smiled when he did.

"Come in," she called.

He walked in and sat down across from her. He ran his fingers through his hair, then grinned at her. Simone couldn't tell if he knew what was coming, if he was prepared for it. She'd have to be careful.

"I'm happy you called," deCostas started. "I very much enjoyed our time together the other night. I was hoping we could do it again."

"I was, too," Simone said. It was practically a purr, but she pulled back. Too much and he'd get suspicious. "I had such a bad day yesterday." She swung her feet off the desk and stood, walking around to him.

"I'm sorry to hear that," he said, smiling. She sat down on the desk, and he put his hand on her thigh. Simone smiled, using all her self-control not to kick him.

"You remember that other detective I told you about, Dash Ormond?" deCostas shook his head. "Sure you do. I said he was the one to go to if you wanted a more forceful approach, right? You looked at his card."

"I remember, right," deCostas said, not meeting her eye but staring at his own hand as it began to stroke her leg. "I didn't want to hire him, though. I knew I had to work with you."

"Mmm," Simone said. "Well, he tried to kill me last night."

"What? That's terrible!" deCostas said, standing, waiting a moment, and then looking her in the eye.

"And he tried to kill my friend Caroline."

"He sounds like a very bad man," he said, his voice teasingly sexual.

"He's more a tool than a man," Simone said. She crossed her legs, letting her foot dig into his leg. "So, I'm trying to figure out who hired him."

"Will dwelling on it really help?" deCostas asked. "Wouldn't it be better to forget all about it? I could give you a massage," he smiled.

"Funny thing is—he tried to drown me. In a dry tunnel under the city." Simone watched him carefully. His eyebrows raised, his eyes opened wider, but his pupils stayed the same, and it took just a fraction of a second too long. "So I owe you an apology. You were right. There was a place where you could walk down under the waves. But it's gone now. I didn't even get a picture."

"I accept your apology," he said, "but I'm sorry you didn't get photos or . . . proof. I could have published with just that—what a discovery!" He sighed—forced, Simone thought. "Perhaps there is a way you could make it up to me?" He pushed a strand of hair behind her ear. Simone was positive now. It was deCostas. deCostas had money and backing from the EU, knew about the painting, and was the one who wouldn't get just a tunnel and some money out of finding the rail. He wouldn't care if the government took it over. He'd get a career, a reputation. There were people all over the city, maybe the world, looking for tunnels, and they'd all drown him in money to find another one once word got out that he'd found the first. And he didn't seem to care that she'd found it.

"Maybe there is," she said. "You see, the police caught Dash. They're hacking his wristpiece now."

"Oh?" deCostas said. Now his pupils shrank.

"Maybe I can find out who hired him, if I can get my hands on the data they extract. And then you can go talk to them and find out how they knew."

"Oh, I don't know if that's very important," he said. His eyes narrowed. "When did they catch him?"

"Last night," Simone said, "maybe early this morning."

"Mmm," deCostas said, and leaned back a little, suddenly relaxed. Simone forced herself to smile. She was losing him.

"Don't you want to know all about it?" Simone said, almost whispering in his ear. She wrapped her legs around his and drew him close, locking him in place. His eyes met hers, and he smiled. It wasn't a nice smile. He wasn't trying to be charming now.

"I think I know enough. Would you like to move this to a more comfortable location, perhaps?" He wrapped his arm around her, ground his hips into her. He was teasing her. He'd figured out it was a setup. Dash must have contacted him sometime recently—after "early this morning." Simone held back a scream of frustration.

"Later," she said. "I'm really caught up in this case. I want to check in with my contact at Teddy. See if they've hacked the wristpiece yet."

"Oh, I wouldn't count on that," deCostas said.

"No?"

"No. These criminals. They always have a way of slipping away. Even when they're caught."

"I suppose you're right," Simone let her legs relax, letting him step away. "It's a real pity," she said with some violence. The charade was mostly over now. She was just keeping it up to make him think she didn't think she'd lost.

"Maybe," deCostas said, stepping away. "But if you're going to be busy with your police friends, I think I'll take my leave. I have some things to wrap up before I head back to the EU."

"Head back?" Simone asked.

"I've been asked to head up an exploration for a tunnel under Barcelona. A small one, not like the pipeline here, but I'll have a whole team."

"Impressive, considering you never found anything here," Simone said, her voice edging cold now. "I mean, *I* found something, but it wasn't because of your little metal balls or your tools. It wasn't even the guy you hired. It was me."

deCostas narrowed his eyes at her and stepped forward. He looked angry—that passion was back, the kind she'd seen spark up violently in his eyes before—the desire to prove something.

"I mean," Simone continued, "you really just stumbled across it. And no one will ever know it existed, unless I tell them. And I'm not going to do that. So how exactly did you get a team? Wouldn't they want to know more? I could call them."

deCostas' eyes were all fury now, and he raised his hands as if to strangle her, but Simone was ready and had her gun to his head before he could squeeze.

"You didn't find a damn thing," Simone said in a near whisper. "I did. Remember that. And you won't find a damn thing without me."

deCostas let go of her neck and swallowed. Then his eyes went cool again, and he smiled.

"Next time, I'll know better," he said.

"So you did hire Dash," Simone said. "You admit it."

deCostas smirked again. "You're recording this?"

Simone rolled her eyes. "Why would I bother?" she asked.

"So you have evidence when you haul me into the police station. Maybe your friend Caroline already made a phone call, got a warrant drafted? Well, maybe you should get this on your recording, then: You know where my funding came from?"

"It comes from the EU, some foundations, your university," Simone said, trying to sound confident. What did his funding have to do with anything?

"Partially. But a very large part of it also comes from right here in New York. From a very prominent family." Simone clenched her jaw. The door to the hall behind her opened, and Caroline stood in the door, Peter just behind her. They had earpieces on, listening to the bug under her desk. Caroline's eyes were hard, but her mouth was soft. Her lips were separated enough to let in thin whistles of breath. deCostas glanced up at Caroline, then back at Simone, and the corners of his mouth popped up like switchblades. "The Khans," he said. "In fact, I probably never would have hired Dash to find Linnea if I hadn't gotten a call from Mr. Khan saying he had just bought a painting he wanted me to look at. I thought that was funny, since Marina told me the painting was still for sale. When I told Khan that, we decided to put Dash on it. He found out who Marina was working for, and then he tried to find the painting and the location on it. You'll find he was paid by Mr. Khan. I believe you told me, Simone, that Dash has a reputation—he's who one goes to for dirty work?" Simone stared at him, silent. Outside the water was calm, lapping at the building, the sound of a slow breeze. "All for the Khans," he said slowly, each word pointed. "Is that the evidence you want? Because if it is, I think, perhaps, the reporters who cover the story may suggest that the Khans were fully aware of Dash's reputation and his actions. Which would be true."

Simone turned to look at Caroline, whose eyes were fixed on deCostas. Behind her, Peter had taken out his handcuffs but wasn't moving.

Caroline stepped forward and slapped deCostas across the face. It left a deep red mark, but it sounded weak, like one drop of water hitting the floor in an empty room.

"It's been lovely," deCostas said, stepping back. "Look me up if you're ever in the EU." He headed for the door and opened it but turned to look at Simone one more time. She saw his real face again, lacking charm and painted over with ambition. She smiled at him, and then he left. She realized she was still holding the gun up, and that her neck was warm as if he'd actually grabbed it. She inhaled deeply, salt and sweat and a touch of cologne, and she put the gun down on the desk.

"We got a confession," Peter said. "I could go arrest him."

Simone plucked the bug from under her desk and crushed it in her hand. Caroline was still staring at the door.

"Not an option," Simone said. "Caroline's career would be over, that kind of scandal. I'm going to go after him, wait till it's dark. Kill him." She started to get down from the desk, but Peter put his hand on her arm and pulled her back.

"I can't let you do that, soldier."

"It's what he deserves," Simone said.

"I . . . I'm a good cop, Simone," Peter said softly. "I've never over-looked a confession before . . . I will if you ask me to. But I can't let you kill him."

"He's right," Caroline said. "Don't kill him. This is my fault. I can weather a scandal like that. Peter, go arrest him."

"Absolutely not," Simone said, grabbing Peter's wrist. "You're not the mayor, Caroline. A scandal this big, no matter how much the mayor needs you, he's going to get rid of you. Your chances for run-ning for mayor will be over. Your career will be over. You know that. We all know that."

Everyone was quiet for a long time. Simone took her gun from the desk and stuck it back in her boot. "I'm going to kill him."

"No," Peter put his hand on her shoulder. "Please, Simone. I can't."

"Then leave," Simone said, pulling away.

"No," Caroline said firmly. "Besides, if he vanishes, or his body turns up, how do we know it won't create just as much of a scandal? This is my fault."

"This is deCostas' fault!" Simone shouted, throwing a hand to-wards the door. "And you're all just going to let him get away with it?"

"Yes," Caroline said, softly. "He gets away with it."

"And Dash vanishes. Maybe becomes someone new but with the same job description in some other city." Simone said. They all stood for a moment in silence.

Caroline finally moved, turning and going over to the sofas in the corner of the room. She fell into one, and looked out the window.

"Sometimes I hate this city," Caroline said.

"Hate it and love it," Simone corrected, coming to sit beside her. "All the time."

"Yeah."

They all sat in silence a moment. Outside, the waves were crashing loudly, almost cheerfully.

"I should go report something to Kluren . . ." Peter said, finally. "I'll say he didn't confess. He was too cool."

"Let me come," Simone said, getting up. "I need to talk to her anyway."

Caroline stood with them. "I should go, too," she said, her voice like metal. "I need to talk with my parents."

THEY PARTED FROM CAROLINE a few bridges from the apartment. She hadn't spoken as they walked, but had looked straight ahead, and the wind had blown her hair back like spilled ink. Simone said goodbye as they split up, and Caroline reached out and squeezed Simone's hand. But she hadn't said anything, and then she'd walked away. Simone and Peter walked in silence for a while.

"So you slept with him?" Peter asked. "I mean, I know it's none of my business. Sorry."

"It was a thing," Simone said. "Which I regret, obviously."

They walked in silence a while longer.

"It's been nice, you know. Hanging out with you again. We haven't really done that in a while."

"Yeah. That's my fault. I thought it would be easier if it was a totally clean . . . you know."

"But it hasn't been bad, has it? Using me for information and not returning the favor? Just like old times."

"Yeah," Simone said grinning. "Just like old times."

They walked a little faster now, their hands in their pockets because though the day was sunny, it had turned cold, and the wind had bite.

KLUREN LOOKED UP AS Peter and Simone walked in.

"What are you smiling about?" she asked. Simone shook her head. She didn't think she'd been smiling.

"It was deCostas who hired Dash," Simone said. "But he won't admit it."

"And you have no proof."

Simone shook her head.

"Then I repeat, what the fuck are you smiling about?"

"I went under, and I came back up," Simone said with a shrug. "Doesn't happen too often."

"I sometimes think it happens too much." Kluren looked back down at her desk, as if done with the conversation. But Simone wasn't done. She didn't want to be Kluren's punching bag anymore.

"I know about you and my dad," Simone said. Kluren's face, already hard as stone, seemed to stiffen.

"Weiss, you leave." Peter nodded and walked out of the office, closing the door behind him.

"You see her when you see me, don't you? The woman you couldn't get my dad to leave for you."

Kluren shook her head, her face almost soft. "I see your dad, who quit the force because both of us fucked up. I didn't quit. I worked hard to get past it. So I see a coward, and, yeah, I see your mom, but I always liked her okay. When I see your mom I don't think about how your father didn't leave her. I think about how she disappeared all of a sudden after your dad confessed."

"Yeah, she left us 'cause she was angry."

"I didn't say left. I said disappeared."

Simone let the words sink in and suddenly realized she wasn't smiling anymore.

"What are you saying?"

Kluren stood and walked around the desk so she was close to Simone.

"I was never in love with your father," she said, her voice gentler than usual. "Maybe you have some fairy-tale idea that he was perfect and no woman could resist him, but it wasn't like that. It was time together, boredom, stakeouts, restlessness." Simone thought maybe she'd seen her dad as irresistible as a kid, but now she remembered what he'd spent his life teaching her, and it made her think that he had been lonely. Lonely, sad, and angry.

"It wasn't love," Kluren continued. "I don't know if he even liked me very much. Hell, I didn't like him. So when he said we should stop, I said fine, and applied for a new partner. He said he was going home to tell his wife. Next thing I know he's retired and your mom is gone. He was a cop. A good cop. He always got the evidence, even if he had to put it there. You can't be that good a cop without having a little darkness in you. Not out here. So, yeah, I wonder sometimes where your mother went. She ever write to you? Did she leave you a goodbye letter?"

Simone crossed her arms.

"Didn't think so. Makes you wonder about how he went out, doesn't it?" Simone willed herself not to blink, to keep staring forward. "When I look at you, I see all that. But that's not why I'm hard on you, Pierce. I'm hard on you 'cause you're sloppy. You follow your instincts, but nothing else. That's why deCostas is getting away. That's why people are dead."

Simone opened her mouth but had nothing to say and closed it again.

"Right." Kluren walked back around to her side of the desk and sat down, looking at the papers in front of her while Simone stared, waiting for something, though she couldn't say what. "You should go now."

Peter was outside, waiting for her. She tried to smile at him but then realized she looked angry and shook her head. He followed her out of Teddy.

"What did she say?"

"That the ocean is deep and dark and we're all just a few feet from drowning," she said tonelessly. She could feel Peter stepping forward, reaching out to put his hand on her. Ten minutes before she would have wanted that, but now the thought of it made her sick. She didn't know who he was. She didn't know who anyone was. Her dad had been a corrupt cop. She was probably dirty, too, in some way, and she didn't want to get that on Peter, if he was clean. And if he was dirty, she didn't want to know.

She turned around before he could touch her and locked her eyes with his. She sidestepped his hand. "I should go," she said. "I'm supposed to meet Caroline and Danny. I'll see you later."

"Sure," he said. He looked confused and sad and Simone knew it was her fault, but she couldn't fix it.

"We can all drown together," Simone said. Peter nodded, though he clearly didn't understand, then went back inside. But Simone stayed on deck a few minutes longer, staring up at the sky, where the seagulls flew like dirt in the wind. The air was getting even colder, and the salt smell was stronger now, burning her nose and eyes.

She remembered the day she'd poured her dad into the water. She'd found him dead in his office armchair one morning, gun in his hand, bullet in his skull. She'd taken his body to the recycling center herself, wrapped up in sheets in the back of a taxi boat with a driver who kept staring at her. She asked them to take care of it as quickly as possible, but when they saw the red button on his temple, the entrance and exit wounds, they asked her to wait in the other room.

She'd sat alone there, didn't call anyone, didn't cry, didn't check her messages. The room was small and white and brightly lit like a freezer. Eventually, one of the attendants had come back in and brought her back to the room where her father was. She was led in as Kluren was walking out. They stared at one another as they passed in the hall, and Simone looked back as she went into the room. Kluren stood outside, arms crossed, waiting.

They had burned her father and handed her the ashes in a black plastic cylinder. She'd held it in both hands as she walked back out, as though it held something more than dust. Kluren was still there. They looked at each other from across the room, and Simone felt her eyes water up but then swallowed, deeply, and forced her face straight. She'd never spoken to Kluren alone. It had always been her dad who handled things when they got hauled in to the police.

Simone walked across the room to her. Kluren's golden eyes seemed to dilate slightly, taking her in. They'd stared at each other, Simone trying to figure how to ask what she wanted to ask.

"Clearly a suicide," Kluren said, as if reciting to a judge. "No need for investigation. Case closed. File sealed."

Simone let out a deep breath and stared down at the black cylinder.

"And you won't tell anyone?" she asked.

"No," Kluren said.

"Then it was a heart attack," Simone said, looking back up. Kluren's expression didn't change, but she leaned forward very slightly.

"You have a lot of potential. You should join the force. I could make sure you moved up the ranks quick, lose some bad habits."

Simone shook her head, her eyes watering again, though she didn't know why. "Dad always said the cops had too much red tape to deal with. Couldn't get things done."

Kluren let out a disappointed sigh. "Look around, Simone. You're alone in the middle of the ocean. We all are. Do you really think it matters what color the tape is, as long as it holds us together?"

"My dad—"

"Don't be him." It wasn't so much an order as it was a warning. "Be better."

Simone realized how close they were now, how she could feel the heat off Kluren's body, almost see the circuits in her eyes, and she stepped backwards. She stroked the black cylinder in her hands and looked down at it. It was made of cheap plastic. It felt like if she squeezed it, it might crack and explode in her hands, sending ashes everywhere in a cloud.

When she looked back up, Kluren was gone. Simone told everyone it was a heart attack. Her dad hadn't taken great care of himself. No one doubted it. They told her how sorry they were and offered to cook for her and take her in and make everything better. She smiled and shook her head. She was fine. Never trust anybody. Not even Dad.

There had been clouds on the horizon that day, and the water had been choppy. It had looked to Simone like the waves were reaching out to pull the ashes down, to sink them as low as they would go, to the blackest part of the water.

Her mother had never left her a note, but that didn't matter much anymore. It didn't even matter if what Kluren was implying was true or if when she met Simone at the recycling building that day, she'd been unsurprised. Relieved. However her mother had gone, she'd gone.

Simone turned and walked off Teddy. She tapped her earpiece and called Caroline.

"I hate my parents," Caroline said, when she answered. Simone laughed at this and found she couldn't stop. She laughed as she walked down a rickety bridge and the water reached up to grab her. "What's so funny?" Caroline asked over her laughter, and Simone stopped.

"Nothing," she said.

"You okay?" In the background, Simone could hear Caroline walking through City Hall Plaza, her footsteps on the solid wood, the fountain in the background. She pictured her there, staring up at the city, about to go into work after an awful morning, and still as poised and put together as a statue.

"Let's have dinner. I want to tell you some things." She stopped next to a large cruise ship and lit a cigarette.

"Okay," Caroline said. "But not out. I'm sick of eating in public."

"So come over. I'll grab some food from one of the noodle carts or something."

"Get the pad thai from Suzy's," Caroline said. "I'll be by after work. I'll complain about my parents some more."

"Me too," Simone said, exhaling smoke. It spread out into the air like vanishing ghosts.

"Okay, see you then."

"Yeah," Simone said. "And thanks."

"For what?"

"For listening, I guess."

"Sure," Caroline said. "Later, stalker." Caroline hung up. Simone stood where she was for a long moment. There were no other people in sight, and she could hear the waves underfoot and the way they hit the boat's side. She could smell the salt and the vague gasoline smell of boats. She took another drag on her cigarette. There were a lot of bodies under her, their ashes piling up to make underwater trenches and caves. Tunnels, maybe. She smiled at that. Tunnels made of ash leading all the way back to the mainland. But she was still floating. She threw her cigarette into the water. Its burning red end went out immediately, like the final flash of lightning in a storm. She watched the cigarette bob there for a moment—just another bit of trash in the ocean. Then, she put her hands in her pockets and started walking home.

ACKNOWLEDGMENTS

———

I owe so many people so many thanks for their help with this book—the first and foremost being my parents, for their incredible support and, as my dad is a big mystery fan and my mom loves sci-fi, for their inspiration. They both read this book multiple times and gave me such great feedback, too. I could not have done this without them and there are not enough ways to thank them for everything.

I pretty much wrote this book for my agent, Joy, and followed her lead on every revision and decision. She's always pushing me in new directions and to try new things and I cannot thank her enough for all her love and support. This book would not exist without her.

My editor, Ron, has been totally amazing throughout this entire process, with a fantastic eye for refinement. He's made this book so much stronger than it was when he got it, and he's been funny and kind and wonderful to work with. Thank you, Ron, for being an awesome guy and an awesome editor. And thank you to the entire team at Regan Arts, especially Emi, Richard, Lynne, and, of course, Judith.

My readers! My amazing writing group and readers who are incredibly supportive and inspiring: Laura, Robin, Schmergel, Margel, Stella, Paula, Holly, Ryan, Rebecca, Adam, Angela, Leslie, and Sarah.

They've all been vital to honing this book into what it is and I'm appreciative to all of them for taking the time to help me.

I also need to thank so many other people: Luke, for his thoughts and advice and helping out Joy when she was off having a baby. He really went above and beyond. My father-in-law, Mark, who provided me with stories, information, and some really disturbing photos from his time as a diver for the sheriff's department. And Jens, my munitions expert, for talking me through all the gun stuff.

And Chris, for being Chris.